# The Rising

## BECA LEWIS

PERCEPTION PUBLISHING

# Contents

# *Prologue*

S eventy-six years earlier...

He was late. He'd promised to come. And yet she didn't want him to. What they were doing was wrong, and she knew it. So did he. So why? Why pretend no one would care, that they weren't hurting anyone?

As long as they never find out, Annie thought. And they never would. Because they were careful. The only place they met was at the old cabin by the river. No one ever went there. From the outside, it looked like it was falling down.

Inside told a different story. Inside, he had propped up the beams and fixed the broken floorboards. She had swept and cleaned and polished the few pieces of furniture in the room. The oil lamp cast a warm glow over the space that seemed to exist outside of time, outside of Lazy Rivers with all its judgments and expectations.

There was a mattress, and that was enough. They brought food to eat and took it away. They wrapped themselves in the blankets they had both brought from home, the ones that wouldn't be missed.

Sometimes she would trace the pattern on his blanket and wonder who had made it, who had stitched love into its seams for a man who now shared it with her instead of his wife.

A fire would have been nice, but the smoke would give them away. Instead, they huddled together for warmth on the colder nights, their breath visible in the air between whispered promises neither could keep.

Outside, they let the weeds fill the yard, and vines climbed the sides of the cabin so it was almost invisible. The river ran not twenty yards away, its constant murmur covering their voices, its waters washing away their footprints in the soft bank.

Tonight it smelled of spring mud and possibilities, the current running faster than usual after the recent rains. She sometimes thought the river kept their secrets willingly, swallowing their whispers and carrying them downstream, far from Lazy Rivers and the people who knew them.

Why the one-room cabin was there was a mystery. There was only a faint path leading to it. One that only they knew about. There was no record of it on any town map she'd ever seen. It was as if it had grown from the riverbank itself, appearing just when they needed it.

He had found it one day while walking along the river. His eyes had lit up describing it to her, as if he'd discovered buried treasure. And in a way, he had. He'd convinced her it was their place, all the while knowing it was wrong.

Maybe that's why he hadn't come yet. Maybe he never would again. And that was probably best. It was time for them to stop.

Now that he had married, they were both committing adultery. Before it had just been her. And she hated herself for it.

But it had been so easy to believe him when he said she deserved these stolen moments of happiness, away from the daily misery of her life. He had a way of making the impossible seem inevitable, of making wrong feel right.

A farmer's wife. Not what she would have chosen for herself. But she had been told she had no choice. It was her duty to marry, be a good wife, work from morning to night with no pleasure that belonged to her. The bruises from her husband's temper were easier to hide than the emptiness inside her.

If she could run away, she would. But there was nowhere to go. And he'd find her anyway. She was unpaid help. *Like most wives,* she thought. Her husband made sure she knew how lucky she was that he had chosen her, damaged goods that she was.

Which is how she ended up doing this. She told herself she deserved it. He was gentle, kind, and careful with her. It was all new. To be loved. If this was love. She wasn't sure. And she hadn't cared.

Until now. Now she felt a flutter, and her hand went to her stomach. She knew. The secret they'd kept would soon become impossible to hide.

Yes, she had to tell him this was the last time. She would have someone else to love now. Her baby. Their baby. She knew it was his. Her husband had been away when it was conceived. She hoped she could hide that fact when the time came because this baby would be her new life without him, and that would have to be enough.

As darkness fell, and the cabin disappeared into the night, she made a decision. She would create a hiding place beneath the floorboards, a space where she could leave a letter for her child, should they ever need to know the truth. A letter. The letter would tell them it had been made from love, however flawed.

By lamplight, she found a loose board near the corner where the mattress lay. Her fingers trembled as she worked it free, revealing the dark earth beneath. She dug carefully, scooping soil with her bare hands, creating a small cavity just large enough for the metal box she'd brought with her.

Inside it, she placed a letter she'd written over many sleepless nights, and the only photograph they'd ever taken together, his face half in shadow. She wrapped the box in oilcloth before nestling it into its hiding place, then carefully replaced the board, ensuring it looked undisturbed. This secret would wait here, patient as the river, until it was needed.

Outside, an unusual spring storm gathered strength. Heavy raindrops pelted the cabin roof, and through the cracks in the walls, she could see the river swelling, creeping higher up its banks as if even now it was trying to reach the cabin, hungry for the secrets they'd buried here.

But the waters would recede by morning. Their secret would stay safe—for now.

The sound of footsteps snapped Annie out of her thoughts. He was coming after all. One last time. She'd give herself this gift of one last time to be loved, not knowing that some truths remain buried only until the waters rise.

# One

"Do you think this rain will ever stop?" Serenity asked her mother as they sat at the kitchen table having coffee and toast spread with the jam Pete had given them last fall.

The rich aroma of fresh coffee filled the kitchen, creating a pocket of warmth and comfort against the gloomy day outside. Steam curled above their mugs, mingling with the scent of the toast and raspberry jam, making the kitchen feel like the safest place in the world.

Pete had a bumper crop of raspberries last summer and had passed out jars of jam, saying he'd never get to all of them before he died.

"Not that I'm intending to do that anytime soon," he would add as people's faces fell at the prospect of not having Pete in their life.

"I should call him today," Lizzy said, as if reading Serenity's thoughts about the jam and its maker. "His farm sits so low near that bend in the river. The last time we had this much snow and then rain, the water came right up to his porch."

Serenity frowned. "And he's alone out there. Maybe we should drive out to check on him once this rain lets up a bit."

"At least it's not snow," Lizzy replied. They both laughed at that.

Just a few months before they had been buried in snow, the biggest storm in years. Now the snow was melting, big piles of it that were slowly disappearing. And despite, or maybe because of the rain, they could see daffodils bobbing in the breeze, their yellow heads ducking as if trying to shelter from the deluge.

Lizzy paused, her gaze drifting toward the window where the sound of the river carried faintly over the drumming rain.

"The river's higher than I've seen it in years," she observed. "Pete said the snowmelt alone would bring it to the banks, but with this rain..." She let the thought trail off, taking another sip of coffee.

The rain fell in relentless sheets, drumming against the roof like impatient fingers. It streamed down the windows, distorting the world outside into watery smudges of gray. The gutters overflowed, creating miniature waterfalls that carved channels into the soft earth below. Each rumble of thunder seemed to vibrate through the floorboards beneath their feet, as if the storm itself was trying to reach them.

*Spring in Lazy Rivers is maybe the most beautiful time of the year,* Serenity thought. At least it would be after the rain. It competed with autumn in her mind, but spring also carried the promise of new beginnings.

And that was surely what they were in the middle of after the year they had. It felt as if everyone around them was throwing off the past and embracing their new reality.

Lizzy had discovered that Joseph was her half brother and Tyler, Iris's grandson, was her half nephew. They were two secrets she wished had come to light years before so she could have enjoyed more time with them as family.

But Iris had never told Lizzy about her and Big Mike. And Lizzy had refused to look at the clues that would have revealed Joseph's relationship to her when she first gave Mama Ruth the lockets that Big Mike had given to her and her mother after her mother, Mae, passed away. She had asked Mama to hide them away, not wanting to know what was sealed inside.

Lizzy sighed. So much of her life had been caught up in not wanting to know. Pushing people away. People she loved. Like Matthew, whom she could hear moving around upstairs and who would soon come down to join them for breakfast.

That she could have had him with her all these years, but had made him leave before he even knew about his daughter, brought fresh grief every time she thought of it. In fact, grief lay in wait for her at every turn. Grief and happiness now lived inside her like twins, entwined together.

Some mornings she woke with grief's hand on her heart, mourning the decades wasted in isolation. Other moments, joy would suddenly flood through her without warning—watching Matthew's smile, hearing her daughter Serenity laugh, feeling her granddaughter Sam's arms around her. The twins of grief and joy traded places throughout her days, one always waiting in the shadow of the other.

She'd learned to welcome them both, understanding that her capacity for joy existed only because she could also feel the depth of her loss. They were two sides of the same heart that was finally learning how to love without fear.

And there was a lot to love. It was as if the universe had been keeping all these gifts for her, just waiting for her to receive them. Despite the sorrow, and sometimes the anger at herself that she felt, she was also proud of herself. She had opened her heart; she had reached out for help, and now she was surrounded by family and friends.

Looking across the table at Serenity, who was staring out at the rain, Lizzy knew she was seeing the rain as something she could paint for her next gallery opening. This one would be in Spring Falls at a gallery that Sam had found for her last fall.

They were all planning to go, and Lizzy figured the falls would be spectacular after this rain. It had been years since she had visited that town, and she was looking forward to it.

Touching Serenity's hand, Lizzy said what she often said these days: "Thank you for coming home."

And Serenity answered as she always did: "Thank you for bringing me home."

The two of them smiled at each other, Serenity hiding the fear she lived with. Her mother had pretended to be sick last summer to bring her home, but Serenity had never lost the fear that Lizzy hadn't been pretending to be sick; she really had been. And now she was pretending to be well.

Watching her mother's face, Serenity noticed the shadows under her eyes that seemed to deepen despite the happiness in their lives. There was a fragility to Lizzy's movements that hadn't been there even a month ago—a slight hesitation when she reached for her coffee, the way she seemed to tire more quickly in the evenings.

Serenity made a mental note to talk to Alex about it. He had been spending more time with them all, and she wondered if he'd noticed the subtle changes too. For now, though, she pushed the worry down and focused on the warm kitchen, the rain outside, and the precious moments with her mother.

Both of them knew how quickly life could change, sometimes for the better, and sometimes not.

# Two

Matthew and Sam came down the stairs together, laughing at something, and Lizzy's heart swelled. She wanted to enjoy every single moment of her time with them, because they would be off soon on an adventure together.

"Morning," Matthew said, crossing to Lizzy and kissing the top of her head. His hand lingered on her shoulder, a gentle reassurance that though he was leaving, he'd always return to her.

Thunder crashed, and lightning flashed outside the kitchen window.

"Randy and I saw Pete yesterday at the diner," Sam announced as she poured herself a cup of coffee. "Pete said that we can expect the river to really flood this time."

Before sitting down at the kitchen table, she gave her mother and grandmother a hug. Lingering a little longer with her grandmother. She knew they were breaking her heart a little by leaving.

"He said the snowmelt has already raised the river to almost record levels, and this rain will definitely cause a flood at his place."

"That river," Lizzy murmured, her eyes drawn to the window. "It's been keeping Lazy Rivers' secrets longer than any of us have been alive. Every time it floods, it seems to rearrange things—brings something to the surface that's been hidden."

Serenity gave her mother a curious glance. "Like what?"

"Oh, just old things. Artifacts from the town's early days. Once the foundations of an old mill nobody remembered surfaced after the river receded. The river has its own way of making sure nothing stays buried forever."

Lizzy shivered slightly, though the kitchen was warm. "Pete told me once that the river doesn't give up what it takes until it's ready for the truth to be known."

"Well, I'm ready for the truth about where my father lives to be revealed," Sam said, "and I'm sure he's not in the river." There was a beat of silence around the table as everyone thought that was a weird thing to say.

Trying to make light of her remark, she unfolded a map she had brought down from her room. "I've marked three locations where my father might be." Sam's fingers traced the route on the map, following the imaginary journey that would lead her to a stranger who shared her DNA.

"I keep wondering what I'll say when I actually see him," she admitted, her voice softer now. "Or what he looks like—if I have his eyes or his laugh."

She glanced at Matthew, guilt flickering across her face. "And whether he'll even want to know me. Thirty years is a long time to suddenly spring a daughter on someone."

She didn't add her deeper fear—that finding Lucas might somehow diminish what she'd built with Matthew, this grandfather who had chosen her, who had stepped into her life with such natural affection. The thought of disrupting their newly formed family made her stomach twist, even as she knew she needed to find the missing piece of herself.

"You'll find him," Serenity said, squeezing her daughter's hand. "And whatever happens when you do, you've got us."

"Always," Matthew added. "Even if Lucas turns out to be living as a nomad on the Mongolian steppes, we'll track him down."

Sam laughed, the tension in her shoulders easing slightly. "Better pack warm clothes then."

Lizzy silently watched their exchange, cataloging each smile, each gesture, storing them away for the quiet days ahead.

She'd become so accustomed to their presence—Matthew's deep voice in the mornings, Sam's footsteps on the stairs, the sound of their laughter filling rooms that had been silent for too long. Soon those sounds would be gone, she and Serenity would be home alone, and the house would feel empty.

Lizzy knew that Serenity, too, was already missing the two of them. But then Serenity had Alex. In the past few months, Serenity and Alex had spent more time together, and she thought they were finally admitting to each other that there was a bond of love between them.

Like Sam and Randy Carter. They too were spending more time together, but Lizzy figured Sam wasn't making any promises to anyone until they tracked down Lucas and let him know he had a daughter.

*Ah, secrets,* Lizzy thought. *When will they end?* She wondered who was keeping them now, because she was sure that there was one somewhere that remained to be uncovered.

After another clap of thunder and flash of lightning, they all stood and went into the living room to look at the river. They could barely see it through the gray sheet of water that sluiced down. But they knew it was many feet above its bank.

The house was built high enough up on the hill that they felt safe, but they knew Pete's farmland would take the brunt of it. It was low and very flat.

"Has anyone heard from Pete this morning?" Matthew asked, peering through the streaming windows with concern.

Lizzy frowned. "I tried calling, but he's not answering. That's not like him—Pete's always up with the chickens, even though he doesn't have any anymore."

"His place sits awfully low," Serenity said, getting worried now too. "And he's been talking about his bad knee acting up. What if he can't get to higher ground?"

"He's probably fine," Lizzy replied, though her voice lacked conviction. "That man's survived everything this river and life have thrown at him. This is probably just one more rain to him."

Matthew shifted uncomfortably. "I don't know, Lizzy. When I saw him at the diner yesterday, he mentioned something about the river acting strange—said it was 'pulling at things that should stay buried.' I thought he was just being poetic."

"Should we drive out there?" Sam asked. "Make sure he's okay?"

Lizzy shook her head reluctantly. "Not in this. The road to his place dips down by Miller's Creek. It's probably underwater already." She didn't add what they were all thinking—that Pete lived alone on that sprawling old farm.

"Alex probably already checked on him," Lizzy said, more to reassure herself than the others. "And his farmland is probably the safest place to flood. Pete no longer farms it himself—he leases it out, and it being spring, the crops haven't been planted yet."

But as they all stared at the rain, no one looked convinced.

"Maybe he is already in town," Lizzy added. "At the diner, most likely. He knows that the town fathers built the town much higher from the river, and that the waters have never flooded the town. It's safe there."

"Sure," Serenity said, her thoughts easing a little, thinking how much the river was part of the town. The area really. Lazy Rivers wandered around until it reached Spring Falls and then ended in Silver Lake.

The three towns were connected by the river, but by other things too. Silver Lake was where Iris had been for the last five years before passing away, and Spring Falls was where her next art showing would be. Sam had found the gallery when she had spent a few days there before returning to Lazy Rivers.

And Jan, her agent, had contacted the owner and made the arrangements. Serenity was looking forward to seeing the town again. It had been years since she had been there. Which reminded her, she had some paintings to finish.

"Well, since we're not washing away yet, I have work to do," she said, hugging her mom and smiling at her father and Sam.

She left the three of them at the window, staring at the rain, and headed to her studio to paint what spring and the river rising together felt like. A combination of amazement at the power and beauty of the river and anxiety about what it could do.

# Three

L izzy was right. Pete had already moved himself to the diner, determined to stay there as long as he could. Not only was he worried about the water rising, but he was also lonely. This was not something he admitted to anyone. Ever. But he was. It had gotten worse each year ever since his wife had died.

*Truth be told*, Pete thought to himself, *he had been lonely most of his life.* His mother, Annie, had died when he was just a boy, and that meant he and his dad did most of the farm work together.

Work that started before the sun came up, and kept going until they fell into bed at night. Too busy working to be talking or socializing. His dad was a hard taskmaster and even more distant after his wife died.

Sometimes they had a woman or two from town come help in the house, make food, keep it reasonably clean, and a few of them took the time to give Pete extra attention.

But mostly, he was alone. Which is why he had loved going to school. There were people there. And he'd see Lizzy, Iris, Joseph, and John at school. Which was good because he didn't get to go over to Lizzy's house to play with them as much as he would have liked to.

Now completely alone at his house, he had slowly closed up one room at a time, too much work to keep them up. He rarely went upstairs; it hurt his knee too much. He lived mostly in the kitchen and bedroom. What else did he need?

So as soon as he could each day, he'd come to the diner. There were people to talk to, or at least to watch. Today he'd stay as long as they let him stay. He didn't think they'd mind. Hardly anyone was coming out in this weather.

Sipping his coffee, Pete thought back on his life. Even though his father was disappointed in him, Pete had a good life with his wife. Why didn't he have children? "We need kids to help on the farm," his father had told him more than once.

Pete had never bothered to remind his father that he was an only child, and if he wanted kids, why not have more himself? Besides, that made him feel guilty. His mom, even when she was alive, seemed to be sick all the time. Maybe she couldn't have more kids.

Still, sometimes he indulged his anger at being the only one helping his dad. Would he have chosen to be a farmer if he had had a choice? Probably not. For sure, his wife hadn't wanted to be a farmer's wife, but she had chosen him and that meant choosing the farm.

And he didn't want to tell his dad that not having children was Pete's fault. His wife, Nancy, had wanted them. After years of trying, it turned out that he was infertile. That was something men didn't share with anyone. If you couldn't propagate, what use were you?

There was no consensus about why he was. Measles maybe? Toxins in the ground? No one could agree, and Pete thought it didn't make a difference anyway. He couldn't. That was that. And Nancy stayed with him anyway, despite a lifestyle she didn't enjoy and not having the children she wanted to have. He had been lucky that way. Every day his heart hurt missing her.

And now he was getting old. *Correction*, he said to himself. *I am old*. Every day, something that had once been easy felt a little harder than it had the day before.

Leasing out his land had been a really good decision. Now he wondered if he should just sell everything and move into town.

He was deep in thought about that idea, thinking it was the best one he'd had in quite a while, when the door chimed and he looked up to see Alex Williams, water dripping off of him in sheets.

Amy was right behind him, mopping up the water that spilled off his coat and hat.

"Sorry about that," Alex said, hanging up his coat on the hooks by the door where all the other coats dripped.

"Not your fault," Amy said. "The weather is what it is, but a door opening directly into the diner doesn't seem like good planning. Ethan suggested to Joseph we build an entry into the diner after all this rain stops, and he said he'd think about it."

"That's a good idea," Alex said, wondering why no one had thought of that before. Ethan and Amy, and even Tyler, were changing the feeling of the diner. *For the better*, he thought.

Heading to his favorite booth, he waved at Betty Jean, who nodded and gave him a thumbs up. He knew that meant she would get his favorite breakfast ready. Clapping Pete on the back on the way to his seat, he asked him how he was.

"Dry," was Pete's response.

"Glad you're here," Alex answered. "This way we all know you are safe."

"It seemed a good idea," Pete answered. "The last time we had such a huge snowmelt and this many days of hard rain, it flooded up to my door. This time I left before that happened."

"You can't go back home until the rain stops and the river goes down," Alex agreed, slipping into his booth and gesturing to Pete to join him. "Where will you stay?"

Pete shrugged. "Motel, probably."

"I've got a better idea. Stay at my place. It's big enough. And that way I can assure all the people who have asked me if I've checked on you, that you are with me."

Pete hesitated. Should he? It seemed too much to offer. But he could. He had looked out at the swollen river that morning and thrown a suitcase full of clothes and a Dopp kit with all of his bathroom stuff and headed to the diner. He knew the motel wouldn't be full, or if it was, he'd sleep in his truck.

"Don't be stubborn, Pete," Alex laughed. "You're family. Just say yes."

Pete had to look down to hide the tears that came to his eyes hearing the words, *You're family.*

Had he ever heard his father say any such thing to him? Not that he could remember.

*No wonder the diner had become like a home to him.* Betty Jean, hearing the conversation as she came out of the kitchen, came over and gave Pete a pat on the back.

"Do it, Pete. It will take a load off of everyone's mind. You don't want us worrying about you, do you?"

"No, Ma'am," Pete said, still looking down. Then, gathering his courage, he looked up and said, "Thanks, Alex. I'm honored to take you up on it."

Alex took his house key off his keyring and put it on the counter. "Would you stop by the hardware store and get another one made for me?"

Pete stared at the key on the counter, wondering if anyone had ever given him this big of a gift.

He thought not.

# Four

Since John had moved into her house, Mama felt as if she had stepped into another lifetime. In some ways, it was.

There was her childhood lifetime. Then there was the lifetime with her husband, Ted. And after Ted, there was a lifetime when she lived alone. And now here she was, living with her childhood sweetheart, surrounded by memories from all the previous lifetimes.

She couldn't compare them even if she wanted to. They were all so different. And yet in some ways they were the same. After all, she was the common denominator in all those lifetimes.

Besides, she knew from experience that comparisons only resulted in unhappiness. So, instead, she accepted that she had accumulated lifetimes and now was in this one, and she planned to enjoy it as much as possible.

The four lockets that had revealed so much about Big Mike, Iris, and Lizzy's connection still occasionally weighed on her mind. How long had she kept those secrets, those metal containers of truth, hidden away in her filing cabinet? Decades.

And yet, when the time came to bring them out, everything had changed for the better. It made her wonder what other secrets might be waiting to emerge, what other revelations might rise like the river.

Not that the last few months had been a complete bed of roses. She and John had both had to make adjustments. Their past marriages meant they had habits that worked with those spouses, but not with each other. And then they had both lived alone for years, and that too brought its own adjustments.

But she thought they were doing well. Maybe because they had known each other as children, or maybe because they were old enough to be wise enough to not be bothered by the small things.

She still remembered how, when they were teenagers, John would bring her wildflowers he'd picked by the river. How they'd explored the woods together, discovering hidden clearings and secret places that felt like they belonged only to them.

One spot came to mind—a bend in the river where they'd skipped stones and shared dreams that seemed impossible then. Strange how life had circled back, bringing those dreams within reach just when she'd stopped expecting them.

What she was most grateful for was how John had stepped into the role of both companion and partner with such ease. He worked at the nursery now, and he took over many of the household chores.

He finished the tasks she had left undone for years, noticed things she needed before she noticed them herself, and then did something about them. Sometimes it felt like the shoemaker's elf in Grimm's Fairy Tales taking care of things while she slept. It was wonderful, and she was grateful beyond measure.

This all meant she had time she hadn't had for years to do something with herself. She wasn't sure what that would be, but sitting in her home office surrounded by all the plants, watching the rain pour down, and sipping the coffee John had brought her, she asked herself what she wanted to do with her remaining years.

Had she ever asked herself that? The nursery came with Ted. And she loved it. But it was a life made for her rather than a life she made. It wasn't that she wanted to change anything. She loved her life. She just wanted to add something to it. But what?

"Ready to go?" John asked, sticking his head into her office.

"Sure," Mama replied. They were heading to the nursery. With all the rain, she didn't think there would be much business, but that meant they could spend time cleaning up and taking care of the plants that would soon be snatched up by all the gardeners just waiting for the rain to stop before planting.

Even if they didn't own the nursery, she'd still be working with plants; that she knew for sure. She knew the itch people felt in the spring to get out and work in the dirt, cleaning up after winter, preparing the soil and designing the summer gardens.

As they drove through the downpour to the nursery, even through the rain she could see the red buds on the maple trees and the greening of the willows. It was such a beautiful time of the year. *But the thing about spring,* Mama thought, *is we wait for it all winter, and then it arrives and is gone too quickly.*

If she could slow time down, she would slow it down in spring so she could take in all the blooming trees, the greening leaves, and the spring flowers. But instead of slowing down, it seemed to speed up.

She knew as soon as the rain stopped, nature would produce spring so fast it would seem impossible.

How many springs did she have left? No one knew the answer to that, but she knew she was in the last few decades of her life, and no amount of slowing down time would stop that.

Which brought her back to the question. *What could she add to her life now? What need was going unmet? How could she be useful? Or should she be more creative?*

She'd always been everyone's "Mama," the person people turned to for comfort and advice, for a steady presence when the world felt unstable. It was a role she cherished, even though it sometimes left little room for her own needs and dreams.

Could she continue being Mama Ruth to the town while also discovering what Ruth—just Ruth—wanted for herself?

All those thoughts vanished as they pulled up beside the nursery's back door and made a quick dash to the door that her son, Tom, held open for them. His husband, Brad, took their wet coats and hats and hung them by the door.

Inside, the nursery was dry, warm, and smelled of earth and growing things. Mama's heart swelled with happiness that here she was surrounded by so much beauty and three men who thought the world of her.

*Really, what more could she ask?* And yet, something was bothering her. Was it the relentless rain? The threat of flooding that the snowmelt and rain brought? What was it?

Perhaps it was knowing that Pete's farm would be underwater by now. Or maybe it was that strange feeling she'd had since the rain started—an unsettled sensation in her chest, like something long forgotten was trying to surface.

The river had been part of her entire life, flowing alongside all her memories, but today it felt different somehow. More purposeful. As if it had waited all these years to reveal something important.

"You're quiet today," John said as they moved among the seedlings, checking for signs of dampness or disease.

"Just thinking," she replied, not ready to share her uneasiness. Not when she couldn't even name it herself.

# Five

*Almost there,* the man said to himself. Because of the rain, he had forced himself to stop the night before at a motel just outside of Spring Falls. Part of him wanted to keep pushing through, to get to Lazy Rivers as fast as possible.

But the wise part, the patient part, the part that had waited months to make this trip, took over, and he had stopped for the night.

The rain was just as bad as the night before, but at least it wasn't pitch black outside. So although it was still hard to see, it wasn't impossible.

The landscape had changed as he'd crossed into this part of the state, with more hills, denser forests. And although the car windows were up, he thought he could hear the rush of the river. *Probably imagining it,* he thought.

Still, it was possible. On the car's GPS, he could see that the river followed the road in many places, and if it weren't raining so hard he'd probably be able to glimpse it through the trees once in a while.

He would have known it was there even without the GPS, having studied maps of the area for weeks, memorizing the bends in the river, the location of certain properties, all the places that featured in the documents he'd found. He couldn't wait to see them for himself. But now he was worried that they were buried under rushing water. Now, what would he have to prove what he knew?

None of this was how he thought this trip would be, and it wasn't how he planned to arrive in Lazy Rivers. He had imagined himself driving into town, the sun shining, birds singing, flowers nodding their heads. Maybe even people waving at him as he came to town as if they knew him.

But that was all fantasy. No one knew him. No one would wave at a stranger coming into town. And they especially wouldn't be waving if they knew why he was coming to Lazy Rivers.

He was coming to take what was his. What he didn't even know he owned until just a few months before.

He was still angry about how he had found out. Why had his parents keep that secret from him? Neither of them had been brave enough, or in his mind, wise enough, to tell him while they were alive.

No, he had to find it in a letter. *Cowards.* That's what he had been saying to them for months now, wondering if when you were dead you could still hear people talking to you.

His anger had faded a bit towards them. After all, they had been wonderful parents, and his mother had lost her mind, literally, in the last ten years. Dementia had destroyed everything that she might have wanted to tell him.

Sometimes when he'd visit her in the nursing home, she'd recognize him, but mostly not. Sometimes she'd call him a different name. A name he had never heard before until he found the papers.

Once, during a moment of unusual clarity, she'd grabbed his hand and said, "The river keeps everything, you know. Everything we tried to hide." He'd dismissed it as another confused rambling, but now those words haunted him. What else had the river kept hidden all these years?

"Cowards," he whispered to himself again as he drove. But now that the anger had faded, he thought they might have simply wanted him all to themselves. Out of love, probably. Because he had felt loved all his life.

Then, people started dying around him. First his wife. Then his dad. Then his friends. Then his mother. It was the worst part of getting old. Losing people.

No wonder he felt as if he were losing his mind. All the grief all at one time. But he had carried on. What else could he do? Who could he turn to? There was no one left. Which is why he had to make this trip, no matter what he might find.

For months he had carried the extra worry that he might carry the gene for his mother's illness. He thought about getting tested, getting the worry over with. Knowing would be better.

He had put off going through all his mother's things, not being able to face it. Finally, one day, he had tackled the job. It wasn't much after all. Much of what she owned, including his parent's home, had been sold to pay for the nursing home.

Yes, he had worried about inheriting the heart disease that had killed his father, or his mother's dementia. But all that worry had vanished, to be replaced instead with anger when he found the letter and the papers, and learned the truth.

A birth certificate with a name that wasn't his, and a location he'd never heard of before: Lazy Rivers. How had his parents kept this from him all these years? He wasn't their son. Never had been. Someone had given him away.

Months passed. More grief, more anger. Finally, he decided he couldn't take it anymore. He had to see for himself what had been taken from him. And that was why he was going to Lazy Rivers—to get answers.

And to claim what was rightfully his, the property by the river that according to the internet had been in his actual family for generations. A family he didn't know he had. This was the place where it all began. With all the rain and flooding, he wondered if there would be anything left to claim. But it didn't matter. He'd come too far to turn back now, and he was too angry to care what it would mean to others.

# Six

In her studio, Serenity stood before a blank canvas, mixing blues and grays on her palette. In her mind's eye she could see the swollen river, its usually lazy meandering now a purposeful surge. She understood the river. How many times had her own emotions risen like floodwaters, bringing to the surface feelings and memories she'd tried to bury?

Her art had always been about revealing—taking what lay hidden beneath the calm surface and giving it form, color, life. She knew the river was doing the same thing now, reclaiming whatever secrets had been entrusted to its depths. There was honesty in that process. The river was impartial in what it revealed.

She dipped her brush and made the first stroke—a curve that echoed the bend in the river where Pete's land met the water. The canvas would hold whatever emerged, just as the town would have to face whatever the river revealed.

Serenity didn't know why she was thinking that way. Why would she be thinking the town would have to face something? Shrugging, she accepted it as a premonition that may or may not come true.

These intuitive flashes had been happening more frequently lately. Small nudges of awareness that often turned out to be accurate, as if her gift was evolving beyond just seeing other people's memories into something more predictive.

Like how she'd known Alex would call seconds before her phone rang last week, or how she'd felt compelled to check on her mother the night before she'd found her struggling with a stubborn jar lid, frustration building in her weakening grip.

As she painted, she allowed memories to come through her onto the canvas. Some were her memories. Some were other people's memories she had seen. Nothing tangible, just the feelings.

As her brush moved across the canvas, a memory surfaced—not fully formed, but sharp enough to make her pause. The memory wasn't hers, and she couldn't place whose it might be. But it settled into her painting, a shadow beneath the water's surface that wasn't quite visible but somehow essential to the composition.

For years she had hated the fact that she could see other people's memories. Only recently had she acknowledged that it was that gift that also fueled her as an artist, and when she allowed herself to appreciate it, her art became better and better.

It was a Rivers woman's problem or gift depending on how you looked at it, passed down from generation to generation. It had branded them, haunted them, and isolated them.

But times had changed. Not only had she, her mother, and her daughter chosen to live life instead of hiding from it, they had all found it easier to deal with the gift, and also to accept its blessings.

Their gift had helped find a missing boy and convey a dying woman's wishes. And now, perhaps because she had stopped hiding from what she could do, she was better able to separate herself from other people's memories, and contain them in separate rooms in her mind. At least that's how she imagined it.

And now she had learned how to slowly open those rooms and let out what she wanted in order to paint the way she was painting now.

This was the last painting she wanted to finish before her show in Spring Falls. She thought that her agent, Jan, might choose it as the one to highlight in the marketing campaign. As soon as she finished it, she'd send her pictures.

On the table by the door, her phone buzzed instead of pinging. She had forgotten to unsilence it from the night before. Glancing over at it, a paintbrush still in her hand, she saw the message was from Alex asking if she wanted to have lunch with him.

A new restaurant had opened in town, where the bakery used to be. It was such a small town that a new restaurant opening was a big deal. Plus it was Thai, her favorite.

Glancing over her shoulder to see outside, she could see the rain was letting up a little. Besides, it was only a few miles away. "Yes," she texted back with one finger, trying not to get paint on the phone. "Of course," she wanted to add, but it wasn't necessary. He knew how she felt.

What she was grateful for was his willingness to let their relationship move along at a pace she was comfortable with. A snail's pace, she knew. Still, it was moving. Slow and steady, like the river was most of the time.

A few hours later, Serenity put the paintbrush down, happy with the results so far. *Almost done*, she thought. Something was missing, but she couldn't see what it was yet. She knew if she waited, it would reveal itself.

Her bedroom was on the other side of the studio, so it didn't take long to change out of her paint-spattered clothes. Taking a minute, she checked herself in the mirror. She thought that each day she could see another line on her face, but that was because she had it an inch from the mirror, checking to see what had changed.

If she thought of herself as a painting, she might see the changes in her as an evolution instead of something she didn't like. But she was proud that she was much fitter than she had been when she first came to Lazy Rivers almost a year ago. Except in really terrible weather, she walked a few miles each day, and had started an exercise program that she did each day.

Plus, her eating habits were better. Matthew liked to cook, and instead of snack foods, she ate at least one good meal a day. She'd miss his cooking when he and Sam started traveling.

*But then there is always the Thai restaurant,* she thought, hoping it would be a good place to go.

Brushing her still very red hair that had only a few streaks of gray, she applied a bit of mascara to bring out her blue eyes—still thinking of herself as a painting—and headed into the living room.

Sam and Matthew weren't there, but her mother was sitting in her favorite chair reading a book.

"I'm running a few errands and then going to lunch with Alex," Serenity said, bending down and giving her a peck on her cheek. "Do you want me to bring you anything?" she asked.

"I'm good," her mom said, barely lifting her eyes from the book she was reading.

Serenity was glad her mother couldn't hear her thoughts because she immediately thought to herself, *I hope so.*

Her mother looked fine on the surface, content with her book and the quiet morning. But lately there had been moments—a hesitation when reaching for something on a high shelf, a slight breathlessness after climbing the stairs, the way she sometimes paused mid-sentence as if searching for energy to continue—that made Serenity watchful.

She'd mention it to Alex at lunch, see if he'd noticed anything during his frequent visits. She didn't want to worry unnecessarily, but after last summer's "pretend" illness that had brought her home, she couldn't shake the feeling that this time something might actually be wrong.

Outside, the rain was still falling. No longer the heavy downpour that had been going on for days, but still much more than a drizzle. Puddles lay everywhere. It would be a long time before the ground dried out enough to plant the vegetables and flowers she knew her mother was dying to get into the ground.

As she drove toward town, evidence of the flooding became more apparent. A section of Old Mill Road was barricaded, water lapping at its edges. The baseball field had become a shallow lake, its backstop rising from the water like a strange metal island.

Near the bridge, town workers in bright yellow raincoats monitored the water level, which had risen to just a few feet below the roadway. Emergency vehicles were parked at strategic points, their lights creating eerie patterns through the rain-streaked windshield. Lazy Rivers had weathered floods before, but this one seemed determined to test the town's preparations.

With windshield wipers beating out a steady rhythm, she headed into town. Passing Tate's nursery, she beeped her horn, two short beeps, hoping Tom heard her as she drove by.

A car she hadn't seen before drove around her as she had slowed down to honk, and she glimpsed the man behind the wheel. Even though it was a backcountry road, it seemed dangerous to her. He had passed her when it was hard to see what was coming.

As the car passed, she didn't see a memory, she just felt anger. Raw and potent, it struck her like a physical force, making her grip the steering wheel tighter.

This wasn't the typical impatience of someone stuck behind a slow driver—this was deeper, older. She glimpsed the profile of the driver—a stranger, his jaw set in determination—and felt a chill despite the car's warmth.

Not knowing who he was, it worried her that he was that angry, and she hoped he was just passing through. She also hoped the anger was temporary. Maybe he was just angry at the weather.

The song, "The Sun Will Come Out Tomorrow" popped into her head, and she hummed it to herself all the way into town, and forgot about the angry stranger.

# Seven

T om was in the middle of rearranging the store when he heard the car horn. Pausing, he smiled to himself and waved in the direction of the road. He knew who it was. Serenity.

It was hard to imagine life without her in it. Although she had moved away and only returned last year, they had picked up their friendship where they had left off. Now it was stronger than ever. They would turn to each other when either of them needed to talk something through and they needed an impartial opinion.

Well, as impartial as they could be as friends. As kids, they had only touched on the possibility of a deep friendship. They were both wary of the world. She barely let herself exist in it, fully aware there were people in town who said that the Rivers women were witches and scary. They had told their children to stay away from them. And those kids either did that, or tormented her.

Everyone had known that the Rivers women saw their memories, and that frightened them. What they didn't know is that it frightened Serenity too. She didn't want to see people's secrets.

Tom remembered how she'd described it once—like having strangers constantly whispering in your ear, telling you things you never asked to know. The weight of carrying other people's pain, their shame, their regrets.

"Sometimes," she'd told him, sitting by the river where they'd often escape to talk, "I feel like I'm drowning in everyone else's lives while trying to hold on to my own."

She had told him that too often they were horrible memories, and because she was helpless to do anything about them, she hated the experience. Once in a while she saw something lovely, and that helped. But still she wanted it to stop, and it wouldn't. He'd understood then why she'd built those walls around herself, why distance became her protection.

Everyone knew about the Rivers women, but no one knew his secret. Except his mother and Serenity. His mother had simply said she had always known, and what difference did it make? Except she understood it made the world harder for him to live in. That worried her, because she loved him.

He didn't have to tell Serenity. She knew. She never told him how she knew. But she did. And she said that meant she could be his friend without ever worrying about him wanting something from her except friendship. That had made him love Serenity even more than he had before, and he understood then just a little more about how hard it was to be a woman in the world they lived in. How misunderstood and undervalued one can be as a person.

One time she had shared with him that she hated that she was beautiful. She wanted people to appreciate her because she was an artist, and a thinker, and a kind person. And that felt to her as if it were impossible.

So she had left town to make one of her problems easier to bear, and became the artist she had always wanted to be. But he had missed her wisdom, and courage, and the talks they used to have as they sat by the river. She stood up for him, and he stood by her. And now she was back. And dating an emotionally wounded, but wonderful, man. He thought they were perfect for each other. Lately, life had felt as if it was almost too good to be true.

He wasn't superstitious, but did that mean they were being prepared for a new problem to deal with?

The rainy day was giving him a chance to do something he had been wanting to do since last spring. Reorder the store, and give everything a good scrubbing.

The inside of the nursery's store looked almost the same as it had when he was a kid. He wondered when someone looked at it as something new. The wooden shelves still held the same earthy scent of peat and fertilizer, mingled with the sweeter notes of seed packets and the subtle plastic smell of pots.

The old bell above the door hadn't changed either, its familiar chime announcing each customer. Even in the rain, light filtered through the window panels, creating that distinctive greenhouse glow that had always made this place feel magical to him, like stepping into another world where everything grew and thrived.

Last fall they had a new greenhouse built, and that had sparked anew the desire that he had since he was working in the nursery as a child alongside his father, to make it better. Now that his mother had actually turned over the nursery to him, he and his husband, Brad, had spent the winter happily planning the new look.

They would leave his mother's office as it was. John had his own workspace in the new greenhouse. Both of them were on board with the changes. It was strange that he was now paying his mother to work there rather than the other way around, but he saw the wisdom of doing this now.

It gave his mother and John the chance to spend more time with each other, and there was no worry about what would happen to the nursery at their passing. *Please God,* he said to himself, *make that be many years from now.*

He missed his father, as he knew his mother did too, but he thought John was the perfect new man for his mother. Two happy couples, he thought to himself as he looked over at Brad carefully restocking the new shelves that John and his son Randy had installed in the store.

He was grateful for everything. Even the rain. He was quietly celebrating his good fortune when he heard Serenity's car horn. All was well in their world, and he hoped it would stay that way forever. But knowing that it wouldn't, because that was how life was, he cherished the lovely moments even more.

Through the windows, he could see the rain had eased slightly, but the ground was saturated, water pooling in every depression. The flood warnings had been constantly on the radio all morning.

Brad had mentioned that the old creek behind the nursery—usually just a trickle—was now rushing like a miniature river. Nature had its own rhythm, its own way of clearing out and making room for fresh growth. Sometimes the process was gentle; sometimes it was destructive. Tom wondered which this would be.

# *Eight*

After texting Serenity to ask her to lunch, Alex felt on top of the world. He shouldn't, really. The town was under a flood warning. But compared to the past years of his life, he thought he could deal with a flood. Living with an abusive father, a dead mother, distant and sometimes abusive siblings, and missing the one brother who cared for him, life had been hard.

When Serenity returned to Lazy Rivers, it was as if the tide had turned. Other people started coming back to Lazy Rivers, too. Serenity's daughter, Samantha, and Serenity's father, Matthew, were first. Then Alex's brother, Zach, returned, solving the missing boys mystery. Although Zach had died last fall, Alex had months together with him, thanks to Serenity and her ability to see memories. Even when Zach was too ill to speak, she told him stories about the life that Zach had lived, seeing them through Zach's memories.

After that, John joined his son, Randy, in Lazy Rivers and rekindled his childhood love affair with Mama Tate—now called Mama Ruth because of John, who called her by her real name, Ruth. Other things had changed too. When Lizzy's childhood friend, Iris, briefly recovered from her coma to whisper the names of Big Mike and his wife Sarah, Lizzy had stepped in and a buried secret had come to light. Joseph's father, Big Mike, was also Lizzy's father.

There was more. It turned out that Big Mike was also the father to Iris's son Snags, and that meant Tyler was Joseph's nephew. Joseph was shocked, but also delighted to learn he had siblings, something he had longed for as a child.

Alex sighed to himself. He worried about what was going to happen to Tyler's father. Snags was still in prison, but now on murder charges since Iris had eventually died after he had hit her on the head five years before.

But good things had come out of that secret being revealed. Joseph, Lizzy and Tyler had become closer in the past few months. Alex could see Joseph in the kitchen with Tyler teaching him how to cook. As far as he could tell, Tyler was thriving under the care of Joseph and his wife, Betty Jean.

Everything had changed for the better. Yes, it had been a mess for a while, but the last few months had been peaceful, and everyone had settled into their new reality while waiting for spring.

Now spring was here, roaring in with the river. The piles of snow that had been taller than him were almost gone. The massive winter storm they had endured was going down as the biggest one in over fifty years. Which is why a swollen river didn't seem like such a big deal to Alex. Except when he allowed himself to worry about it. But everything was in place to take care of whatever was coming.

Flood warnings were issued. Emergency vehicles were standing by. What else was there to do but wait, and take Serenity, the woman he had secretly been in love with his whole life, to lunch?

As children, they lived in entirely different worlds, both of them isolated. Besides, he was five years older, and as kids that was a big difference. Now it was nothing. Alex didn't know where their relationship would go. All he knew was that he wasn't going anywhere. She was the one. Whether he was the one for her, time would tell, and he would give her as much time as she needed to decide.

Sometimes he marveled at how their paths had finally converged. They'd both suffered in different ways—his pain visible in bruises and broken bones, hers invisible but no less real.

They understood each other's caution, the careful way they both tested the ground before stepping forward. When she looked at him, he felt truly seen, past the badge and the authority, to the person beneath. That alone was worth waiting for, however long it took. If nothing else, living by a river taught him that time flows on with no effort. And it brought to the surface whatever needed to be dealt with when it was ready.

A few hours later, closing his computer, Alex glanced at Pete, who had returned to the counter so he could chat with whomever came in the door, and beckoned him over.

"I'm heading home for a minute. Do you want to follow me there, and I'll show you around the house?"

Although Alex had given Pete his key, it was still hard for Pete to process that he would live with Alex until the river went down. Why would Alex do that for him?

Seeing his hesitation, Alex added, "Seriously, Pete. I want you to stay with me. Come."

Nodding, and turning aside so Alex wouldn't see the tears in his eyes, Pete left a tip on the counter for Amy, and followed Alex out the door. His coat still felt wet from when he first came in, and he shivered. Cold didn't use to bother him so much. But in the last few years, it got to him. Getting old was hard. And good at the same time. It gave him perspective, making the important things clearer.

Pete had outlived most of his contemporaries, watched the town change, felt himself become a kind of living history. He knew people valued that because they told him. His knowledge of the river, the land, the weather patterns—it meant something. He might not have children to pass his legacy to, but he had the town.

And right now, he had Alex's kindness, unexpected but just as welcome as the new buds on the maple trees.

Pete felt that being old gave him options. Options like selling the old farm. There was no one to take it over. But old also meant he shuffled more than walked sometimes, and things that never used to ache did. *Still,* Pete smiled to himself. *Life was good. He had friends all over town.*

On the way out of the diner, a man coming up the steps bumped into Pete, and he had to grab the handrail to keep from falling. The stranger wore a city coat—too light for this weather—and his eyes had a searching quality, taking in everything around him with an intensity that seemed out of place.

Out of habit, Pete said, "excuse me," even though he hadn't been the one to do the bumping. The man said nothing, barely acknowledging Pete's presence as he brushed past. But something in his expression—a flash of recognition quickly masked—made Pete pause. Had he seen him somewhere before?

"Who was that?" Alex asked as they walked to their trucks.

"No idea," Pete answered. Both of them were too busy trying to avoid the worst of the puddles to say more.

As they drove through town, Alex noted how the creek that ran behind the elementary school had overflowed its banks, water lapping at the edge of the playground. They passed the public works crew sandbagging around the drainage culverts on Elm Street, their movements practiced and efficient. The town had its flood protocols, rehearsed year after year, even though the river rarely made it to the town's streets.

But Alex couldn't shake the feeling that this time the coming flood was bringing something else for the town to deal with. After navigating the wet streets, by the time they arrived at Alex's house, they had both put the rude man out of their minds.

Alex's home sat on a quiet street near the edge of town, a modest bungalow with a wide front porch. It had belonged to one of the deputies who had worked for the sheriff before him. A man who had helped him see he could be the sheriff that the town needed.

When the deputy and his wife retired to Florida, they'd practically insisted Alex buy the house, giving him a price far below market value, saying that it still made them money.

"Because," they had said, "a police chief needs a proper home."

Alex had maintained the exterior's classic art déco charm but had gradually made the interior his own over the years.

The house had always felt too big for just him—something that he hadn't cared about until recently, when thoughts of a different future had begun to take shape.

But Alex knew that life, like the river, was constantly ebbing and flowing, and it was best to move with the current whenever possible and let it take you where it wanted you to go.

# Nine

Jan Patton stared at the picture that Serenity had just emailed to her. Serenity was right. It was the perfect piece to highlight in their marketing program. Especially since her next gallery opening would be in Spring Falls, a town named for where the river fell a few hundred feet before heading to where it ended in Silver Lake.

Spring Falls was a place she would love to see in person, but that would mean she'd have to travel, and that wasn't going to happen.

Jan sent Serenity's picture of her painting off to the woman who put together their marketing along with a few suggestions for the copy. She was the facilitator, not the doer, for her clients. As an agent, she prodded and poked until her clients got their work done. She helped them make decisions and then passed the doing of it all to a team of people she had worked with over the years.

*How many years?* Jan asked herself. *Maybe too many.* She was thinking of retiring, having saved up money over the years for the day she made that decision, but then what would she do with herself? Knit? Watch TV? Garden? Read? She already did that. Would she really want to do more of it?

For a fleeting moment, Jan contemplated getting out into the world. Maybe join a gardening club, or something. But it passed quickly. She loved her life. Alone. Well, not alone; she had her cats. Three. Each one different from the other, but they were her comfort and entertainment. If she had a client who had cats, they would share precious cat stories and cat pictures. At least half of her clients had cats, so that actually gave her plenty of cat appreciation time.

*No,* she decided, *I will not retire.* Instead, she wouldn't take any more clients. And there was one client she had never liked, so she'd lie to him and say she was retiring. Since none of her clients knew each other, there was zero chance that he would find out that she was actually firing him. *Or,* she thought, *you could grow a pair and tell him the truth.*

That she was afraid of firing him outright was strange given that she was famous for telling it like it is to her clients. After all, that was her job.

If her clients didn't listen to her, they wouldn't achieve the success she guided them to. She didn't make her clients successful; they were on their way to success when they found her, or she found them. She wasn't a starter agent—she was an expansion agent.

The more she thought about it, the more she knew she wouldn't retire. She loved her work. Instead, she'd tell the client that she couldn't work with him anymore, and stop taking new clients. That would work. And with that extra time, maybe she'd do something different that she hadn't tried before. As long as it didn't take her out into the public for long, she'd be okay.

Getting up from her computer, grunting from the effort, she headed to her favorite chair, where Miss Toes, her oldest cat, would be waiting for her to cuddle while she read a book. First, she grabbed a bowl of snacks and a drink. Her eReader was charged and waiting for her.

But she didn't pick it up. Instead, as she played with her cat's feet—which had earned her the name Miss Toes because she loved it so much, purring so loudly that she vibrated—Jan contemplated what to tell Serenity about Lucas. Would she lie, be evasive, or tell the truth?

The rain tapped gently against her windows, creating a soothing backdrop to Miss Toes' rumbling purr. Her apartment was exactly as she liked it—shelves lined with art books and novels, walls decorated with small original pieces from her clients, everything in its place.

The soft lamp beside her chair cast a warm circle of light that held the gray day at bay. This was her sanctuary, perfectly arranged to keep the messy outside world at a comfortable distance.

At Serenity's request, she had been looking for Lucas for months. Before Serenity had told her that Lucas was the father of her daughter Sam, she had known Lucas only as one of the first buyers of Serenity's paintings.

But then, a few years ago, he had stopped buying paintings from any of her clients. Jan knew Lucas purchased paintings for his clients, not himself, and she had assumed he had retired from that work.

Why Serenity had decided to let Lucas know thirty years after the fact that he had fathered a child, Jan didn't know. It seemed weird to her. Why not let things be as they were? *But wasn't that Serenity's right,* she asked herself. Maybe something had changed. Or maybe her daughter wanted to know her heritage, or Serenity was finally feeling secure enough to reach back into the past.

Jan knew from representing artists that timing was everything. Some truths couldn't emerge until the right moment, like a photograph developing slowly in a chemical bath. Perhaps this was simply Serenity's time for this particular truth.

But she had said none of that and simply started looking. She talked to other agents and buyers, and after months of looking, had found him. But what to do next was where she was stuck.

And she was well and truly stuck. The information she'd uncovered sat like a weight in the locked drawer of her desk. The obituary had been from just three months ago—Lucas Ng had died after a brief illness. The photograph showed an elegant man standing beside a much younger woman identified as his wife. There were no children or other relatives mentioned.

It saddened her to know that Lucas had died never knowing he had a daughter. It was tragic. But since there were no siblings for Sam, did it matter if she found her father now? How could she tell Serenity that her search had ended at a grave?

Sensing her distress, her other two cats hopped onto her chair. Copper almost knocked over her snacks before settling into her lap along with Miss Toes. Blackie stayed on the chair arm, declaring her independence from the other two.

Addressing all three, Jan asked them what she should do. How long could she keep the secret of what she had found?

Finding Lucas hadn't been in her job description after all. And how could she tell her this news over the phone? But Serenity was one of her favorite clients, and if she was ever going to meet one face-to-face, it would be her.

Their relationship had evolved beyond the typical agent-client dynamic over the years. Jan had watched Serenity's art transform as her life changed—the early pieces filled with isolation and longing, then the gradual opening up, colors becoming more vibrant, spaces more inviting.

She'd heard the change in Serenity's voice when she spoke about returning to Lazy Rivers, about reconnecting with her mother, about watching her daughter blossom. How could she be the one to punch a hole in that newfound happiness?

All three cats stared at her, but none of them gave her an answer. Instead they put their heads down and went to sleep. Not wanting to disturb then, Jan closed her eyes and willed herself to relax, hoping that if she fell asleep, when she woke up, she'd have her answer as to when and what to tell Serenity about Lucas.

As she drifted off to sleep, she thought that the truth would find its way to Serenity eventually—truths always did. But did it have to come from her? And did it have to be now, when Serenity was preparing for her gallery opening, when everything in her life seemed finally to be falling into place?

Jan's phone lit up with a text. Serenity again, asking if she'd had any luck finding Lucas. The question sat there unanswered, as insistent as the rain on her roof.

# Ten

B etty Jean wondered what was going on in the world that she had two strangers in the diner within days of each other. Lazy Rivers was not a town that people headed to as a destination. She thought it was a bit tragic since it was such a beautiful town, but on the other hand she loved that it was a town so small, she figured she knew everyone.

But she didn't know the man who had bumped into Pete, nor had she known the man who had stopped in the day before for coffee and pancakes.

The first man—the one who'd come in yesterday, wearing a black stocking hat—had ordered with the precision of someone who knew exactly what he wanted. No substitutions, coffee black, a nod of thanks and a small smile. She'd noticed his careful gaze taking in every corner of the diner, lingering on the old photographs on the wall.

The second stranger, the one who'd bumped Pete, had a different energy altogether—hurried, almost desperate, and angry, his eyes darting around as if searching for something specific. Both men carried themselves as if they didn't belong, but somehow felt entitled to be there.

It was a fluke that she was at the diner both times. She and Joseph were spending more time at home than ever before. Well, maybe not Joseph. He was loving teaching his new-found nephew Tyler how to cook, and guiding Ethan through the mechanics of managing the diner.

Ethan's girlfriend, Amy, now fiancée as of a month ago, was an excellent waitress and had an eye for detail. Between Ethan, Tyler, and Amy, the diner was running better than it ever had. So well, in fact, she and Joseph were planning a road trip in a few weeks. Exactly where hadn't been decided yet. But they would probably stay within a few hours of town just in case they needed to come back. She had already declared that Falling Waters was a destination, and they would plan the trip with that in mind.

The other change in their life was Lizzy. Instead of someone they knew but rarely saw, they now had Sunday dinners together with Lizzy's family, which often included Alex and Randy, and of course, Tyler, too. Finding out Lizzy was his half-sister had opened Joseph's heart. He'd always had a kind heart, but he had protected it. Only Betty Jean had been allowed into that space. Now, their entire world had expanded.

No longer was Joseph the hulking presence who hung out in the doorway between the diner and the kitchen. Now he moved through the space with a new ease, remembering customers' usual orders, asking about their families, even occasionally sharing a quick laugh.

It was as if discovering his connection to Lizzy had somehow freed him from an invisible burden—the weight of thinking he was alone in the world except for Betty Jean. She loved watching this transformation, loved seeing others finally recognize the warmth she'd always known existed behind his quiet exterior.

The only thing that clouded their days was that he now knew that Snags, Tyler's father, was his half brother. And that fact haunted him. Should he get to know him? Ignore him? Snags would remain in prison all his life for killing his mother. He had lashed out in anger when Iris had told him who his father was. That anger had been with Snags all his life. Would it have been different if he had known that Big Mike was his father?

Joseph knew that anger. Sometimes he felt it inside himself, and he knew it was because of Betty Jean it had never festered and erupted the way that Snag's had. And what Joseph had that neither Lizzy nor Snags had, he grew up with Big Mike acting like his father. And although Big Mike had been a taskmaster, he'd had a big heart, wanting to help as many people as he could.

Which he had. But obviously his big heart had extended to loving more than one woman. Joseph didn't really think that had been just his heart talking, but still he knew his father had also loved Lizzy's mother, Mae.

Joseph had seen it when he and his father would go over to help Mae out around the house and garden. When the work was over, he'd be allowed to play with Lizzy. That is until his mother, Sarah, had put a stop to it. Big Mike hadn't gone over just to be kind, Joseph could see even then that his father wanted to be there.

Joseph wondered how his father had handled the fact that Mae could see his memories. Did that make it better or worse for him?

Betty Jean knew all this about how her husband Joseph felt about what he had learned and how it changed his life, because they had spent many hours talking things over. Working through the revelations. Growing together. The revelations could have split them apart, but they didn't.

Instead, it had strengthened an already strong bond between them. They'd weathered it together, like they had everything else in their decades, side by side. The revelations had been shocking, yes, but there was also something oddly comforting about seeing the pieces fall into place—understanding why Big Mike had made certain choices, why certain names had always caused a tension in the air.

The truth had a way of making the past make sense, even as it complicated the present. Betty Jean sometimes wondered if this was how archaeologists felt, uncovering layer after layer, each discovery both answering questions and creating new ones.

Betty Jean could not see how someone could love anyone else more than she loved Joseph. So, seeing him happy in the kitchen or taking time to speak to someone in the diner made her heart swell with joy.

Still, there was that nagging worry that perhaps Big Mike had loved even more women. And if that were true, were there secrets still to be uncovered?

Through the diner window, Betty Jean could see how the rain had slowed to a steady drizzle, but the damage was already done. The creek that ran behind the post office had jumped its banks, creating a shimmering pool in the side parking lot. The news on the radio that morning had warned that the river would continue to rise for at least another day as the water from upstream made its way down.

*Secrets, like the coming flood,* she thought, *had a way of traveling downstream, building momentum until they could no longer be contained.* Which is why two men she'd never seen before coming to town worried her. She needed to find out who they were and why they were there.

Her instincts, honed by decades of watching people come and go through the diner's doors, told her these men weren't just passing through. They had come to Lazy Rivers with a purpose. And given how recently the town had finally settled into its new understanding of the past, she couldn't help but worry that these strangers might be carrying yet another piece of history ready to surface, that may or may not be something they wanted to know.

# Eleven

In the end, Jan chickened out and sent Serenity an email with Lucas' obituary attached. She wrote, "So sorry," in the email and hoped that was enough.

She'd debated including the photograph that had come with it—Lucas in a tailored suit, his arm around a younger woman identified as his wife. The resemblance between Lucas and Sam was unmistakable in the image: the same high cheekbones, the same slight tilt of the head when smiling.

Her fingers had hovered over the keyboard afterward, wanting to add something more meaningful—some profound wisdom about loss and missed opportunities, about how time was crueler than anyone ever admitted. But what could she possibly say that wouldn't sound hollow? No platitude could soften the blow of learning your search had ended before it began.

She knew that saying sorry wasn't enough, but what else could she do? She couldn't bring Lucas back from the dead, could she? No one could. At least an email was better than the text she was going to send but hadn't because the three cats had all simultaneously given her the look of disapproval that only cats can give as she took out her phone to send the text.

Looking at the three of them watching her so intently that she thought they were seeing right through her, she had stopped and said, "Okay, you're right," had gone to her desk and written the email instead. Afterwards, she had returned to her chair and her cats and thought about the sadness and joys of life. She had her share of both. Didn't everybody?

She supposed the important part about life was what each person did about their sadness and joy. For her, she had found her place in life, which meant her life was mostly filled with the various shades of joy.

Each day she made a difference in her clients' lives. Being an agent meant being a buffer between artists and the harsh realities of the business, between their creative impulses and market demands. She'd become skilled at delivering difficult news over the years: rejected submissions, lukewarm reviews, disappointing sales. But this was different. This wasn't about art; it was about life and death and possibilities forever extinguished.

Jan liked to think that when someone bought one of her clients' paintings and hung it on a wall, each time they looked at it they found inspiration, or peace, or pleasure. So didn't that mean she was okay?

Didn't that mean she was doing what she was supposed to be doing? Not everyone needed to stand on a soapbox and preach their particular brand of gospel. Jan shuddered at the thought. What a noisy world that would be. Well, maybe it was.

But when her cats, Miss Toes, Copper, and Blackie settled back down in the chair with her, she imagined they had given her their blessings. She had chosen the right thing to do. The Lucas thing was done and dusted on her part. Selfishly, she thought that maybe a wonderful painting would come out of it as Serenity dealt with Lucas' death. Or maybe a new book from Samantha Rivers.

She had been a fan of Sam's books from the very first one Sam wrote, and she had only gotten better over the years. So young, and so very talented. Just like her mother. Her mother painted feelings, and Sam wrote to produce and understand feelings. Jan sighed, thinking how Sam's father would have been proud of his daughter if he had known about her.

It never occurred to Jan that Lucas might have already figured out that he had a daughter named Samantha Rivers. After all, Lucas could have seen Sam's picture on the back of one of her books and figured it out. Because, there for all the world to see was a woman with the same hair and eyes as his.

And if he had been curious enough and looked up more information on Sam, he would have discovered that she was

Serenity Rivers' daughter. After that, it wouldn't be such a leap of imagination to think that Sam might be his.

But that would have meant he had picked up one of her books out of the millions of books. And although he might have cared enough to watch Serenity's career, she had never mentioned that she had a daughter.So it was much more likely that he had never known. Besides, if he had, wouldn't he have confronted Serenity?

*Perhaps it was time to do that*, Jan thought. Put the two of them together. Why not tell the world that they were mother and daughter? Why not make that part of the show in Spring Falls? A mother and daughter show. Paintings and books. Why not?

The symmetry of it appealed to her sense of narrative: mother and daughter together professionally, just as they'd reconnected personally. Both women creating from the same wellspring of emotional depth, just through different mediums. And now, with Lucas gone, there was a certain poetic completion to it—the two Rivers women standing together, their artistic lineage unbroken despite the missing branch that was Sam's father.

She'd wait until Serenity got over Lucas's death before bringing it up to her, but in the meantime she'd float it by the gallery's owner. Cindy might just go for it. It was a quirky gallery in a charming town. Perfect for this kind of gathering.

Jan could feel her skin prickle with excitement, which meant it was a great idea. Spring Falls was a small enough venue to try it in. She wasn't expecting a big crowd at the opening since they weren't in a big city, although they may get people from Pittsburgh, PA, which wasn't that far away.

That part didn't matter anyway, because most of the sales would take place online. *Yes,* she thought, *this would be the perfect venue to try out this idea of a mother and daughter show.*

The whole idea of it was so delightful to Jan that the tragedy of Lucas' death faded into the background. After all, she had never met him in person. Well, she had never met most people in person. But still. Serenity hadn't seen him in thirty years, and Sam—well, she had never even met Lucas.

She dashed off a quick text to her marketing team about the idea, asking what they thought about it, silenced her phone, and while her cats purred softly on her lap and chair, lay her head back and took a nap, letting the creative juices flow while she rested, grateful that she had chosen this life. Some might call it lonely. She called it blissful.

She was drifting toward sleep when her phone buzzed, despite being silenced. A text notification from Serenity, the subject line simply: "Are you sure?" Jan's eyes flew open, sleep suddenly far away. What an odd question! Of course, she was sure—obituaries didn't lie. Did they?

# Twelve

They were waiting for the bill at the Thai restaurant when Serenity checked her phone and saw what Jan had sent her. She had gasped and turned pale, turning to Alex as if he would know what to do, the phone nearly slipping from her fingers. Her mind refused to process the words on the screen, rereading them three times as if they might somehow rearrange themselves into different news.

Lucas Ng, 65, after a brief illness... The photograph stared back at her—older than she remembered, his hair now silver at the temples, but unmistakably the same man who had once spent afternoons discussing art theory with her, whose laugh had filled her small apartment, whose genes had combined with hers to create Sam.

"What's happened?" Alex asked, rising from his seat as if there was something he had to do. Emergencies were part of his life. He took action.

But Serenity just shook her head and motioned for him to sit down.

"You can't fix this one, Alex," she said.

The lunch had been perfect. Outside, the rain continued, no longer a sheet of water but a steady stream. If it hadn't been raining for days, and there wasn't the threat of a flood, it would have been a delightful sound. A welcome spring rain.

Instead, everyone shook their heads as they came into the restaurant. They were wet and miserable, wishing the rain would stop. Inside, it was warm and cozy and smelled of curry and spices, with colorful tapestries on the walls and soft Thai music playing just loud enough to be heard but not so loud as to interfere with conversation. It didn't take long for the atmosphere and food to transform everyone's mood.

The restaurant was small, with just ten tables, most of them occupied despite the weather. The owners, a husband and wife who had moved to Lazy Rivers just six months ago, circulated among the tables, genuine smiles on their faces as they asked if everything was satisfactory.

Serenity had been happy, and the food, and the time with Alex had only increased her feelings of contentment. Everything was finally going their way. Once the rain was over, the floods would withdraw.

Her paintings were getting better. Matthew and Lizzy were happy. Sam and Randy were in love. And she was finally admitting that she loved Alex and that he loved her. Words had not yet been spoken, but she knew it to be true.

Everything was right in her world. Her mother would get better, the rain would stop, the sun would come out, and flowers would bloom. She had been smiling with that thought, thinking that her green curry was the best she had ever eaten and looking forward to returning, then she checked her email.

"Lucas died," she said, wishing it weren't true.

Alex knew who Lucas was. Serenity had told him the story months before. He knew Matthew and Sam were planning a trip to find him once Jan gave them a place to start. It hurt his sense of rightness that for a moment, a very brief moment, he was relieved. Had he really thought that if they found Lucas that Serenity would resume their relationship? It had been over for thirty years.

The shameful relief was immediately followed by guilt, then genuine sadness—not for Lucas himself, whom he'd never met, but for what this would mean to Sam. Another door closed before she could even approach it. Another loss for this family he'd grown to love.

Recovering, he took Serenity's hand in his. He loved her hands. Long and elegant, as if they were designed to hold a paintbrush.

No matter how careful she was, there was always a spot of paint somewhere on them, and today it was the color of the sky outside.

"What will I tell Samantha?" Serenity asked. She knew the answer. She'd tell her the truth. What she meant was, how could she tell her? She was the one who had kept that secret from her for all this time, and now it was too late.

Serenity's look, pleading with Alex for the answer, broke his heart. If he could fix it, he would. He knew how to fix things. But not something like this.

"Do you want me to be with you when you tell her?"

Serenity's first impulse was to say no. She was used to doing everything on her own. But that was the problem. She had done everything on her own. This year had taught her it was important to be part of a family, a community. And Alex was family.

"Yes," she said. "Do you have time now?"

The last thing she wanted to do was tell Sam the news. But it was better to do it now rather than carry the secret around hoping it wasn't true. It was. It was a stupid response to Jan, asking, "Are you sure?" Of course she was sure. There was an obituary. Not much of one. No real information. And only a few months old.

The obituary had been frustratingly sparse: "Lucas Ng, 65, passed away after a brief illness. A respected art consultant, Mr. Ng is survived by his wife."

No mention of a funeral service, no details about the illness, nothing about his life's work or passions. Just a few clinical sentences and that photograph. Had he been happy? Had his life been fulfilling? Would he have wanted to know about Sam? These questions would now remain forever unanswered.

And they had missed him by months. That knowledge was what was going to hurt the most. If only she had told Sam earlier. Years ago. But she hadn't.

Jan hadn't responded to her text. Why would she? There was nothing more to say, nothing that could make it right.

"I'm all yours," Alex answered, meaning it in all the ways it sounded.

The bill came, and Alex paid, saying he had invited her when she tried to pay half.

As they headed for the door, people looked up and smiled at them. The people of Lazy Rivers actually liked their sheriff, and they were learning to appreciate the woman he was with. They often forgot that she could see their memories.

Now she was the woman who painted beautiful pictures, had come home to help her mother, and in the process brought healing to their town.

Alex smiled back at them. Serenity was in too much of a daze to notice. Neither of them noticed the man sitting in the dark corner of the restaurant, his back to them, in the shadows by himself. If they had, they wouldn't have known him anyway. He had made sure of that.

But as they passed, the man turned around, and his gaze followed them intently, lingering especially on Serenity. His hands tightened around his chai latte.

Without realizing it, he had started to stand as if to approach them, and then remembered what he had come to Lazy Rivers to do and settled back into his seat

He pulled out his phone, scrolled briefly, then studied something on the screen—a photograph, perhaps—before looking back at the door long after they had gone.

*Soon,* he thought. But first, he needed to know more.

# Thirteen

Raymond Harmon studied the diner from where he sat at the counter. It had obviously been around for a long time. The worn but polished counter, the faded photographs on the walls, the menu that looked like it hadn't changed in decades, all spoke of a place steeped in history.

And everyone seemed to know each other. Conversations flowed across tables, the waitress called customers by name, and the cook occasionally emerged from the kitchen to chat with regulars.

Which meant they didn't know him. Would they all be talking about the stranger in town? If so, what did he want them to say about him? That he was pleasant but forgettable? That he seemed like he might have business here? Or would he be memorable in a more specific way?

He knew his anger was putting people off. The hostility he'd carried for months had become so much a part of him it leaked into every interaction, like the time he'd nearly knocked over that old man on the stairs.

The waitress—Amy, according to her name tag—had been noticeably cool to him when he came in and as she poured his coffee. Had she seen what he had done? Was that what he wanted? Or did he want to pretend to be part of this little shit-hole of a place?

He knew the answer. If he wanted to get what he came for, he needed to fit in. The information he'd found online told him what he wanted to know about property lines, but property records could be disputed, especially ones as old as these. He needed allies, not enemies. At least until he secured what was rightfully his.

Once he got it, he'd be out of there as fast as humanly possible. The town was everything he'd expected and feared—quaint, insular, trapped in the past. The kind of place he might have once liked, but not anymore.

The photos on the wall caught his attention—particularly one from what looked like the 1950s, showing a group of men standing proudly in front of the diner. His eyes lingered on one face in particular, a tall man with a confident stance. Something about the set of the jaw, the way he held himself apart from the others while simultaneously being their obvious center, stirred something uncomfortable in Raymond's chest. Was that him? The man who owed him everything?

Sipping his coffee and studying the diner, he tried to figure out whom to suck up to. Who was the top dog, the big cheese? In places like this, there was always a hierarchy, always someone whose opinion mattered more than others.

It wasn't the cook, Joseph—he'd heard the name called out several times. The man was respected, certainly, but he kept to himself too much to be the center of influence. The young woman waiting tables had pull with the younger crowd, but she was clearly new to her authority.

Which meant the actual power probably lay elsewhere. The sheriff, maybe—whoever that was. Or perhaps the mayor. Small towns like this often ran on invisible networks of influence built up over generations.

He adjusted his approach accordingly. He would start with the waitress, Amy. Smooth over that first bad impression. Leave a good tip. Ask casual questions about the town, framing them as admiration rather than curiosity. People loved to talk about their hometowns to outsiders, especially if they thought the outsider was impressed.

Raymond knew that patience would be his best strategy. Towns like Lazy Rivers didn't reveal their secrets to outsiders quickly. The river was rising, according to the people in the diner. That might make things a little more difficult. But would it matter?

The property had been there long before he was born. It could wait another day or two while he positioned himself properly and made plans. Tomorrow, he would visit the county records office, verify what he had found on the internet.

Then he would take a drive out to get the lay of the land. That is if he could. He might have to wait for the river to go down. But that wouldn't happen until it stopped raining, and the weather forecast wasn't encouraging about that.

All the more reason to make a better impression in town since he might be here longer that expected. One that didn't have people talking about the old man with the bitter attitude. Even though that was exactly who he was.

As Amy approached to take his order, Raymond straightened up and offered her his most charming smile. "Beautiful town you've got here," he said, meaning none of it. "I might just stay a while."

Amy nodded and politely answered, "That would be nice."

*So far,* Raymond thought, *I haven't redeemed myself.*

Betty Jean had watched the old man as he sat at the counter. She watched as he appeared to decide to change from a grumpy old man to a pleasant old man. She didn't buy it. So when Amy went to serve him, she joined her.

"I'll be your waitress, sir," she said, tilting her head at Amy to let her know it was okay. She knew Amy would understand that Betty Jean needed to check the guy out.

Betty Jean had developed a system over the decades—a series of casual questions that revealed far more than newcomers realized they were sharing. Where they were from, what brought them to town, how long they planned to stay—innocent inquiries that painted a picture of intentions. She'd honed this skill over years of working at the diner. Now it was second nature.

"Would you like to see the menu, or would you like to try my husband's famous pancakes?"

Raymond forced himself to smile, ran his hand over his grizzled gray beard enjoying the feeling of it, and said, "I'll try the pancakes."

To himself, he noted he had just met the influencer in the town. And now he knew the cook was actually her husband. That meant they were probably the owners. When he got back to the motel, he'd look them up. It was something he should have done in the first place rather than being a hothead and coming into town blind to what kind of place it was. He wouldn't make that mistake again.

The anger that had fueled him since finding those papers wasn't just about property or inheritance. It was about belonging. About the life he might have had, about the family connections he'd been denied.

The land was just a tangible representation of everything else he'd lost—his birthright, his history, his place in a continuous story rather than the standalone chapter he'd lived. But he wouldn't let himself think about that now. Focus on the practical. The rest was just sentimentality he couldn't afford.

Betty Jean wasn't fooled by his smile. She'd seen too many genuine smiles to be taken in by someone who wanted something. And considering what she already thought of him, she doubted it was something he should have. But being better at pretending than Raymond could ever be, Betty Jean smiled sweetly and said, "Good choice," and went into the kitchen to tell her husband that this stranger was someone to watch out for.

She didn't know about the other one yet, the one who had come in a few days ago. She'd keep an open mind about him. But this one was so obvious that it was almost as good as wearing a blinking sign that said, "Don't trust me."

What bothered her most wasn't just his transparency—it was the calculated way his eyes had lingered on the old photographs, particularly the ones with Big Mike in them. She'd seen that look before, on the faces of people who'd come looking for something they believed the town owed them.

Betty Jean had protected Lazy Rivers and its secrets for too long to let some stranger with a grudge disrupt the delicate peace they'd finally achieved.

Raymond watched as the woman named Betty Jean took his order and headed into the kitchen. He was pretty sure he'd fooled her. But he'd watch and make sure. No one was going to get in his way. He came to get what belonged to him, and nothing and nobody was going to stop him.

# Fourteen

Serenity had texted her daughter Sam to let her know she was heading home and had something to tell her, not trying to soften the message, because what good would that do? Sam had texted back that they were all home. Serenity assumed that whatever she had to tell her, Sam wanted everyone to hear.

*Probably better that way*, Serenity thought. Get it over with all at once. For Matthew and her mother, it wouldn't change their world the way it would for her daughter. Sam would never get a chance to meet her father. *And it's all my fault,* Serenity thought.

A thousand "if only" ideas went through her head. If only she hadn't sent him away. If only she had told him. But the truth was, she had barely thought of him in the last thirty years. Once in a while she looked at her beautiful daughter and was grateful to the man who had given her the black hair and green eyes, but that was it. What kind of person did that make her?

On the way to the house, she and Alex didn't talk. Serenity was grateful that he was giving her the space to just be. The thump of the windshield wipers, the rain on the car roof, and the car going through the puddles on the road were the only sounds in the car.

*It will be okay*, she kept telling herself over and over again. She couldn't allow herself to think anything differently. At least not until the telling was done.

At the house, her daughter, Matthew, and Lizzy were waiting for her in the kitchen. It's where they told each other the news of the day. If they were surprised to see Alex, they didn't show it.

"Okay, what?" Sam said.

"I need to tell you about your father," Serenity answered, the words tumbling out before she could second-guess herself. Just say it, she thought. No preamble.

"Jan found him." She took a deep breath. "But we're too late. He died three months ago."

The kitchen fell silent. Outside, the rain continued its steady drumming against the windows, filling the space where words should be.

Sam's face remained perfectly still, a skill she'd developed as a child to hide when she was seeing someone's memory. But this wasn't about a memory. This was about a future that would never happen, questions that would never be answered.

"How?" Sam finally asked, her voice steady.

Serenity pulled out her phone, opened the email from Jan, and handed it to her daughter. "An illness, apparently. The obituary doesn't say much."

Sam stared at the screen, at the photograph of a distinguished-looking man with silver-streaked black hair and familiar green eyes—her eyes. A stranger who had contributed half her DNA and then vanished from her life before she'd drawn her first breath.

Her fingers touched the screen briefly, as if trying to make contact across time and death. For an instant, her writer's mind cataloged the details—the slight tilt of his head that mirrored her own, the shape of his hands, the way his smile seemed to hold back as much as it revealed.

"Lucas Ng," she read aloud, testing the name on her tongue. Her father's name. A name she'd known but had never connected to a face until now.

Matthew moved closer to Sam, his hand hovering near her shoulder, uncertain whether she wanted comfort or space. "I'm so sorry," he said. "I was looking forward to our trip."

Sam nodded, still studying the photograph. "He had a wife," she observed, her voice detached, analytical. "No mention of children. And now it's too late." Sam handed the phone back, her movements precise, controlled.

Alex stood quietly by the door, an observer of this family moment but respectful of its boundaries. He caught Lizzy watching him, with an unreadable expression on her face. Lizzy had lived with the consequences of secrets for decades.

She'd seen how they shaped lives, how they created absences that were felt even when they weren't understood. Now, watching her granddaughter face this particular absence, she felt a familiar ache—the Rivers women's legacy of choices made, of paths not taken, of connections severed in the name of protection or freedom.

"I need some air," Sam said suddenly, pushing back from the table. The carefully maintained composure was cracking around the edges. "I'm going for a walk."

"It's pouring," Matthew pointed out gently.

"I don't care." She moved toward the hall closet for her raincoat. "I just need to process this."

Serenity started to follow, but Alex touched her arm lightly. "Let her go," he said softly. "She'll come back when she's ready."

"He's right," Lizzy said. "Sam's like you. She needs space to sort through her feelings."

Sam paused at the door, raincoat half-buttoned. "I'm not angry," she said, looking directly at Serenity. "Not at you. I know you just did what all the Rivers women have done. Send the men away. Not telling them about their children. But I need to... I don't know. Make sense of this, of this feeling like I've lost someone I never had."

After Sam left, the kitchen felt emptier, all the joy and comfort that had been there sucked away. Serenity sank into a chair, the weight of the revelation settling into her heart.

"You did the right thing," Matthew said, placing a cup of tea in front of her. "Telling her right away."

"Did I?" Serenity stared into the steaming cup. "I could have told her years ago about her father. We could have found him while there was still time."

"You couldn't have known," Lizzy said. "None of us knows how much time we have."

Alex pulled up a chair beside Serenity. "Sam will be okay. She's strong."

"Like her mother," Matthew added.

Serenity nodded, grateful for their support but unable to shake the feeling that something about this situation wasn't quite right. The obituary had been so brief, so impersonal. Almost as if it had been designed to communicate only the essential fact of death, without revealing anything of substance about the man himself.

And the photo—professional, posed, nothing candid or revealing. The kind you'd use when you wanted to be recognized but not truly seen.

She shook her head, dismissing the thought. Grief often made people search for alternative explanations, for ways out of the finality of death. But the truth was simple enough: Lucas was gone, and with him, the possibility of answers, of connection, of completion.

Through the window, she could see Sam standing on the porch staring at the rain. The water was everywhere now—falling from the sky, pooling on the ground, rising in the river beyond. Like grief itself, flowing through and around them, impossible to contain.

# Fifteen

P ete stood in the entryway of Alex's house, his small suitcase
at his feet. Alex had dropped him off before heading back to
meet Serenity for lunch, leaving Pete with a key and instructions
to make himself at home.

"Kitchen's stocked, guest room's upstairs, second door on the
right," Alex had said, clearly in a hurry, but still taking time to tell
Pete about the house. "I'll be back after lunch. Just settle in."

Now alone, Pete took his time exploring. He'd driven past
this house countless times over the years, watching it change
hands from one of the past deputies to Alex, noting the subtle
transformations.

The flower beds that the deputy's wife had planted were filled
with daffodils, their yellow and white heads bent against the rain.
Two Adirondack chairs replaced the porch swing that used to be

there. Someone had repainted the trim from white to a subtle blue-gray.

Inside, the house had the feeling of a place that had been carefully attended to but not fully inhabited. Clean lines, comfortable furniture, nothing excessive or out of place. A bachelor's home, but one with taste and intention.

Pete carried his suitcase upstairs, his knees protesting at each step. The wood creaked pleasantly underfoot, solid oak planks that had been recently refinished.

The walls were a warm beige, decorated with framed photographs of Lazy Rivers through the seasons, many of them looking out over the river—the river that right now was threatening to overflow.

The guest room surprised him. It wasn't just a spare room with a bed, but a thoughtfully-arranged space with a quilt that looked handmade, a reading lamp, and a small desk by the window. From here, Pete could see down to the street and out toward the western edge of town.

"This is nice," Pete said aloud, setting his suitcase on the bed. "Real nice."

He noticed the closet stood empty, hangers waiting. A fresh bar of soap sat wrapped on the bathroom counter. Alex had prepared for a guest. The thought warmed him more than he cared to admit.

After unpacking his few belongings, Pete wandered back downstairs. The rain continued its steady drumming on the roof, but inside it was warm and dry. He settled into an armchair in the living room, looking around at the space that would be his home until the flooding subsided.

His thoughts drifted, as they often did these days, to his farm. He'd been thinking about selling it for months now. Since Nancy had passed years ago, the place had felt too big, too empty, too full of memories.

The farm had been in his family for generations. His great-grandfather had staked the original claim, built the first structures with timber from the property itself. Pete had been born in that house, just like his father before him.

"Nancy always tried to make that house nice even though she hadn't wanted to live there," Pete murmured to the empty room, the memory of his wife warming him. "Kept it looking nice despite not wanting to be a farmer's wife. Made it a home anyway. She'd always kept fresh flowers on the table, even in winter. Said a home needed something alive in it besides the people."

Pete sighed. After all these years, he still missed her, and he knew he always would. He was counting on seeing her again. He couldn't imagine a universe that would keep him apart from her forever.

Nancy Miller had been the town librarian when he'd met her, pretty and smart and far too good for him, everyone had said. Including him. But she'd loved him anyway, stuck with him through the lean years and the good ones.

His mother had lived there too, of course. Annie. Dead when Pete was just eight. Heart gave out, they said. But he always thought it was more that her spirit gave out. She'd never seemed happy, his mother. He remembered how pretty she was, how she would sing when she thought nobody was listening.

His father had changed after she died. He wasn't meaner; he had always had a mean streak. But he was more withdrawn and distant. It was as if part of him went with Annie. The farm had felt emptier after that. Just him and his father, working side by side but rarely speaking. The kind of silence that grows heavier with each passing year until it becomes its own presence in a room.

Pete thought about his mother, about how she always had a sadness about her. Perhaps, like his wife, she hadn't wanted to be a farmer's wife either. Farming's a hard life even if you like it. Maybe it was too hard for a woman like his mother. She was... delicate somehow. Like she'd been broken and put back together, but not quite the same.

What Pete never said to anyone was how sometimes he'd catch his mother staring off toward town with a look of such longing it had made his child's heart ache. Or how she'd kept a small box locked in her dresser drawer that he'd found after her death, empty except for a pressed flower. Nothing that told him why she kept it.

Looking around Alex's living room, Pete suddenly saw it with fresh eyes. Maybe this was the answer. Not just a temporary refuge from the flood, but a glimpse of a possible future. A smaller place, manageable, within walking distance to the diner and the town center. Somewhere he could age without the constant reminder of all he'd lost, all that had never been.

"I think it's time," he said aloud, making the decision final in his mind. "Time to sell the farm."

He had no kids, no family to leave it to. He had been leasing out the land for farming these past few years anyway. Might as well make it official. Turn it over to someone who'd work it proper.

Maybe he'd talk to John and Randy about it. They'd done good work at Lizzy's place. The two of them knew how to pull the best out of something. Maybe they'd know someone who had a place like this to sell to him. Something in town where he could be closer to people all the time.

The river would keep rising overnight. He didn't need anyone to tell him that; he'd been through too many spring floods not to know what was coming. But at Alex's house, Pete felt safe. Protected. For the first time in longer than he could remember, he felt like he belonged somewhere, even if just temporarily.

Pete walked to the kitchen and put on a kettle for tea, opening cupboards until he found Alex's collection of mugs. He smiled at how neatly they were arranged. The man had a place for everything.

And as the rain continued its steady rhythm on the roof, Pete allowed himself to imagine a different kind of future than the lonely one he'd resigned himself to. He'd wait for Alex to return from his lunch with Serenity to share these thoughts. Alex would understand. He always did.

# Sixteen

Stepping out of the house, Sam felt numb. She contemplated just walking away. Right through the rain. To somewhere else. Anywhere. The news that her father had died before she could meet him left a hollow ache in her chest.

*It's not fair,* she said to herself. She wanted to scream it into the wind, but she also didn't want to scare the people she knew were watching her from the house. Four people who loved her. They didn't kill him. It wasn't their fault.

She could blame her mother, though. Part of her thought she had a right to do so. If Serenity had only told her sooner. But the rational part of her wouldn't let her go there. Her mother was only following the River's women's protocol.

It was no one's fault, actually. She could even blame herself for not insisting earlier in her life, for not stopping everything the moment she learned his name and going off looking for him.

But that wouldn't help. Jan, with all her resources, had just found him. The fact was, they were too late. Their timing sucked, but it was no one's fault. She could just as easily blame her father for dying. For not knowing he had a daughter. *He should have felt that he did. Right?*

*Wrong,* she replied to the voice in her head that wanted someone to blame. *No,* she repeated to herself. *It was no one's fault.* But that didn't make the grief any less real. She had lost someone she never had the chance to know.

But she could still be angry, couldn't she? Angry that she never met him. Angry at the stupid Rivers women's policy of not telling the men who fathered their children that they had a child. She would not follow this absurd idea. That was the one thing she could do.

Which brought her to Randy, and knowing that it was time for a little truth telling to herself. Plopping herself down on the swing on the porch, she bowed her head, hearing raindrops splattering on the driveway. Yes, the swing was wet. She could feel it seeping into her pants, the chilly dampness a fitting match for her mood. But she didn't care.

With all her ranting about stupid traditions, wasn't she holding onto them herself? The moment she had seen Randy, she had known he was the one. Even just seeing his eyes in her rearview mirror had made her run away to Spring Falls for a few days.

But love at first sight was such a ridiculous cliché she couldn't bring herself to admit it had happened to her. Besides, she wanted to be free. She wanted to go off at a moment's notice and see the world.

*Or,* she asked herself, *is it I want to run whenever things get too intense?* When people noticed she knew things she shouldn't, or she naively told them she could see memories. It scared people. First they were intrigued. But then they realized what that would mean for them, and they'd pull away. And she'd leave town.

But Randy had none of those reactions. Even when she told him some of his childhood memories, just to see what he did with them, he did nothing at all. He simply said that it was nice to see his memories again from someone else's perspective.

She remembered telling him about the time he had fallen from the oak tree behind his house when he was nine. Rather than being spooked, he'd smiled and said, "I'd forgotten about that. Dad brought me ice cream after the doctor put in the stitches."

Like Matthew, he let it be just one of the things the person he loved could do. And she knew that he loved her. He told her in countless ways. Told her he'd wait. Told her she was the one for him.

*I'm an idiot,* she mumbled to herself. She knew that if she still wanted to go off on a trip, he wouldn't mind. He'd be waiting for her to come back. Perhaps she and Matthew wouldn't be looking for her father, but maybe they'd still take a trip and Matthew would write his story about it, and she'd write hers.

"I'm wet, and I'm an idiot," Sam said to herself.

Getting up, she walked back into the house to change her clothes, announcing to the people sitting in the living room pretending to read that she was changing her clothes and then going to see Randy.

Seeing her mother's worried face that she was trying to hide behind a smile, Sam walked over and hugged her.

"I'm really not mad, Mom. But it's time to change how we've always done things."

To her surprise, tears started running down her mother's face, a rare sight that made Sam realize just how much Serenity had been holding inside.

"Really, it's okay, Mom," she said, hugging her tighter.

"Tears of agreement," Serenity said, glancing over at Alex, who was standing in the doorway between the kitchen and living room.

Sam looked at her mom and Alex and whispered, "Do it, Mom. I'm going to."

Then she bounded up the stairs. Within minutes she was back, waving at them as she went out the door. All four of them walked to the window and watched her drive away.

Serenity felt Alex beside her and reached out to hold his hand. She felt him startle, and then relax, and a smile spread across his face. She'd talk to him later, but she knew he understood the message. And that was enough for now.

Sam didn't bother calling Randy to tell him she was coming. She knew he was at home; the rain kept him in more than he wanted. He had told her he'd be using the time to work on his own house while he waited to start the next project he and his dad would work on.

She knew one project was helping Tyler fix up the house he had bought with the money his grandmother had left him. Tyler worked at the diner, but he also helped Randy and John in construction. Sam thought Tyler was just drinking in as much male-father-friend energy that he could, having missed out on it all those years.

Pulling into Randy's driveway, she turned off the engine, pulled down the mirror and checked to make sure she looked decent.

How he knew she was coming didn't matter. It was that he was there, an open door waiting for her. She stepped through the door into his arms, the scent of sawdust and coffee enveloping her as she sighed, thinking that she had finally come home. Not to a place, but to a person.

# Seventeen

Tyler Clarkson sat watching the news, the endless reports of flooding and road closures across the county. He didn't know what else to do with himself. After his grandmother died, he had a choice: keep moving on, be a wanderer looking for something. Or stay in Lazy Rivers.

He chose to stay. It was the first time he'd chosen to root himself anywhere since he was twenty. The feeling was both comforting and terrifying. After all, he had discovered that he had family. And friends. Joseph was his uncle, and Lizzy was his aunt. How he could end up with a family like that was a miracle, because they both came with an entire set of friends and opportunities.

Sam had taken him under her wing and helped him in ways he didn't know he needed help. She called, stopped by, brought food, took him shopping, and introduced him all over town. She'd even dragged him to the library to get a library card, insisting it was 'a basic necessity of civilized life.

The town had known who he was. After all, he was the son of the man who killed his mother. Snags was famous for all the wrong reasons. But Sam and all of her family reminded Tyler constantly that he was not his father, the man who had put his grandmother in a coma, and who was now in prison for her murder since she had died. Or his grandfather, Big Mike, for that matter.

He was the grandson of Iris Clarkson, a warm, loving, strong, and capable woman. And he could be that, too. Or was already as Sam kept telling him. And Sam was not the only one who was watching out for him. Lizzy was acting as a grandmother to him. Joseph was teaching him how to run the diner, just in case he wanted to end up owning it.

Ethan, who could have been jealous of him, wasn't. Instead, Ethan was helping him too. He had already mastered the breakfast rush, learning the rhythm of orders and the precise timing needed to keep everything flowing smoothly.

And Sam's friend Randy—well more than a friend—and his father John were showing him the construction business. They had also helped him buy the tiny cottage where he was now living. It was a fixer-upper, but they promised to help him fix it up. His grandmother had left him enough money to buy the house and repair it, but he still needed to earn a living, which is why the diner and the construction jobs were helping him.

When he first moved into the cottage just a month ago, it felt as if a swarm of ants had helped him. Every person he knew showed up. All the Rivers women. Alex, Joseph, Betty Jean, Mama Ruth, Brad, Tom and of course Randy and John.

Each of them took on a project for a few days, and when they retreated, he had a warm, comfortable place to live. The cottage smelled of fresh paint and new wood, nothing like the musty apartments he'd drifted through over the years.

Yes, it still needed some repair work, mostly on the outside, but it was already better than any place he had ever lived.

What he liked most about it was that it was out of town, on a few acres of land. That's what he wanted. A place where nature was the focus. And since Pete's land and the Rivers women's land, bordered his property, he knew he would never be surrounded by a development.

He wasn't on the river, but he could walk there within minutes. He was already looking forward to doing that once the weather cleared. The old path would take him through Pete's land, but Pete said he was welcome to use it anytime he wanted. And if he felt like it, he could clear the path since it was so overgrown.

*A project for the summer,* Tyler thought. Pete had mentioned that the path was one that Big Mike himself had helped clear. The thought of walking in his grandfather's footsteps gave Tyler mixed feelings.

But he needed projects. Something to keep himself busy. Because sometimes doubts crept in. Worry about his future. Worry about his father, now in prison for murder. Should he go see him? What would he say? Was it required of him? Every time he thought about facing Snags, his stomach knotted. The man had stolen his grandmother from him, but he was still his father—his blood.

And then there was his future. Would he live out here all alone for the rest of his life? Did he want to own the diner? Did he want to build things? What did he want?

Samantha had caught him biting his nails one day and made him tell her about the worries that sometimes overtook him. She had laughed a little, then taken his hands and said, "Tyler, you are only twenty-five. Your whole life is in front of you. And everything you knew has been upended. Of course, you are not sure. You don't have to be.

"This is your time to explore and experiment, not the time to worry about your future. You have a big family now. No matter what you choose, we will support you."

The concept of unconditional support was still so foreign to Tyler that sometimes he found himself waiting for the catch, the moment when they'd all decide he wasn't worth the trouble. It had taken all of his willpower not to cry in front of her. Sam had wisely headed into his kitchen to make coffee, giving him the chance to collect himself.

Still, he couldn't shake the feeling that he should be doing something. He wasn't due at the diner today, and there were no construction jobs because of the rain, but the drive to be useful made him edgy. But the rain kept coming down. His nonexistent yard was a muddy mess. The weather forecast on the TV droned on about how much rain there was and the possibility of flooding everywhere.

What could he do? He had to do something. He was bored. Making up his mind, he decided to go to the diner and help if they needed it, and if not, just sit there until someone came along that needed some help. He threw a change of clothes into his backpack, just in case he was needed out in the rain, and headed to his truck.

The cottage actually had an attached garage, so for once in his life he didn't have to step out into the weather to get into his truck. The garage needed a massive amount of work, but it had a roof and walls, and that was enough for now.

As he drove the short, muddy, rutted lane to the highway, the rain pounding on the truck's roof making the windshield wipers work overtime, Tyler smiled to himself. Doing something made him happy. That was good to know. It was a place to start. And maybe that's all anyone really needed—somewhere to begin.

# Eighteen

After Serenity and Alex had left the Thai restaurant, the man in the corner, who called himself Philip Brown, motioned to the waitress, paid his bill in cash, and left a generous tip, but not so much he'd be remembered. Over the years he'd perfected the art of being forgettable.

Watching Serenity's face, he had a good idea of what had just happened. Which meant he hadn't timed this trip exactly right. He was a little too late. Now he had to decide what to do next.

He stepped out into the rain. Heading to his car, he pulled his stocking hat closer over his ears, and flipped his raincoat hood over his head. He didn't need to follow Alex and Serenity. He knew where they were going.

The question was, where was he going? What was his next move? He thought he had this all planned out. That was his thing.

Planning. Being careful. But life had surprised him, and all his careful plans lay in tatters.

He wasn't even sure what he wanted the outcome of his plans to be anymore. *Maybe the best thing to do is drive away and let things be,* Philip thought. It was probably the wisest move, but he still hadn't done what he had come to Lazy Rivers to do.

Laughing to himself as he sat behind the wheel of the car, with the windshield wipers doing their best to wipe away the rain, he realized another thing keeping him in town was the rain. The universe seemed to conspire with fate to make him do what he was supposed to do.

When he had looked at his phone in the restaurant, he had seen the warning that the roads were flooding. The safest place was where he was. At least the safest physical space. Not necessarily the safest emotional space.

Philip hoped he could handle the emotional stuff. He thought he had done that well in his life, but now he wasn't so sure. He found himself daydreaming, asking "what if" to himself, much too often.

*Regrets aren't worth it,* he said to himself. That's what his father had always said, one of the few pieces of wisdom the man had offered. "Looking back only gives you a stiff neck."

Then, with the windshield wipers still running, he asked himself if regrets weren't worth it, why was he in Lazy Rivers at all? "You're just tired," he said out loud. Talking to himself in the third person had often helped in the past; maybe it would help now.

"Go back to the motel, get some sleep; you haven't slept well in a long time." Philip nodded to himself. Yes, in months. Ever since he had gotten the news, and regrets had come to live with him. The constant reminder that time wasn't something he could control.

And it was true. He was tired. Maybe if he got some rest, he'd think better. Besides, at the moment, he'd have to let things play out a little.

Pulling his car into the motel parking lot, he noticed a truck idling outside the motel's office. Watching from his car, he saw an old man come out of the door, get into the truck, and pull it in front of a room a few doors down from him.

*Nice of them not to rent the room right beside me,* he thought. He knew the motel was mostly empty. The other day, the man behind the desk told him that people didn't stay in Lazy Rivers for long. It was just a drive-through town.

"That's what people think anyway," he had continued. "But to the people who live here, it is a beautiful, kind, safe place to live. Unless the weather is bad," he had chuckled, as he looked out the window.

"This rain is going to mess with everything. Combined with the snowmelt from the huge storm we had this winter, we are definitely headed for a flood."

Seeing Philip's face, he added, "Don't worry about here though. We're too far from the river and on a slight hill, so we've never had a problem. Still," he had added as Philip had taken out his wallet to pay, "if you don't want to be stuck here, you might want to keep going."

It was an offer that Philip almost took. He didn't really want to be in Lazy Rivers. It was something he was making himself do. A final errand, perhaps. A loose end to tie up.

"Thanks for the warning," he'd answered, and taken out enough cash to pay for a few days.

"I have nowhere I need to be, so I'll just take my chances here."

The man nodded, put the cash in the drawer and handed Philip his keys.

"Have you ever been here before?" he asked.

"Nope," Philip answered truthfully, glad he didn't have to lie. "Where do you suggest I get some good food?"

And that's how he had ended up at the diner the day before and at the Thai restaurant today.

Philip stepped out of his car just as the old man, even older than him, was unlocking his room. They glanced at each other, did the head nod that men do to acknowledge each other, and stepped into their rooms.

The first thing Philip did was strip off his wet clothes and head to a hot shower. The motel's shower was surprisingly wonderful.

He made it as hot as he could stand it, trying to get warm. He was always cold these days.

Afterward, wiping the steam off the mirror, he acknowledged that the man in the mirror was someone he didn't know. Now bald, too thin, the only thing he recognized were his eyes.

His grandmother would have said they were "dragon eyes"-the only part of him that visibly showed his heritage. Otherwise, the man he used to be was no longer there. He barely knew himself, so how would anyone else know him?

The thought was both comforting and terrifying.

Pulling on sweatpants and a sweatshirt in an attempt to stay warm, he climbed into bed—where he had added all the extra blankets in the room—and turned on the TV, praying that it would lull him to sleep.

Maybe after sleeping he'd know what to do next. Leaving town was probably no longer an option. The memory stick with all the information lay on the nightstand, a reminder that it was something he had said he was going to do.

The question that circled around and around in his head was, did it have to be him that did it? He could take the coward's way out and have someone else deliver it.

I'll figure it out in the morning, he told himself, and then lay still listening to the rain pounding on the roof, and the murmur of the TV turned down low, until finally, sleep came for him.

# Nineteen

R andy was on his way out the door to help with the flooding when Sam pulled up. He'd been watching the weather reports all morning, knowing Alex would need every able-bodied person he could get. He opened the garage door so she could pull her car in and then went to meet her.

Even before Sam opened the door, he knew something was wrong. First, she hadn't called. She always did. Even if it was just a quick text saying 'on my way.' And she looked like she'd been crying, her eyes red-rimmed and puffy.

His heart started beating faster in fear as he rushed to open her car door. *Please don't let anything be wrong, please,* he begged in his heart. He didn't think he could take it. Not when he'd just found her, not when everything was finally falling into place.

Without thinking, Sam stepped into Randy's arms and started sobbing. The sound was raw and broken, nothing like the composed woman he knew. He had never seen Sam shed a tear. She was always so careful to keep her emotions at bay. All he wanted to do was beg her to tell him what was wrong, but instead he helped her into the living room, and settled them both on the couch where she continued to sob against him, holding on as if he might float away if she didn't.

He wondered whether she really understood that he would never leave. No matter what happened, he'd be there in whatever way she wanted him to be. He had known the moment he had glimpsed her in his rearview mirror when she had first returned to Lazy Rivers. Until that moment, he hadn't believed that people found each other in this lifetime, but then he knew without a doubt that they did.

So as she sobbed, he waited. Just letting her cry, wishing he knew what was wrong and wanting to do something about it. Instead, he forced himself to be still, and finally when the sobbing eased, and she leaned back to look at him, he pushed her hair away from her face and kissed her on the forehead.

"What's wrong?" His voice was gentle, patient. He'd wait all night if that's what she needed.

Grabbing a tissue from the box on the side table, she blew her nose, for once not caring how unappealing that might be, and dabbed the last of the tears off her face.

"Sorry. I had no idea how upset I'd be."

"Nothing to be sorry about. Why are you upset?"

"I found out that my father died," Sam said, the words catching in her throat, barely able to say them without wanting to collapse into tears again.

Seeing Randy's face as he absorbed what she said made it even worse. She knew he knew how it felt to lose a parent.

"Oh, sweetheart, I'm so sorry," Randy said, his own memories of losing his mother flooding back. The hollow ache, the regret of things unsaid. But at least he'd had twenty-five years with her. Sam never had a chance.

Sam, seeing the truth of what he said, and feeling the weight of loss, took his face in both her hands and said, "I love you, Randy."

For a moment, Randy thought he was dreaming. He had waited so long for her to say it that it didn't seem real. The phrase hung in the air between them, precious and fragile. Only for a moment though, and then he said what he'd been waiting to say to her, afraid it would push her away, "I love you too, Sam. And always will!"

A horn honked outside, and they looked to see John in his truck, the bed already loaded with shovels and emergency supplies.

"Helping Dad with sandbagging. I mean, Dad and I are helping with the sandbagging."

Sam laughed, her heart overflowing with the joy she'd been holding it in for so long, that releasing made her feel like crying again.

"Go," she said, pulling him up. "I'll be here when you get back. And I'll stay if you'll have me." The words carried more than just tonight's promise. They carried a future, a choice to stop running.

"Yes, yes, yes!" he answered as the horn sounded again. He pulled out his keyring, removed the extra house key he'd had made just in case, and handed it to Sam. "In case you need to go home to get more things."

For Sam, that was the crowning touch. He had prepared for her and this moment. Had hope when she'd been too scared to hope herself. *It only took losing my father* for me to *see what I was missing,* she thought, as she accepted the key.

Grabbing the coat he'd left by the door on his way to get Sam, he opened the door and then turned back to see Sam smiling at him with the biggest smile he'd ever seen. It was a dream come true.

When the door opened, John saw Sam standing in the house's doorway, waving at him, and he knew. The way she fit into that doorway, into Randy's life, looked so natural it was like she'd always been there. And he felt his heart burst with joy for his son. Sam and Randy had both found the loves of their lives. Could life get any better?

So for the rest of the day and into the night as they battled floodwaters, Randy and his father, John, smiled despite the icy rain and backbreaking work. Love had a way of making even the hardest tasks feel lighter. If anyone had asked them why they seemed so cheerful while sandbagging in a storm, they would have told them, but everyone was too busy fighting the river to notice.

# Twenty

A lex left not long after Sam. He knew he'd be needed at the station. Flooding was not new to Lazy Rivers, but this amount of water coming down combined with the rapid snowmelt meant this flood could be a big one. The river had already risen a foot since morning.

On the way to the station, he checked on Pete, making sure everything was fine. Alex said it was possible he'd be sleeping at the station. "Got enough food?" he asked. Pete assured him that the refrigerator was well-stocked.

"Don't forget, help yourself to anything you need,'" Alex said before hanging up, hoping Pete believed him.

On the way to town he passed Tate's nursery, and at the last minute swung in to check on them. Inside he found Tom at the cash register helping the last customer check out. The greenhouse was steamy and warm, the scent of wet soil and growing things a stark contrast to the chaotic weather outside.

"Checking on us?" Tom said, after the customer was gone.

"Yep."

Brad, hearing Alex's voice, came out of the office. "How bad is it out there?" he asked.

"Well, if it gets any worse, I might need to call on you to help with sandbags."

Tom pointed to the corner of the store. "Sandbags ready when you need them, just let us know. John and Randy said they'd help too."

Alex thought about Sam heading to Randy's house and figured the news would be out soon, so he told them about what had just happened. Sam had just discovered that her father had died.

"Ah crap," Tom said. "She never got to meet him."

Brad put a hand on Tom's shoulder, both of them knowing too well how time could run out on important connections.

All three men stood thinking about things that didn't always work out the way they wanted them to when an enormous clap of thunder and an immediate flash of lightning reminded them why Alex was there. The lights flickered ominously. "Power might not hold," Alex said, already mentally adding another problem to his growing list.

"Why don't we close the nursery now? Get the sandbags where you think we'll need them the most. You'll need more than these, but it will get us started," Tom said, glancing at Brad, who nodded yes.

"Great. I think I'll send you to the library; it's the lowest place near town. I'm going to put out an alert for anyone in low-lying areas to go to the high school. They can wait it out there until the river goes down.

"And ask for more help with sandbagging...," he added.

Within hours, the town had rallied. As the water rose, the town worked together to keep everyone safe. Alex directed teams at critical points, his clothes soaked through despite his rain gear. Betty Jean, Joseph, and Amy kept the diner open through the night, serving coffee and sandwiches to the volunteers, while Ethan and Tyler delivered them to those who couldn't leave their posts.

Alex stood at the edge of Main Street, watching the swollen river churning with debris, knowing they'd gotten lucky this time—the water had stopped just inches from breaching the sandbagged barriers.

Now they just had to wait for the floodwater to go down, and everyone knew that would be when the cleanup really started. Junk would be everywhere, things the river had brought with it. Alex knew that some people in town liked it. They said it was treasure-hunting time. And sometimes that happened, but rarely. Still, Alex thought, it was a good mindset to have given what they would be facing.

Last year, the pastor's wife had found an antique silver pocket watch that had traveled miles downstream. Three years ago, a child's toy chest had washed up containing vintage baseball cards worth hundreds of dollars, preserved in pressure sealed plastic. But mostly it was broken furniture, trash, and the occasional dead animal.

Pete had come out to help with the sandbagging, saying there was no way he was sitting this storm out. He had always helped, and he would continue to help until he lay in his grave.

Alex had clapped him on his back, wishing everyone was more like Pete, but had also turned away so that Pete couldn't see how upset his words had made him. Pete was a town constant. The thought of Lazy Rivers without Pete's steady presence and quiet wisdom left a hollow feeling in Alex's chest.

While they were sandbagging, he thought about what he could do for Pete. He could buy his land with the money from the sale of his brother's house, maybe turn it into something for the young people in town. That idea had been nagging at him for a while. Then he'd ask Pete to come live with him. He knew Pete would resist the idea of living with him, but it kept nagging at him, anyway. He could use the company, and even though he'd never say so, Pete was the man he wished his father had been.

He knew Pete didn't have any relatives, so he could adopt him as a dad. *Why not?* he asked himself as he tossed sandbags. On their way back to the house, he almost said something, but the phone rang and disrupted the timing.

It was the prison asking if he'd accept the call. Snags, of course. Alex had been resisting visiting him. Why? What would be the point? But Snags kept calling, asking him to come see him. Reluctantly, he took the call.

Once again, Snags asked Alex to come see him. This time he asked him to bring Tyler.

"I doubt he will want to see you," Alex said.

"It's important. I have to tell him something."

"What could you possibly say to him to make anything better for him?"

"Please," Snags said. And for the first time, Alex heard something true in Snag's voice—something vulnerable that cut through years of contempt. It caught Alex off guard, making him grip the steering wheel tighter.

"Why now?" Alex asked.

"Ask the warden," Snags whispered before ending the call.

The call had gone through the truck's speaker, so Pete heard the exchange.

"What do you think that's about?" Pete asked.

"No idea. I don't want to go, but maybe I should."

Pete paused for a moment before answering. "I would. Something in his voice..."

"And bring Tyler?"

115

Pete nodded. "It's his decision, of course. But if you want me to, I could talk to him. It might be important, it might not be, but he'll never know unless he goes. Besides, it might be good for him to see how different he is from his father, instead of harboring fear that he is like him. Sometimes facing the thing you fear most is the only way to be free of it."

Alex nodded and thought about what he'd seen about Tyler. They had both just watched Tyler working with the men moving sandbags. Volunteering to help. And of course they had seen him working at the diner with Ethan. The two of them worked perfectly as a team. But there was always a pain behind Tyler's eyes, a wariness that might never go away. But a face-to-face with the man who had killed his grandmother might help that.

"Let's get some rest. Then we'll go talk to Tyler."

*And talk to Pete about my plan for him too*, Alex thought. *And eventually talk to Serenity about a life together. But first, get the town cleaned up and back on track.*

What he didn't know was how many things would change during that cleanup, and how it would affect everyone he loved. But even if Alex had known, he wouldn't have stopped it from happening, even if he could have.

# Twenty One

Matthew stumbled through the front door just after dawn, his clothes still damp from the night's work, mud caked on his boots, exhaustion etched in every line of his face. He'd spent the entire night helping coordinate emergency shelters, moving elderly residents to safety, and working alongside volunteers to reinforce the most vulnerable areas of town.

Lizzy met him at the door, her own sleepless night evident in the worried lines around her eyes. She and Serenity had dozed fitfully in chairs by the living room windows, watching the storm rage and waiting for news from the men they loved.

"Everyone's safe," Matthew said, pulling Lizzy into his arms despite his wet clothes. "The library took some water, but nothing that can't be repaired. The elementary school's basement flooded, but no structural damage. Could have been worse."

Serenity appeared in the doorway, her red hair disheveled from her restless night. "Alex?"

"He's fine. He and Pete headed home, too."

Matthew sank into a kitchen chair, accepting the coffee Lizzy pressed into his hands. "Pete was out there all night with the sandbags. That man's tougher than men half his age."

Serenity's phone rang, and she quickly answered it, seeing Sam's number. She put it on speaker so Lizzy and Matthew could hear.

"Mom, you know I'm at Randy's," Sam's voice came through clearly, sounding more settled than she had the day before. "I'm staying here for now, if that's okay."

Serenity caught Lizzy's eye across the kitchen and saw her own relief reflected there. Both women had worried about Sam's grief over her father, but hearing the contentment in her daughter's voice eased something tight in Serenity's chest.

"Of course it's okay, honey. Are you both safe?"

"Yes Randy's amazing, Mom. He and John worked all night sandbagging."

There was something in Sam's tone—a warmth that made Serenity smile despite her exhaustion.

"Get some rest. We'll talk later."

As Serenity hung up, her phone buzzed with a text from Alex: "Everything under control. River cresting now. How are you?"

She typed back quickly: "We're all fine. Matthew just got home. You need sleep."

"Soon. Will call later."

The simple exchange warmed her more than the coffee in her hands. The way Alex checked on her, included her in his thoughts even in the middle of a crisis, felt like coming home to something she'd never known she was missing.

Outside, the rain had finally stopped. The sunrise filtered through the clouds for the first time in days, casting everything in a golden light. The silence felt strange after so many hours of pounding rain and howling wind.

"It's over," Lizzy said, settling beside Matthew and taking his hand. "The storm's passed."

"This part, anyway," Matthew agreed. "But the actual work starts now. The cleanup's going to take weeks."

Serenity walked to the window, looking out over their property toward the swollen river in the distance. She could see debris caught in the trees along the banks, piles of branches and unidentifiable objects that the floodwaters had carried from upstream. She could see a red cooler suspended in the lower branches of an oak tree, and what looked like part of a wooden dock was up against the bank.

"There's no point in going out to assess the damage today," Matthew continued, his voice heavy with fatigue. "The snowmelt upstream is still feeding the river. It'll be another day before the water recedes enough to see what we're dealing with."

"Then today we rest," Lizzy decided. "And prepare for whatever comes next."

The three of them settled into the living room, the exhaustion of the night finally catching up with them. For the first time in days, the house felt peaceful, protected. They were safe, their family was safe, and that was enough for now.

At Alex's house, both men finally walked through the door, equally exhausted from the long night of sandbagging. Pete immediately headed to the kitchen to start fresh coffee, his movements slower than usual, the night's work showing in the careful way he was moving. Alex's phone buzzed again.

"He's calling back," Alex said, seeing the prison number. After the conversation they'd had in the truck on the way home, where Pete had heard Snags asking both Alex and Tyler to visit, Alex was even less inclined to deal with this now.

"You going to answer?" Pete asked, pouring two cups of coffee.

Alex reluctantly accepted the collect call. "I told you I'm not ready, Snags."

"Don't wait too long." Snags' voice carried the same odd urgency they'd both heard earlier. "What I have to tell you and Tyler, it matters. And time isn't something any of us have as much of as we think."

Alex ended the call and looked at Pete, who was setting a steaming mug in front of him.

"Still think I should go?" Alex asked, remembering Pete's earlier advice about bringing Tyler to see his father.

Pete settled into his own chair, considering. "Something in his voice..." He paused, sipping his coffee. "But you're right. When the town's cleaned up, not before. The boy's got enough on his plate right now. Besides, whatever Snags has to say has waited this long. It can wait a little longer."

"My thoughts exactly." Alex rubbed his tired eyes, thinking about Tyler working so hard to build a new life. "Right now, I just need some sleep. Today's going to bring enough surprises of its own."

# Twenty Two

At the motel, Philip woke to sunlight streaming through his window. For the first time in weeks, the constant ache in his body had dulled to a manageable throb. Surprisingly, after finally falling asleep to the pounding rain and howling wind, he had slept through the night. A rare occurrence for him.

He wished he could bottle whatever it was that let him sleep, but knowing that wasn't possible, he accepted it as a gift that he might never get again.

His body didn't want to get out of bed, but he forced it to anyway. He had something he needed to do, and he couldn't be wasting time now. The doctors had been clear about timelines, even if they'd been vague about everything else. Months, not years. Maybe less. And that had been months ago. He knew he was on borrowed time.

Why had he made it so complicated? Why had he felt as if he had to sneak around, check things out, before doing what he had come here to do? There was no point in berating himself about it now. It was done. He had started the ball rolling months before when he had heard the news. No, it had been years before really when he had decided to retire from the world.

Not that he hadn't had a good life, but he had wanted something else. Something away from the world of social media, constant attention, the fighting between people, competing belief systems. The business world had consumed him for decades, but in the end, he'd needed to just get away.

So he had. Left the world as he had known it and disappeared, to everyone but himself. Those years of quiet and solitude had been everything he had wanted. He had thought there would be months of adjustment, but instead, he had fallen into his new life, with his new name, as easily as floating in a pool of warm water.

And that's when he started reading. Everything. Classics, romance, mysteries, new age non-fiction. Months of reading everything until he started narrowing down what he liked.

The small town he had picked to live in thought of him as the hermit in the hills, and that's exactly what he was. He had shaved his head, easier to take care of that way, and wore a black stocking hat everywhere he went.

Seeing Serenity with another man in the restaurant had shaken his resolve more than he'd expected. She looked happy. Content.

The way she smiled at the man beside her tore at his heart. He could just leave everything as it was and leave town.

And do what? Philip asked himself. He didn't have an answer. He wasn't even sure why he had come to Lazy Rivers. Taking out the bag that had all his medication in it, he portioned out what he needed to take that day. The little plastic organizer was marked with days of the week, each compartment a reminder of how regimented his life had become.

Part of him wondered why he bothered. None of it was going to save him. But it wasn't in his nature to give up something he had started. And in this town was something he had started but didn't know he had until he read that book.

Digging through his suitcase, he pulled it out, and looked at the picture on the back. As always, his eyes teared when he looked at it. The resemblance was unmistakable once you knew what to look for. He hadn't been a weepy man, but now it seemed that he was. He blamed it on the medication. Or the illness. Either way, the picture never failed to move him.

A few months before, he had read the entire book, and then he had liked it so much that, rather than donating it to the local library, which was his habit, he had kept it. And read it again, delighted that he had found an author that he liked so much.

One day, he turned the book over to read the blurb, and noticed the picture of the author. At first, it had been a quick glance. Nice looking woman. Then later, as the book lay on his dresser with the picture facing up, he had glanced at it again and it caught his attention.

And it was that picture that had brought him to Lazy Rivers. But the question he was asking himself this morning was why. Why not leave it alone? Why not leave today and forget the whole thing?

*Might just do that,* he said to the man he saw in the mirror. But first, some food. Then decide. He packed his bag just in case. Took the memory stick off the nightstand and put it into his pocket. The files on it contained everything he'd gathered over the past months. Photos, documents, proof. Maybe he'd do something with it. Maybe he wouldn't.

But he'd put his bag in the car, just in case he wanted to leave town. He'd paid for a week, so the manager wouldn't care. He could call from the road. Just making that decision settled him down.

He had choices. Small ones maybe, but just knowing that he had them made him feel better. As he closed his door, turning to lock it, he saw the man he had seen the night before. Something about him seemed familiar, though Philip couldn't place why. They glanced at each other and nodded.

Philip wondered if they were the only ones at the motel, and for a moment wondered what the man was doing in town. Then he let it go. It was none of his business. It was still wet outside, but the sun was shining, and he let himself feel the joy of still being alive.

His stomach rumbled, and that made him happy too. He hadn't been hungry for a while. It was a good sign.

He turned the car toward the diner. He'd decide what to do next once he had some food. Maybe he'd see her again, the young woman who looked so much like the photo. Maybe that would help him decide what to do next.

# Twenty Three

Raymond wondered who the man with the black stocking hat was, but only for a moment. He had more important things on his mind. The rain had thrown a wrench into his plans. Everyone was busy keeping the town from flooding.

Of course, that was a good thing, but it made things a little more complicated. *Or maybe not*, he mumbled to himself. *What difference did it make? He was here to take what was his, flooded or not.*

How he was going to do it was still not something he was sure about. The lawyer had been clear about the inheritance laws, but putting theory into practice was another matter entirely. He needed more information first. *And food,* he said to himself as he got into his truck after nodding to the man.

A few months ago he would have marveled at the sun shining on all the raindrops falling off trees, taken a moment to breathe in the clean fresh air. But that was before. Before his parents had died. Before he'd found the paper. Before he searched out the truth of who he was. Before he discovered he was owed something. And he was going to get it.

It didn't matter now that life before had been a good one, as far as lives go. He'd been married to a nice woman, but then she died. Cancer. Before his parents even, so he had no one to turn to in his grief when they died. No kids. She hadn't wanted any. And he had agreed. Why not? He was busy.

He owned his own construction company. He knew how to read land, assess property values. Skills that would serve him well now. He took time off and fished and hunted. Traveled a little. Enough to say he had done more than just stay in town, as so many of the friends he had grown up with had done.

Everything had been enough. He had loved enough. Had fun enough. Been loved enough. Emotions had not been something he had much to do with. Why? Everything was good enough.

But now, it was as if a switch had been turned on. Now he was filled with emotion. Frustration. Anger. A sense of being cheated out of something that should have been his from birth. Not love, though. He'd had that. But his inheritance. At first he had questioned whether being so filled with emotion was a good thing, then he had stopped that nonsense.

He felt alive. For the first time in his life, he felt alive. He marveled at how much being angry had turned him from the just-enough man to the I-want-and-deserve-more man. So he had nodded at the man in the black stocking hat out of habit. Not because he cared. Unless that man could bring him back the life he missed out on, he didn't give a rat's ass about him one way or another.

*Hungry*, he reminded himself, and remembered the diner and that old woman who knew everything. Maybe he'd get her on his side and get the information he was looking for. He used to be good with people. He could find that part of himself and bring it back. It might be an act at the moment, but so what? All that mattered was that it worked.

Pulling into the parking lot, he saw the stocking-hat man's car. Was he following him? *Of course not*, fool, he said to himself. *He was here first. And how many places in town were there to eat anyway?*

He could practice being polite with him. Maybe he'd learn something.

Inside the diner, he saw the old woman, and two men working behind the counter who looked vaguely alike. But then it was a small town; probably everyone was related somehow. He'd have to be careful about that.

He found the man with the hat at the counter and sat down beside him.

"Imagine seeing you here," he said. "I'm Raymond." The man looked up at him, and Raymond noticed how drawn his face looked, and wondered what was the matter with him. The only color in his face were his green eyes.

"Philip," the man answered after hesitating a beat. Raymond, now a fully suspicious man (after all his life had been one thing and then it had been turned upside down and was now another thing) wondered why he hesitated.

Then, the old woman was there asking if he wanted coffee.

"Sure," he said, "and those pancakes you served last time. I'm Raymond, this here's Philip."

"Betty Jean," she answered as she poured.

"We just met," Philip added. "We both are staying at the motel just outside of town."

"Oh," Betty Jean replied. He had answered the question of how two such different men were friends. They weren't. The only thing they had in common was that they were strangers in town.

"What brings you both here?"

"Business," they both said at the same time. Looked at each other and laughed.

Betty Jean doubted that they were there for the same kind of business, but since no more was said, she headed into the kitchen to give Joseph the order. She also wanted him to look at the two men and see if he knew them. One thing was certain—neither man was telling the whole truth about why they were in Lazy Rivers.

Joseph took a second to glance at the two men, said, "No, I don't know them," and went back to work. They were busy this morning. The crew, who had worked all night, had come in for breakfast, and she was grateful that Tyler and Ethan had stopped by to help.

She knew they both had worked sandbagging, so they must be exhausted, but they appeared to be doing fine. She noticed how Ethan and Tyler worked together as if they'd known each other all their lives.

*Ah, the resilience of youth,* she thought, and smiled at them both. They seemed to get along well, and that made her happy. She knew Tyler could use a friend close to his own age.

Maybe Tyler would learn more about Ethan than she had. All she knew was he had been raised by a single mother who had passed away a few years ago. His mother had mentioned the town Lazy Rivers to Ethan, and he had come to see it and stayed.

Maybe because of the diner at first, but now she knew it was Amy who would keep him in town. She was a local girl; she had watched her grow up.

If she had been Ethan's mother, she'd have been happy to see him with her. Amy was bright, cheerful, hardworking, and kind. And she obviously loved Ethan. No one could ask for more than that.

Glancing at the two strangers at the counter, she wondered once again who they were. Something about both of them made her nervous. And worried. When the man called Raymond had come in the other day, she had taken an immediate dislike to him. His attitude. But something about him seemed familiar.

The other man she did like. But he worried her. Maybe because he seemed so burdened with something.

Either way, she knew they were bringing change. That, combined with the town almost flooding, had put her on edge. She'd ask the boys to keep an eye on the two of them.

Maybe she could figure out what they were up to before they did it. Whatever that 'it' was, she didn't think it was going to be a good thing. Her instincts had kept her and Joseph safe for decades. She wasn't about to ignore them now.

# Twenty Four

At first, Raymond tried to make conversation with Philip. But that hadn't worked. So instead he gulped his coffee, ate his pancakes at record speed, and left, not aware that every single person in the diner unconsciously sighed in relief.

Not everyone knew that they had been uncomfortable or why, but Philip did, although he had done his best not to show it. Raymond had given off such negative energy, Philip had been tense and afraid the whole time he had sat there with him.

Philip didn't consider himself someone who noticed such things, but it was hard not to feel the anger coming off the man. He wondered where he was going to eat breakfast if that man was always going to be at the diner.

Betty Jean came over to clear Raymond's plate and smiled at him when he looked up. When Philip smiled back at her, Betty Jean decided once again that she liked him.

"That man was a hard man to sit beside, wasn't he?" she whispered. Philip nodded.

"I'll tell you what. If that happens again, I'll figure out a way to get you away from him. And I'll let the rest of the crew know too. Although I'm sure they would have figured it out on their own. We take care of our own here, even the ones just passing through."

When Philip didn't confirm that he was just passing through, she continued. Pointing towards the kitchen, she said, "That's my husband, Joseph, cooking away. He's the one who owns the diner. Then the two boys, well young men are Ethan and Tyler."

Just then Amy came out of the kitchen, and Betty Jean added, "and my replacement, Amy, Ethan's future wife."

Everyone waved and smiled at him, and Philip felt at peace for the first time in months. He thought that if he had time, he might actually enjoy living in this town. However, it wasn't just time that was the problem—it was the question of whether he would be welcome if they knew why he was there.

Smiling at each of them, he said, "Thank you," and went back to eating his pancakes and enjoying the hum of the conversations in the diner and the sense of well-being that permeated the air.

When the doorbell chimed, he glanced up and stiffened, seeing who had just walked into the diner. Amy, who had taken Betty Jean's place because she and Joseph were heading home, whispered to Philip that the man who had just come in was Alex Williams, the police chief.

Philip was grateful to learn his name, but it made him nervous that Alex was there. At least he was alone, but what if he hadn't been? What was he thinking eating in such a public place?

The moment of peace had vanished and now he was afraid. "Are you alright?" Amy asked, wondering what had happened. She didn't think that Philip was even aware that he was trembling.

"Yes, thank you," Philip answered, pushing his now empty plate away and putting twenty dollars on the counter—far more than the meal cost—and hurrying out the door. He was heading down the stairs, his head bowed, moving as quickly as his condition would allow, just as Serenity pulled up outside the diner.

By the time she had parked and stepped out of her car, Philip was in his and driving away. All she saw was a man with a black stocking hat on his head, but a memory flashed by.

It had been a glorious few days of not seeing memories, so it surprised her. It also surprised her that she knew exactly where the memory took place—not just the location, but the specific moment in time.

After hugging Alex, now a regular thing they did, which just last summer would have shocked them both, she sat down and thought about the man in the car.

As Amy filled her coffee, she asked if she knew who that man had been, "such a nice man," Amy answered, "a little quiet and, I don't think he's well. I heard him say that he's staying at the motel just outside of town."

"His name?" Serenity asked.

"Oh, he said his name was Philip."

"Thanks," Serenity said. Looking at Alex after Amy had walked away, she said, "It was weird. I saw a memory as he drove away."

Alex wondered what she meant. It wasn't weird that she had seen a memory; that's what the Rivers women did. It was part of the package of loving one. Knowing that at any moment they could see one of your memories.

Not that they had a choice. It just happened. It was only recently that they had learned to live with it, and the town in general had come to terms with the fact that they could. No longer was the word "witch" whispered behind their backs, although some people still crossed the street when they saw one coming, thinking that would protect them. It wouldn't.

"What was weird about it?"

"I knew the place. It was a gallery in SoHo where Jan had placed some of my paintings. I even know when it was because I was there for that show—my very first New York opening."

"So you could have been in the room at the same time as that Philip?"

"It's possible."

"How long ago?"

"A long time ago. It was at the beginning. That's why I remember it so well. I couldn't believe that I was having an art show in New York and that people were buying the paintings.

"Up until then, I was an artist in my mind only. Selling a painting or two at those weekend craft fairs, thinking that was all I'd ever amount to. I thought I would do that kind of selling the rest of my life, but someone who saw a painting knew an agent and gave me her number."

"Jan?" Alex asked.

"Jan." Serenity confirmed. "I sent her pictures. She said she'd give me a try. Got me into that gallery, and we've been together ever since."

"How long ago?" Alex asked.

"Over thirty years."

"'Wow. So you're telling me that man was at your first showing in New York over thirty years ago?" Alex's police instincts were kicking in. "That doesn't seem like a coincidence."

Serenity nodded. Not understanding how that could be true. "Of course, there were hundreds of people walking through that show. Jan had done her usual amazing marketing campaign to get them there."

Then Alex said out loud what she had been thinking. "What was a man who'd been at the art gallery thirty years ago doing in Lazy Rivers now? Do you think you know him?"

The question hung between them, heavy with implications neither wanted to voice. In Alex's experience, when the past showed up unexpectedly in Lazy Rivers, it usually brought secrets with it. And not all of them were good.

# Twenty Five

When Amy brought Alex and Serenity their orders, Alex asked Amy to ask Tyler to come sit with them for a moment. A few minutes later, Tyler appeared at their table, and Serenity slid over so Tyler could sit down beside her. She looked at him with pride in her eyes. He had grown so much in the last few months.

Even if he wasn't officially a member of their family now, Snags being the half brother of her mother Lizzy, she would still have thought of Tyler as family, and she was grateful that she was actually his cousin. She thought that gave her the extra right to watch over him.

"What's up?" Tyler said. He'd spent the night sandbagging and then working at the diner. He was afraid that if he sat down too long, the exhaustion would sink in, and he didn't want to leave Amy and Ethan alone in the diner while it was still so busy.

"Snags keeps calling."

Alex knew not to call Snags Tyler's father. Tyler had made it clear that he would never call him Dad. Not ever.

"Crap," Tyler said, shaking his head. "Can't he leave it alone? I don't want to see him. I thought I made that very clear."

"You did. And I did. But that hasn't stopped him. He swears that he has something to tell you, and that there isn't much time left."

"Not much time left? Does that mean he's dying?"

"It does. I talked to the warden. Snags has terminal cancer."

"So he didn't escape the death penalty after all," Tyler said, his voice flat. "I suppose it wouldn't be kind of me to say, 'good,' but that's the first thing that occurs to me. Does that make me a terrible person?

Serenity wanted to reach over and hug Tyler, but was fully aware that he didn't want that. He was working hard to be strong, and not fall apart. He needed to work this out on his own.

"Listen," Alex said, 'I understand how you feel. I don't have any good memories of my father either. He was cruel and violent, and I spent years wishing he was dead."

"But if he were alive, and in jail for killing your mother, would you go see him? Even if he was dying?"

Alex leaned back in the booth and imagined what he would do. It took a few minutes before he moved forward and answered.

"Yes. If that were happening now, I would go. Not for him, but for me. Otherwise, I think I'd regret not hearing him out, and wondering what he thought was so important. The not knowing would eat at me forever."

Tyler looked down at the table, took a deep breath, and looking directly at Alex—thinking that Alex was a man he admired and trusted—said, "Okay, when?" The answer cost him, but he meant it.

Serenity watched the tension drain out of Alex and was grateful to Tyler for making the brave choice.

"I'll set it up for tomorrow. That gives you some time to get some rest, but not to put it off. Let's get it over with."

Tyler nodded and stood.

On his way to the kitchen, he stopped and looked at both Alex and Serenity. "Thanks," he said quietly, "for not making me feel like I have to do this alone."

In the kitchen, Ethan was finishing up a batch of pancakes for a family with two kids who had just arrived.

"What was that about?" Ethan asked, seeing how drained Tyler looked now.

For Ethan, having Tyler working at the diner had at first made him mad. Tyler was Joseph's nephew. That probably blew his chance of ever owning the diner himself. He had been rehearsing a speech to Joseph and Betty Jean for months, telling them how much he loved working there. He and Amy had talked about it, and they wanted to know if Joseph and Betty Jean would ever think of selling the diner to them. When they were ready, of course.

But now, he didn't think he had a chance. Unless Tyler wasn't interested. Maybe he wasn't, but he sure worked at the diner a lot.

However, his initial resentment of Tyler had faded away. There was something about working alongside Tyler that felt natural, like they understood each other without having to explain things. It wasn't Tyler's fault that he was the grandson of Big Mike.

Ethan wished he could have met the man. He sure put his mark on the town of Lazy Rivers. *In more than one way,* Ethan thought. Fathered three children to three different women. Part of him wondered if there was more out there. It didn't seem likely. No one had come forward, and after all these years, why would they?

Besides, there had only been four lockets. One for Sarah, Mae, and Iris, and one of them was for his grandchild, Lizzy. So no, Ethan thought, Big Mike's children were all present and accounted for.

All of which made him think about his father. He had often wondered who he was, but his mother had refused to talk about him. When he asked, she would say some stories were better left untold. Finally, she told him never to ask again. And then she died. Ethan missed her every day. She had been kind and generous.—the kind of mother anyone would be lucky to have. Still, he hadn't had a father, and despite hearing about Alex and Tyler's inadequate fathers, he thought it was possible he had a good one, who just didn't know that he had a son.

Maybe someday fate would intervene and give him a clue where to find him. He hoped his mother would forgive his still needing to know.

# Twenty Six

When Tyler stepped away, Alex made a call to the prison and arranged for their meeting the next day. After paying his bill, he called Tyler over and told him he would pick him up in the morning.

"Best to get this over with," he said, shaking Tyler's hand.

He wanted to hug him, show some paternal support, but was that appropriate for a police chief? The answer was "maybe," but he still couldn't bring himself to cross that line, even though Tyler clearly needed the comfort.

Watching Tyler's face go even paler, he added, "Go home and get some rest. You don't want to show up exhausted."

Tyler nodded, saying he'd stay just a little longer until Betty Jean and Joseph returned.

Leaning against the counter for support, Tyler watched Alex and Serenity leave, wondering if Alex would be mad if he changed his mind. Serenity turned at the last minute to smile at him, and Tyler caught something in her expression—not pity, but understanding. She'd faced her own difficult family truths.

He gave her a small smile in return, doing his best to stay positive. He knew what she was saying with that smile. He had family to come to after it was over. He'd have to do it.

"What's wrong?" Ethan asked.

Ethan had watched the exchanges between Alex and Tyler and noticed how Tyler's face had shown even more fatigue. And something else. A cross between sadness and anger.

At first, Tyler just shook his head, thinking, why burden someone else with this problem. But seeing Ethan there, ready to listen, he blurted out, "I have to go see my father in prison tomorrow."

Although Ethan didn't know the entire story of Tyler's life, Betty Jean had filled him in enough to know that Tyler seeing his father was not something that would be easy for Tyler.

"Want company?"

Tyler's head snapped up, startled. In all his twenty-five years, no one had ever offered to accompany him to something difficult.

"What?"

"Want company?"

Tyler stared at Ethan. He had never thought about making friends. People he knew, maybe. But he had always kept moving on, and when he was young he hadn't wanted any. They would find out about his father, and it both scared him and embarrassed him. The idea that someone might want to be his friend despite knowing the truth felt revolutionary.

Ethan just waited, knowing how hard it was for Tyler to accept that he wanted him to be there. For Tyler it felt like another pivot point in his life. And this was a good one, because having a friend was a gift. One he hadn't thought of asking for, but now that it was being offered, he realized how desperately he'd wanted it.

Ethan, although slightly standoffish at first, had warmed up, and then been kind and helpful to him. He and Amy had taught him a lot about working at the diner. *Was that a friend?*

"Really? Why would you want to go to such a terrible place?"

"Isn't that what friends do? Help each other out when they have to go to a terrible place?"

"Actually. I don't know. I never had a friend."

Ethan clapped him on his back. "Well, now you do. I'm going. I'm curious anyway. I won't go in with you to talk to your father if you don't want me to, though."

"Snags. He doesn't deserve the name of father."

"Got it! I never had one, so not sure how this all goes." Ethan's voice carried no self-pity, just matter-of-fact acceptance of his circumstances.

"You let me know what you need from me, and I'll do it. I heard Alex say what time he'll pick you up. I'll be at your house a little before then. Do you think he'll mind that I'm going?" Ethan asked, wondering if he should have asked permission first.

"He won't. He's cool that way," Tyler answered, thinking how lucky he was to have found people like Alex and Ethan in his life.

"Okay. Go home now, though. Amy and I have this. Get rest. I'll see you in the morning."

"You're sure?" Tyler asked, trying to give Ethan a chance to change his mind gracefully.

"Yep, I'm sure. Now get going!"

Tyler's still wet coat was on the hook at the back door of the diner, along with his muddy boots. As he opened the door, sunlight streamed through the opening, landing at Ethan's feet.

It seemed symbolic to him somehow, if that wasn't too woo-woo. His grandmother Iris had often told him to look for symbols, to trust that the universe sent messages in small moments. He thought it was foolish, and yet helpful.

"Thanks, man," Tyler said, before shutting the door.

Ethan waved him away with a smile and turned back to flipping pancakes on one griddle and hamburgers on the other.

Tyler marveled at Ethan's skill, at the way he moved around the kitchen with natural grace. There was something about watching Ethan work that reminded him of his grandmother—the same focused competence, the same way of making difficult tasks look effortless.

He wondered if Betty Jean and Joseph had thought about selling Ethan and Amy the diner. He thought they would be great at running it. Maybe he could return the friend favor and make that suggestion to all four of them.

It didn't even occur to Tyler that he would probably end up inheriting the diner since he was Joseph's nephew. Having family and friends was all so new to him that he hadn't thought through the implications. Besides, even if it had occurred to him, he wasn't sure he'd want it.

Although he wasn't sure what he wanted to do with his life, he knew that working at the diner forever wasn't it. But having friends like Ethan? That was something he definitely wanted to keep.

# Twenty Seven

S am woke to the smell of coffee and something that might have been pancakes, though she couldn't be sure. Randy wasn't exactly known for his cooking skills, but the effort warmed her heart more than any gourmet meal could have.

She found him in the kitchen, standing over the stove with a look of intense concentration, his hair still tousled from sleep. A stack of slightly lopsided pancakes sat on a plate beside him, and he was flipping what appeared to be his masterpiece—one that actually looked round.

"Success," he said without turning around, somehow sensing her presence. "Only burned two this time."

Sam laughed, wrapping her arms around his waist from behind. "Even Mom's pancakes aren't this wonderful."

She paused, realizing how easily the word "mom" had come out. Before she moved back to Lazy Rivers, she'd been calling Serenity by her first name, keeping that careful distance.

"Well, I can't promise they're edible, but they're made with love." Randy leaned back into her embrace. "Sleep okay?"

"Better than I have in months."

It was true. Despite everything that had happened yesterday—her father's death, the emotional upheaval, even the flooding—she'd slept deeply and peacefully. Something about being here with Randy made the world feel safer somehow.

Randy turned in her arms, studying her face in the morning light streaming through the kitchen window. "You look... different. More settled."

"I feel different." Sam reached up to touch his face, marveling at how natural the gesture felt. "I've spent so many years running from anything that felt permanent. Now, I can't imagine wanting to be anywhere else. It's like I was afraid of the wrong things all along."

A memory flickered then—Randy as a young boy, maybe eight or nine, sitting at this same kitchen table with his mother. Mary was bandaging a scraped knee while Randy fought back tears, trying to be brave.

"Home isn't just a place," she was telling him gently. "It's where people love you no matter what."

Sam blinked, the memory fading as quickly as it had come. Randy was watching her with concern.

"Memory?" he asked, no judgment in his voice, just understanding.

"A good one," Sam assured him. "Your mother—when you were little. She was telling you that home is where people love you."

Randy's expression softened. "I remember that day. I'd crashed my bike trying to impress some older kids. Mom always knew exactly what to say. She would have loved you, you know. She always said I'd know when I found the right person because everything would finally make sense."

His voice caught slightly. "I just wish she could have met you."

"Does it? Make sense?"

Instead of answering with words, Randy kissed her forehead, then her nose, and then finally her lips. "What do you think?"

The pancakes were only slightly burned, and they ate them sitting cross-legged on Randy's bed, sharing coffee from his favorite mug—a chipped blue one his father had made in a pottery class years ago. The morning felt lazy and perfect, like they had all the time in the world.

Outside, the sun was working hard to dry up yesterday's rain, sending steam rising from the wet ground.

"I should probably call my mom," Sam said eventually, though she made no move to reach for her phone. "Let her know I'm okay."

"She knows," Randy said, stealing a bite of her pancake. "You texted her yesterday, remember? Besides, I think she's a little busy with her own romance right now."

Sam smiled at that. "It's about time. Alex has been looking at her like a lovesick teenager for months."

"Speaking of which," Randy set down his coffee and turned to face her fully. "Are you sure about this? About us? I know everything happened fast, and with your father and the flood and—"

Sam silenced him with a kiss. "Randy Carver, are you trying to give me an out?"

"I'm trying to make sure you're not here because you're sad and need comfort. I want you here because you want to be here."

Another memory surfaced, this one more recent—Randy working alongside Tyler and John during the flooding, his shirt soaked through, exhaustion written in every line of his body.

But every time someone had needed help, he'd been the first to volunteer. There was something about his steady kindness, his willingness to show up when things got difficult, that made her chest tight with emotion.

"I see your memories sometimes," she said softly. "The way you helped Mrs. Peterson fix her fence last month when she couldn't afford to hire someone. How you always check on Pete when the weather's bad. The way you worry about Tyler fitting in." She touched his face again. "I see who you are, Randy. And I choose this. I choose you."

Randy was quiet for a moment, then reached over to his nightstand and pulled out a small wooden box Sam had never seen before.

"I was going to wait," he said, his voice uncertain. "Maybe months, maybe a year. But yesterday, when you showed up at my door grieving your father, I realized how quickly things can change. How we might not have as much time as we think."

He opened the box to reveal a simple silver ring with a small, perfect diamond. "This was my mother's engagement ring. Dad gave it to me before he moved in with Ruth, said I'd know when the time was right."

Sam's breath caught. "Randy—"

"I'm not asking you to marry me tomorrow," he blurted. "I'm asking if you'll consider a future with me. If you'll let me love you the way you deserve to be loved. If you'll help me build something that lasts."

Sam looked at the ring, then at Randy's hopeful, terrified face, and felt something click into place. Not the desperate grab for security she'd seen in other relationships, but a quiet certainty that felt like coming home.

"Yes," she said simply. "To all of it. Yes."

Randy's smile was brighter than the morning sun as he slipped the ring onto her finger. It fit perfectly, as if it had been waiting for her all along. "My hands are shaking," he admitted with a laugh. "I've been carrying this around for weeks."

They spent the rest of the morning in bed, talking and dozing and planning a future that felt both thrilling and inevitable.

Sam called her mother briefly to let her know what had just happened, and Randy called his father to share the news. Both conversations were met with joy and relief, as if everyone had been waiting for them to figure out what was already obvious to the rest of the world.

It wasn't until later, as they were getting dressed to face the day and help with flood cleanup, that Sam caught one more memory—Randy standing in his father's garage just last week, polishing his mother's ring and whispering to himself, "I hope you approve, Mom. I hope she says yes."

"She did approve," Sam said suddenly. "Your mother. I saw the memory of you cleaning her ring. She would have been happy for us."

Randy stopped buttoning his shirt and looked at her with wonder. "How do you do that? See exactly what I need to hear?"

"I don't choose what I see," Sam said, then paused, considering. "But maybe the memories I catch are the ones that matter most. The ones that help us understand each other better."

As they prepared to leave Randy's house—their house now, Sam supposed—she felt a contentment she'd never experienced before. Yesterday had brought loss and change and uncertainty. But it had also brought this: a love that felt solid and real and worth all the Rivers women's fears she'd finally abandoned.

She didn't know what the cleanup would bring, what secrets the floodwaters might have churned up, or what revelations might be waiting in the bright morning ahead. But for the first time in her life, she wasn't afraid to find out.

Because now she had Randy to face it with. And that made all the difference.

# Twenty Eight

Alex drove straight to the police station after leaving the diner, his mind still turning over the conversation with Tyler. The kid had more courage than most grown men Alex knew, agreeing to face the father who'd destroyed his life. He just hoped that whatever Snags had to say would be worth putting Tyler through that ordeal.

The station was quieter than it had been during the flood crisis, but there was still cleanup coordination happening. Alex settled at his desk and called the prison to confirm the next day's appointment.

"We'll have Clarkson ready," the guard confirmed. "Fair warning though, Chief—he's been asking for a chaplain. Might want to prepare the boy for that. Terminal cases sometimes get... philosophical."

Alex grimaced. The last thing Tyler needed was Snags trying to play the repentant father on his deathbed, using religion to manipulate one final conversation.

"Thanks for the heads-up."

He was updating his notes when Deputy Wilson knocked on his doorframe. "Chief? There's a man here to see you. Says his name is Philip Brown."

Alex looked up, instantly alert. Philip Brown—the man from the diner, the one who'd been at Serenity's art show thirty years ago. "Send him in."

The man who entered was thin, almost gaunt, wearing the same black stocking cap he'd had on at the diner. Up close, Alex could see the pallor of serious illness, but also something else—a nervous energy, like someone who'd made a difficult decision and was committed to seeing it through.

"Chief Williams," Philip said, extending a hand. "Thank you for seeing me."

"Have a seat," Alex gestured to the chair across from his desk, studying the man's face. There was something familiar about him, though Alex couldn't place what. "What can I do for you?"

Philip settled into the chair, his hands clasped tightly in his lap. "I need to tell you something. About why I'm in Lazy Rivers."

He paused, seeming to gather courage. "Philip Brown isn't my real name. I've been living under that identity for a while, but that's not who I really am."

Alex leaned forward slightly. "Go on."

"My real name is Lucas Ng." The words came out in a rush, as if he'd been holding them back for months. 'I'm Sam's father. The father she thinks is dead."

The words hit Alex like a physical blow. He kept his expression neutral through years of police training, though his mind was racing. Sam had just yesterday been devastated by the news of her father's death.

"That's a serious claim, Mr. Ng. Can you prove it?"

Lucas reached into his jacket and pulled out a worn paperback book. Alex recognized it immediately—one of Sam's novels, with the author photo clearly visible on the back cover.

"'I saw this in a bookstore a few months ago. The author bio mentioned she was Serenity Rivers' daughter, living in Lazy Rivers."

Lucas's voice cracked slightly. "She has my eyes, Chief. The same green eyes my grandmother had. And I know the timing is right. Serenity and I had a relationship thirty years ago. Brief, but intense. Then she broke it off with me, and I never knew why."

Alex stared at the book, then back at Lucas. "Sam thinks you're dead. It was in the paper. It said you had died."

"I know. I had to make Lucas Ng disappear when I got sick. I didn't want anyone to watch me die, so I created Philip Brown and let my old identity officially die on paper. I even made up a wife. Seemed kinder than dragging out a long goodbye.'"

Lucas's hands trembled slightly. "But when I saw that book, when I realized I had a daughter... I couldn't leave this world without meeting her."

"You're dying," Alex said, not a question.

Lucas nodded. "A few months, maybe less if I'm unlucky. I've been staying at the motel, just trying to work up the courage to approach Serenity and then Samantha.

"I saw you and Serenity at the Thai restaurant yesterday and then today at the diner this morning and realized you are the man she's in love with, the way she looked at you, it was obvious. I thought about approaching you then, but I panicked."

Alex studied the man across from his desk. The resemblance to Sam was undeniable now that he was looking for it—those distinctive green eyes, the shape of the jaw. And the timing would be exactly right.

"Why come to me first? Why not go directly to them?"

"Because you're the police chief. Because I figured if anyone was going to check out my story and protect them from some dying stranger claiming to be a dead father, it would be you." Lucas managed a weak smile. "And because time is running out. I can feel myself getting weaker each day."

Lucas managed a weak smile. "And because I saw how you looked at Serenity at the restaurant. You care about her."

Alex felt heat rise in his cheeks but didn't deny it. "What exactly are you asking me to do?"

"Help me figure out how to tell them or if I should tell them at all." Lucas's voice was barely above a whisper. "I've spent thirty years wondering if I made the right choice, staying away when Serenity cut contact. Now I'm running out of time to make it right, but I don't want to make it worse."

Alex sat back in his chair, processing everything he'd just heard. If Lucas was telling the truth, this would turn Sam's grief over her father's death into something entirely different. It would give her the chance to meet her father before it was truly too late.

"I'm going to need to see proof of who you are," Alex said finally. "Documentation, anything that verifies your story before I even consider involving them."

Lucas nodded eagerly. "Of course. Whatever you need. I have everything back at the motel—old photos of me and Serenity from when we were together, my real identification, medical records that explain my diagnosis."

"We'll start there. But Mr. Ng," Alex's voice turned serious, "if you're lying about any of this, if you're trying to scam them somehow—"

"I'm not," Lucas interrupted, his voice stronger than it had been all morning. "Chief Williams, I'm dying. I don't have time for scams or lies. I just want to meet my daughter before I go. And maybe... maybe explain to Serenity why I never tried to find her after she told me to leave. I thought she wanted me gone forever. I didn't know she was pregnant."

Alex didn't think it was his place to tell the man that was a Rivers women's tradition. And like most of their traditions, Sam was intending to stop it.

Alex looked into those green eyes—eyes that were unmistakably like Sam's—and found himself believing the man. Which meant he was about to become part of delivering either the most wonderful surprise of Sam's life, or another devastating emotional blow so soon after the first.

"Alright, Mr. Ng. Let's go look at what you've got."

As they left the station together, Alex couldn't help but think about how Lazy Rivers had a way of bringing the past back to the surface, especially after storms. He just hoped this revelation would heal more than it hurt.

And he tried not to think about how he was going to explain to Serenity that the man she'd seen at the diner—the one who'd triggered that memory from thirty years ago—was the father of her child, supposedly dead, but very much alive. Sam's grief would turn to joy, but would Serenity's reaction be the same?

# Twenty Nine

Tyler drove home from the diner in a daze, his mind still processing everything that had happened in the last twenty-four hours. The flood, the sandbagging, Ethan's unexpected offer of friendship, and looming over it all, tomorrow's prison visit. As he pulled into his small garage, the weight of seeing Snags settled heavily on his shoulders.

Inside his house, he kicked off his muddy boots in the entryway, surveying his home. It still needed more work, but it was his, and that felt wonderful. Something he'd never thought he'd have.

He had changed his clothes at the diner, and he carried the wet muddy ones to the laundry John and Randy had helped him put in, started the washing machine they had also helped him install, grateful again for friends who showed up when you needed them most—then he returned to the living room and collapsed onto the couch.

As much as he loved the quiet of where he lived, his house felt almost too quiet after the bustle of the diner and the night of sandbagging. At the moment it was too empty with just his own thoughts for company. He tried to close his eyes, to follow Alex's advice about getting rest, but sleep wouldn't come.

Images kept cycling through his mind: Snags's persistent calling, the way Alex had looked when he'd agreed to go, and Tyler's own reluctance to hear what Snags wanted to tell him. *What difference could it possibly make after all these years?*

After an hour of staring at the ceiling, Tyler gave up on rest. The afternoon sun was breaking through the last of the storm clouds, and suddenly his cozy house felt claustrophobic. He needed air, space, something bigger than these four walls and his racing thoughts.

He remembered Pete mentioning the old trail that led down to the lake, the one that Big Mike had originally cut through the woods decades ago. Pete had said Tyler was welcome to use it anytime, even suggested he might want to clear it out as a summer project. Maybe a walk would help settle his mind.

Tyler changed back into his already muddy boots, grabbed a bottle of water, and then headed out his back door toward the tree line. It took him a while to find the trail—or what was left of it. It was overgrown with brambles and fallen branches and barely visible.

As he pushed through the undergrowth, following the faint impression of a path, Tyler thought about his grandfather. Big Mike had been a complicated man from everything he'd heard—a charmer who'd left his mark on the town in more ways than one. Three children, by three different women.

Tyler tried to picture him—a young man with a chain saw and determination, clearing the way through dense forest. There was something appealing about that image—Big Mike creating something useful, something that would last.

The question was, why would Big Mike need the path? It hadn't been his land. There were other ways to the river. Why cut a trail through these specific woods? Tyler thought, maybe just because he could—it sounded like Big Mike. Doing things because he could, leaving his mark wherever he went.

The trail wound downward through a grove of old oaks, their massive trunks scarred by decades of storms but still standing strong. Tyler had to climb over several fallen logs and duck under low-hanging branches, but gradually the path became clearer as it got closer to the river.

The sound of water reached him before he could see it—the gentle ripple of the river, different from the angry rush of yesterday's flood. As he emerged from the trees, Tyler caught his breath at the sight before him.

The river stretched out like a mirror, reflecting the late afternoon sky. Although the river had receded somewhat now that the rain had stopped, the snowmelt was still keeping it much higher than usual.

Debris floated along the shoreline—branches, bits of plastic, even what looked like someone's patio chair. But beyond the storm damage, it was beautiful. Peaceful in a way that made his chest loosen for the first time all day.

Tyler followed the waterline, stepping carefully around the flood debris, until something caught his eye back in the tree line, half-hidden by overgrown vegetation and almost invisible.

Curious, he pushed through the brush toward it. What he found made him stop short. Old boards were stuck in the weeds. As he pulled one loose, he saw what looked like foundation stones marking the outline of an old structure. The stones were older than he'd expected, smoothed by decades of weather and water.

Most of the wooden structure was long gone, rotted away or reclaimed by the forest, but he could see the outline clearly. A few pieces of the framework remained, weathered gray and covered in moss. In what had probably been one corner, a rusted iron stove sat tilted at an odd angle, its chimney pipe long since fallen.

*This had been a cabin*, he thought. *But when?* Someone had built a home here, close enough to the water to hear the river but hidden from casual view. Tyler slowly walked the perimeter, trying to imagine what it had looked like when it was whole.

Something about it bothered him. The cabin felt older than Big Mike's time in Lazy Rivers. Had Big Mike discovered it the same way Tyler just had? Did he use it as a retreat? Since Big Mike had made that path through the woods, he must have known about the cabin. Did Pete know about it too?

As he stood in the sunshine, Tyler knew he'd have to find out more about the cabin another day. Right now, he had to get some sleep. By the time he returned to his house, the sun was setting, and Tyler was too tired to do anything but head to bed.

Tomorrow would bring whatever it brought. But tonight, Tyler fell asleep thinking not about prison visits or dying fathers, but about the hidden cabin by the river, wondering who had built it, when, and why Big Mike had felt the need to create a path to reach it. He'd ask Pete about it the next time he saw him—and maybe Betty Jean too. Someone in town had to know the story behind that hidden place.

# Thirty

S am pulled into the long driveway down to the Rivers family home, her left hand gripping the steering wheel as she admired the way Randy's mother's ring caught the late afternoon sunlight. The weight of it felt strange and wonderful, a tangible reminder that everything had changed in the span of twenty-four hours.

The house looked the same as always—welcoming and solid, with Lizzy's flower gardens showing the first signs of recovery from the battering rain. But as Sam walked up the front steps, she felt like she was returning as a completely different person than the one who'd left yesterday morning.

Not just because of the ring, but because of the certainty that had settled in her chest. She was going home to tell her family that she'd found her future.

She found Lizzy and Serenity in the kitchen, both looking more rested than they had the day before when they had all learned about her father's death. Serenity was at the stove making what smelled like her famous vegetable soup, while Lizzy sat at the kitchen table sorting through mail.

"There's our girl," Lizzy said, looking up with a smile that faltered slightly when she saw Sam's expression. "Everything alright, honey?"

Sam held up her left hand, unable to keep the grin off her face. "More than alright."

The silence that followed lasted exactly three seconds before both women erupted in delighted exclamations. Serenity dropped her wooden spoon into the soup pot, and Lizzy knocked over her reading glasses in her haste to get a better look at the ring.

"Oh, Sam," Serenity breathed, taking her daughter's hand gently. "It's beautiful. When did this happen?"

"This morning. Randy made me pancakes, and then he just... asked." Sam's voice caught slightly. "Well, not asked exactly. More like asked if I'd consider a future with him. It was perfect. Completely perfect."

Lizzy had tears in her eyes as she examined the ring. "This was Mary's, wasn't it? John mentioned once that Randy had it."

"Randy said his father gave it to him when he moved in with Ruth. Told him he'd know when the time was right." Sam looked down at the ring, marveling again at how perfectly it fit. "I guess he was right."

Serenity pulled Sam into a fierce hug, and Sam felt some of the tension she'd been carrying since yesterday finally release. Her mother's arms had always been a safe harbor, and even now, as a grown woman making her own life choices, that hadn't changed.

"I'm so happy for you," Serenity whispered against her hair. "Randy's a good man. He'll take care of you."

"We'll take care of each other," Sam corrected gently, and Serenity laughed.

"Even better."

Lizzy was already pulling out her phone. "I have to call Matthew. He's over at the nursery helping clean up after the flood, and he's going to be so thrilled. He's been waiting for this almost as long as Randy has."

As Lizzy stepped onto the wrap-around porch to make her call, Serenity guided Sam to the kitchen table. "Tell me everything. Was it romantic? Were you surprised?"

Sam recounted the morning in detail—the burned pancakes, the way Randy had looked both terrified and hopeful, the feeling of everything clicking into place.

As she talked, she watched her mother's face, seeing joy there but also something else. A shadow of sadness that hadn't been there before yesterday.

"Mom? What is it?"

Serenity shook her head, forcing a smile. "Nothing, sweetheart. I'm just... I wish your father could be here for this. He could walk you down the aisle and could see how happy you are."

The words hung in the air between them, and Sam felt her throat tighten. She'd been so caught up in her happiness that she'd almost forgotten about Lucas, about the grief that had consumed her just yesterday morning.

"I know," Sam said. "I thought about that too. How he'll never get to meet Randy, never get to see me married." She paused, then added, "Do you think he would have liked Randy?"

Serenity smiled. "Are you kidding? Randy's exactly the kind of man any father would want for his daughter. Steady, kind, hardworking, and completely devoted to you. Lucas would have loved him."

Her voice caught slightly on his name. "He would have been so proud of you, Sam. Of the woman you've become, of the choice you've made."

Lizzy returned from the porch, her face glowing with excitement.

"Matthew says congratulations. He also says he's not surprised—apparently he and John have been taking bets on when Randy would finally propose."

"They were betting on us?" Sam laughed despite herself.

"Honey, the whole town's been betting on you two. Betty Jean's been saying for months that Randy was just waiting for you to stop running long enough to catch you."

Sam shook her head, amazed. "I thought I was being subtle."

"About as subtle as a freight train," Serenity teased. "But that's okay. Some things are worth being obvious about."

The three women settled around the kitchen table with cups of tea, and the conversation naturally turned to wedding plans. Sam was surprised by how clear her vision was—she'd never been one to daydream about weddings, but somehow she knew exactly what she wanted.

"Something small," she said firmly. "Soon. I don't want to wait a year planning some elaborate event."

"How soon?" Lizzy asked.

"May? June?" Sam looked between her mother and grandmother. "I want it simple. Maybe here in the backyard here. Just family and close friends."

Serenity reached over and squeezed her hand. "Whatever you want, sweetheart. We'll make it happen."

"I was thinking," Sam continued, "maybe Matthew could walk me down the aisle? I know it's not traditional, but he's my grandfather, and with Lucas..." She trailed off, not wanting to darken the mood again.

"I think that's a beautiful idea," Lizzy said softly. "I'm sure Matthew would be honored."

They spent the next hour talking about flowers and food, about whether to have live music or just a playlist, about which, if any, of Sam's author friends she wanted to invite.

It was the kind of conversation Sam had always imagined having with her mother, but better because it was real, because it was happening.

As the sun began to set, painting the kitchen in golden light, Sam felt a contentment she'd never experienced before. Yesterday had brought loss and grief, but today had brought love and hope and the promise of a future she'd never dared to dream about.

"You know what I keep thinking about?" she said suddenly. "How Randy said his mother always told him he'd know when he found the right person because everything would make sense. And it does. For the first time in my life, everything makes sense."

Serenity's eyes were bright with unshed tears. "That's how it's supposed to feel. Like all the pieces finally fit together." She paused, thinking about Alex and how he made her feel the same way.

"My dad wasn't that person for you, was he?"

Serenity shook her head, wondering if everyone knew that Alex was, and perhaps it was time for her to admit it.

"I wish my father could be here," Sam said again, looking at her mother. "But I'm glad I have you. Both of you."

"Always," Serenity promised. "No matter what."

As they sat together in the fading light, making plans for a future that felt bright with possibility, none of them could have imagined that Lucas was less than five miles away, very much alive and agonizing over how to reveal himself to the daughter he'd never known he had.

But that revelation was still to come. For now, there was just the joy of a family celebrating love, and the sweet anticipation of a wedding that would bring new happiness to the Rivers family home.

Outside, the storm debris was being cleared away, and Lazy Rivers was slowly returning to normal. But change was coming, whether or not they knew it. The flood had stirred up more than just mud and fallen branches—it had set in motion a series of events that would reshape their little community once again.

For today, though, there was just love and laughter in the Rivers kitchen, and the happy planning of a future that seemed full of promise. The past could wait. Today was about beginnings.

# Thirty One

Randy pushed through the door of Tate's Nursery just as Matthew was ending a phone call, his face lit up with the biggest smile Randy had ever seen on the older man.

"That was Lizzy," Matthew announced to the room at large, then focused on Randy. "Congratulations, Randy! She says Sam is absolutely glowing."

Before Randy could respond, Matthew had crossed the room and pulled him into a bear hug that lifted him off his feet. Randy found himself laughing, the joy infectious even though he was still catching his breath from Matthew's enthusiasm.

"News travels fast in this town," Randy managed when Matthew finally set him down.

"Fast? Yes! Sam just told Serenity and Lizzy!" Matthew chuckled, his eyes bright with happiness. "She's over the moon, Randy. We all are."

John looked up from the inventory sheet he'd been working on, taking in his son's face and Matthew's excitement. "Well, don't keep us in suspense. What's all this about?"

Randy held up his left hand, wiggling his ring finger. "Sam said yes," his voice full of wonder.

The nursery erupted in cheers and congratulations. Ruth dropped the potting soil she'd been carrying and rushed over to hug Randy, tears already forming in her eyes. "Oh, honey, I'm so happy for you! Mary would be thrilled."

Brad and Tom abandoned their discussion about flood damage to the greenhouse and came over to clap Randy on the back. Customers browsing the garden center had stopped to listen, and they joined in the celebration as if Randy were their own family. That was Lazy Rivers—anyone's good news became everyone's joy.

"When's the wedding?" Ruth asked, already in planning mode.

"Soon," Randy said, grinning. "Sam wants something small and simple. Maybe May or June."

John shook his head in amazement. "I was beginning to think that girl would never stop running long enough for you to catch her."

"Yes," Randy said, his smile getting even bigger. "She finally realized she was running toward something, not away from it."

Ruth was already pulling out her phone. "I better get over to the Rivers' house. Wedding planning waits for no one, and there's so much to do. Flowers, food, decorations..." She trailed off, her mind clearly racing through lists.

"Go," Matthew laughed. "But don't overwhelm them. Sam wants simple, remember?"

"Simple can still be beautiful," Ruth called over her shoulder as she headed for the door. "I'll just offer suggestions!"

As Ruth's car pulled out of the parking lot, the men settled into the comfortable chairs that were scattered around the nursery's main area—an informal gathering spot that had evolved over the years.

"Well," Brad said, settling back with a satisfied smile, "looks like there's going to be at least one wedding in Lazy Rivers this year."

"At least one?" Tom raised an eyebrow. "You thinking what I'm thinking?"

"If you're thinking that maybe it's time for some other couples in this town to stop dancing around each other, then yes," Brad replied with a meaningful look at John and Matthew.

John felt his cheeks warm. "Now hold on."

"Oh, come off it, Dad," Randy interrupted, still riding high on his own happiness. "You and Ruth have loved each other for years. What are you waiting for?"

"And Matthew," Tom added, "you and Lizzy have been circling each other like lovesick teenagers. Maybe it's time to make it official?"

Matthew laughed, but Randy could see the idea wasn't unwelcome. "Lizzy and I have talked about it. Maybe Sam's engagement will give us the push we need."

"Well, what about Serenity and Alex?" Brad asked with a grin. "Now there's a couple that needs a good push."

"Alex looks at her like she hung the moon," John agreed. "And from what I saw yesterday during the flood, the feeling's mutual."

"They just need the right moment," Matthew said thoughtfully, thinking about the death of Sam's father, Lucas. "Sometimes it takes a crisis to show people what really matters."

"Speaking of bringing people together," Tom said, "maybe we should get all the men together. Have a proper game night. Include Tyler and Pete."

"That's a good idea," Randy agreed. "Tyler could use more friends, and Pete's got stories that could keep us entertained for hours."

"We could do it at Alex's place," John suggested. "Give Pete a chance to host, even if it's not his house. Plus, Alex has that big basement with the pool table."

Matthew nodded enthusiastically. "I'll talk to Alex about it. Maybe Friday night, after all the flood cleanup is done. Plus, we need Joseph."

"You're right. And include Ethan, too," Randy added. "He and Tyler seem to be hitting it off. Joseph says they work together like they've known each other for years."

"Good idea. That boy's been working hard to fit in," Matthew said. "Though speaking of new people in town..." He paused, frowning slightly before continuing.

"Betty Jean mentioned there have been a couple of strangers coming to the diner for the last few days. Said they both seemed... I don't know, like they were here for more than just passing through."

The mood shifted slightly, the easy camaraderie giving way to the wariness that small towns developed about outsiders who lingered too long.

"What kind of strangers?" John asked.

"One older guy, kind of sickly looking. Keeps to himself mostly. The other one..." Matthew shrugged. "Betty Jean said he gave her the creeps. Asking too many questions, but not the right kind, if you know what I mean."

"Questions about what?" Brad leaned forward.

"'About the people in town. Property values. Who owns what land? Specifically asking about some of the older farms." Matthew's expression grew more serious. "Betty Jean said he seemed interested in Pete's place."

"And the timing's suspicious," Tom finished. "Right after a flood, when people might be vulnerable. Could be land speculators or scam artists."

Randy felt his protective instincts kick in. "Should we mention it to Alex?"

"Probably. If he hasn't already noticed," John agreed. "He's good at keeping an eye on things. The last thing this town needs is someone taking advantage of folks while they're dealing with flood damage."

"I'll talk to him when I see him," Matthew promised. "Right now, though, let's focus on the good news. Randy's getting married, and there might be more weddings on the horizon."

The conversation turned back to happier topics—wedding planning, the upcoming game night, and gentle teasing about which couple would be next to walk down the aisle. But underneath the celebration, there was a thread of concern about the strangers in their midst.

In a town like Lazy Rivers, everybody knew everybody. Outsiders weren't unwelcome, but they were watched, especially when they stayed longer than a simple overnight visit would warrant. And two strangers showing up during a crisis felt like more than a coincidence.

Still, those were worries for another day. Today was about Randy's happiness, about love winning out over fear, and about a community that took care of its own. Whatever challenges lay ahead, they'd face them together, the way they always had.

As the afternoon sun slanted through the nursery's windows, the men continued their easy conversation, surrounded by the green growing things that represented hope and renewal.

Outside, Lazy Rivers was slowly recovering from the flood, while inside the nursery and the Rivers house, plans were being made for celebrations that would bring new joy to their close-knit community, unaware how important the strangers they'd been discussing would become to all of them.

# Thirty Two

Raymond pushed through the diner's door around dinnertime, hoping to grab a quiet meal and maybe overhear some useful information about the town. What he found instead was Betty Jean practically vibrating with excitement as she bustled between tables, spreading news like wildfire.

"Did you hear?" she was saying to a couple at the corner booth. "Randy and Sam are engaged! Got the call from Matthew twenty minutes ago. That boy finally worked up the courage to propose!"

Raymond slid into a booth near the back, close enough to listen but far enough away to avoid Betty Jean's direct attention. He picked up a menu and pretended to study it while conversations swirled around him.

"About time," called out one of the regulars at the counter. "We've all been waiting for those two to figure it out."

"When's the wedding?" asked another customer.

"Soon, from what I hear," Betty Jean replied, refilling coffee cups as she talked. "Sam wants something simple. Smart girl—no point waiting when you know what you want."

Joseph emerged from the kitchen, wiping his hands on his apron and grinning. "What's all this commotion about?"

"Randy and Sam are getting married!" Betty Jean announced, as if this were breaking news rather than something she'd already told half the diner.

Joseph's face lit up. "Well, I'll be. Good for them. Randy's a good man, and Sam's finally stopped running from happiness. They are perfect for each other."

Raymond's ears perked up at the mention of Alex's name, when Betty Jean continued, "And Matthew says they're planning a men's game night at Alex's place Friday night. All the fellows—you, John, Randy, Matthew, Brad, Tom. And Tyler and Ethan are invited too. And of course, Pete, since he is staying there during the flood cleanup."

Ethan looked up from the grill, a pleased smile crossing his face. "Really? That's... that's nice. I'd like that."

Raymond filed this information away carefully. A gathering at Alex's house, where Pete was staying. This could be exactly the opportunity he'd been waiting for.

"All my favorite men getting together," Amy said with a laugh as she carried plates to a nearby table. "What are you planning—to solve all the world's problems over poker?"

"Wouldn't that be nice?" Joseph replied from the kitchen doorway. "Tyler will probably need something like that after his prison visit."

"The prison visit," Amy said quietly, her voice sympathetic. "I hope Tyler will be okay facing his father."

"It's good that Ethan's going with him," Joseph said. "That boy could use a friend while he hears whatever Snags wants to say so he can move on."

Amy sighed, looking at Ethan, pleased that he was so kind, but worried at the same time. "You sure you want to go through with that?"

Ethan shrugged, trying to look casual. "It will be an adventure."

Raymond watched this exchange with interest. A prison visit? He wondered what kind of family drama was playing out here, but it wasn't his concern. His focus needed to stay on Pete and the property.

Amy set down the plates she'd been carrying and moved closer to Ethan. "You know," she whispered, "listening to all this wedding talk... maybe it's got me thinking."

Ethan's attention immediately shifted from the grill to Amy, his eyes growing warm. "Yeah? What kind of thinking?"

"The kind that maybe we should stop waiting for someday and start thinking about soon," Amy said with a shy smile.

The grin that spread across Ethan's face could have powered the whole diner. "Are you saying what I think you're saying?"

"I'm saying maybe after you get back from helping Tyler tomorrow, we should have a conversation about our future," Amy replied, her cheeks pink but her voice steady.

Betty Jean, who had been listening to this exchange while wiping down nearby tables, smiled to herself, her heart warm at seeing young love bloom. She acted as if she hadn't heard anything, but her eyes were bright with happiness for them.

"We'll talk tomorrow," Ethan promised Amy, his voice soft but determined. "After Tyler gets through the prison visit. Then we can focus on our own future."

Raymond's attention was caught by Betty Jean approaching his table. "Sorry, I didn't mean to ignore you. What can I get you tonight?"

"Just the meatloaf special," Raymond said, handing her the menu. "And coffee."

"Coming right up. You're one of the fellows staying at the motel, aren't you?" Betty Jean's tone was friendly but probing. "We don't get many visitors this time of year."

"Just passing through," Raymond replied carefully. "Nice little town you have here."

"Oh, it is. Been here my whole life, and I wouldn't live anywhere else. Of course, we all know each other, and look out for each other. That's what makes it special." Her message was clear: we notice strangers, and we take care of our own.

After Betty Jean left to place his order, Raymond continued listening to the conversations around him. The talk had turned to wedding planning, flood cleanup, and the upcoming men's night. Perfect. Everyone in one place.

As he ate his dinner, Raymond found himself oddly affected by the warmth in the diner. The easy affection between Ethan and Amy, the way Betty Jean treated every customer like family. For just a moment, he wondered what it would be like to belong somewhere like this instead of always being on the outside looking in.

But sentiment wouldn't get him what he'd come for. He had a job to do, and Pete had something that belonged to Raymond by right. Family sentiment was a luxury he couldn't afford, no matter how appealing it looked from the outside.

Still, as he finished his meal and prepared to leave, Raymond couldn't quite shake the feeling that Lazy Rivers was the kind of place that changed people, whether they wanted to be changed or not. The question was whether he'd be able to get what he came for before the town's particular brand of magic started working on him too.

Outside, the evening air was crisp and clean after yesterday's rain. Tomorrow would bring new opportunities, new information, and maybe the chance to finally confront the past that had brought him here.

For tonight, though, Raymond had learned what he needed to know: Pete was staying with the police chief, and there would be a gathering where Raymond might be able to make his move.

The only question was how to play it. Direct confrontation, or something more subtle? In a town like Lazy Rivers, he suspected subtle would work better.

But he wasn't good at subtlety—his whole life had been about taking what he wanted directly. He'd sleep on it and decide in the morning, though something told him that in a place like this, his usual approach might backfire.

# Thirty Three

Alex gripped the steering wheel a little tighter as they drove toward the state prison, his mind churning with everything that had happened in the past forty-eight hours.

In the passenger seat, Tyler stared out the window with the kind of focused determination that came from steeling yourself for something unpleasant. Behind them, Ethan sat quietly, a solid presence of support that Alex was grateful for on Tyler's behalf.

The morning was crisp and clear, a stark contrast to the storm that had brought so much chaos—and revelation—to Lazy Rivers. Alex found his thoughts drifting between the happiness of Randy and Sam's engagement and the weight of the secret he now carried about Lucas.

Lucas. Philip Brown. The man was very much alive, staying just miles from his daughter, who believed him dead. Alex had spent half the night staring at the ceiling, wondering when and how to tell Sam and Serenity the truth.

The documentation Lucas had shown him was genuine—Alex had verified it all. Birth certificates, medical records, even photographs of him and Serenity from thirty years ago that left no doubt about their relationship. The question wasn't whether Lucas was telling the truth. The question was what to do with that truth.

Should Lucas be at the men's gathering tomorrow night? Pete had been over the moon about the idea and said he'd put the whole thing together. Which was a relief. Alex didn't think he could put anything else on his plate. The thought had occurred to Alex more than once to let Lucas know about the gathering. It would be a natural way to introduce him to the community, to let people get to know him before the bombshell of his identity was revealed.

But that assumed Lucas would be accepted, and Alex wasn't sure how that would go. The man was a stranger, sick and desperate, carrying a secret that would turn at least two lives upside down. And then there was Serenity.

Alex's chest tightened thinking about her, about the conversation they'd need to have. How could he tell the woman he loved that her supposedly dead ex-lover was not only alive but had been watching them from across the Thai restaurant? That he'd been helping Lucas plan how to reveal himself to their daughter?

And if he brought Lucas to the gathering under his fake name of Philip, wouldn't that make it worse?

Besides, why would he invite a stranger to the gathering? If Lucas was going to be there, it had to be as Lucas. And how would that work?

His thoughts were a jumble of questions. Would it be appropriate to ask Serenity to marry him while Lucas was still alive? The thought made Alex feel sick. What kind of man waited for another man to die before proposing to the woman he loved? But the alternative—asking her to choose between her past and her future—seemed equally wrong.

"You okay, Alex?" Tyler's voice broke through his spiraling thoughts.

"Yeah, just thinking." Alex glanced at the young man beside him. "You nervous?"

"Terrified," Tyler admitted with a weak smile. "But also ready to get it over with. Whatever Snags wants to tell me, I just want to hear it and move on."

"That's the right attitude," Alex said, though he wondered if any of them were prepared for whatever revelation was coming. Yesterday had taught him that secrets had a way of being bigger and more complicated than anyone expected.

From the back seat, Ethan leaned forward slightly. "Tyler, can I ask you something?"

"Sure."

"Do you think Snags actually feels bad about what he did? Like, is this some kind of deathbed confession thing?"

Tyler was quiet for a moment, considering. "I don't know. Part of me hopes so, I guess. It would be easier if he felt remorse. But part of me thinks this is just another way for him to control something. Even in dying, he still gets to make people dance to his tune."

Alex nodded. He'd known men like Snags—men who saw every interaction as a power play, even their final ones. "Whatever he says, remember that it doesn't change who you are or the life you've built."

"I know," Tyler said, but his voice carried uncertainty. "It's just... what if it's something that affects other people? What if he tells me something that I then have to decide whether to share?"

The question hit closer to home than Tyler could have known. Alex was carrying exactly that kind of burden right now—information that would affect multiple people, information that wasn't really his to share but that he couldn't ignore either.

"Then you'll deal with it when it happens," Alex said finally. "With help. You don't have to carry tough truths alone." The irony of his own words wasn't lost on him.

They drove in comfortable silence for a while, each lost in their own thoughts. The landscape rolled by—farmland giving way to smaller towns, then to the more industrial area where the prison sat like a gray scar on the horizon.

"Speaking of dealing with things," Tyler said suddenly, turning to look back at Ethan. "I heard you and Amy talking yesterday. You two planning on following Randy and Sam's lead?"

Ethan's face lit up with a smile that transformed his features. "Maybe. We've been talking about it for months, actually. Just waiting for the right moment."

"When is that exactly?" Tyler asked. "The right moment?"

Ethan laughed, but there was nervousness in it. "That's the million-dollar question, isn't it? Amy's amazing, and I love her, and I want to spend my life with her. But there's always been this feeling like... like I should wait until I had everything figured out first. Better job prospects, more money saved, you know?"

"But Randy didn't wait for that," Tyler pointed out.

"No, he didn't. And watching him and Sam yesterday..." Ethan trailed off, then spoke more firmly. "Maybe the right moment is just when you're brave enough to admit you don't want to wait anymore."

Alex found himself nodding along, thinking about his own situation with Serenity. How long had he been waiting for the "right moment"? And now, with Lucas's arrival, the definition of "right" had become impossibly complicated.

"Fear's a funny thing," Alex said, as much to himself as to the other two. "Sometimes we think we're being smart by waiting, but really we're just scared."

"Scared of what?" Tyler asked.

"Of changing things. Of taking the risk that what we have now might not be as good as what we could have." Alex glanced in the rearview mirror at Ethan. "But sometimes the bigger risk is not taking a risk at all."

Ethan was quiet for a moment, then said, "You know what? When we get back today, I'm going to ask her when she wants the wedding."

"Really?" Tyler grinned, and for the first time that morning, his smile looked genuine. "That's awesome, man."

"What about you, Alex?" Ethan asked. "When are you going to ask Serenity?"

The question hung in the air like a challenge. Alex thought about Lucas, dying and desperate to meet his daughter. He thought about Serenity, who deserved to know the truth about her past before she decided about her future. He thought about Sam, whose grief over her father's death was about to become something entirely different.

"Soon," Alex said finally, and he meant it. Whatever complications Lucas's presence created, Alex wouldn't let fear keep him from the life he wanted. "Real soon."

191

As he drove, Alex felt a strange sense of resolution settling over him. Today, Tyler would face his past and whatever truth Snags had to share. He would figure out how to introduce Lucas to the community. And soon—very soon—he was going to ask Serenity Rivers to marry him, regardless of whatever chaos surrounded that moment.

Because if the past few days had taught him anything, it was that life was unpredictable and short, and the people you loved deserved to know it.

# Thirty Four

As they continued toward the prison, Tyler found his mind drifting to the ruins he'd discovered by the lake. The old cabin foundation stones, weathered and mysterious, had been haunting his thoughts since yesterday. Who had built it? When? And why had Big Mike felt the need to create a secret path to reach it?

He had told no one about his find yet. He thought he would wait until after this awful visit was over. Besides, questions about his find felt safer than thinking about what lay ahead at the prison. But they couldn't distract him entirely. Tyler shifted in his seat, trying to ease the knot of anxiety in his stomach.

"You know," he blurted, "I've been thinking about the diner."

"What about it?" Alex asked, grateful for conversation that might ease the tension they were all feeling.

"About Joseph maybe selling it to Ethan and Amy." Tyler glanced back at Ethan, who looked surprised. "I mean, I know Joseph's been teaching me the business, but honestly, I don't think it's what I want to do with my life."

Ethan leaned forward. "Really? You're good at it, though. And Joseph seems to love having you there."

"I am good at it, and I do love working with Joseph. But it's not... mine, you know? Ethan, you and Amy light up when you're working together in that kitchen. You belong there in a way I never will."

"But you're his nephew," Ethan protested. "Family."

Tyler shrugged. "Family doesn't mean you have to follow the same path. Besides, maybe I'm meant to do something else. Maybe after today, after I get this prison visit behind me, I'll have a clearer idea of what that is."

Alex turned to glance at Tyler. "That's very mature of you. Not everyone would be so generous."

"Generous?" Tyler laughed, but there was no humor in it. "Ethan's the one being generous, coming with me today. Being my friend when he doesn't have to be."

"That's what friends do," Ethan said simply.

The prison came into view—a sprawling complex of gray concrete and razor wire that seemed to suck the color out of the surrounding landscape.

Tyler felt his throat tighten as they passed through the security checkpoints, submitted to searches, and were finally led to a sterile visiting room with plastic chairs and tables bolted to the floor.

When Snags was wheeled in, Tyler barely recognized him.

The man, who had once been barrel-chested and intimidating, was now gaunt, his skin yellow-gray and stretched tight over prominent bones. The orange prison jumpsuit hung loose on his shrunken frame, and an oxygen tank accompanied his wheelchair. His eyes, though—his eyes still held that familiar mix of cunning and cruelty that Tyler remembered.

"Tyler," Snags wheezed, his voice barely above a whisper. "You came."

"You said it was important." Tyler's voice was steady, but Alex could see his hands trembling slightly.

Snags' gaze shifted to Ethan, and something flickered across his face.. "And you brought..."

"This is Ethan," Tyler said. "My friend."

"Ethan," Snags repeated, studying the young man's face with an intensity that made everyone uncomfortable. "How old are you, son?"

"Twenty-five," Ethan answered, clearly puzzled by the question.

Snags closed his eyes for a moment, as if calculating something. When he opened them again, he looked directly at Alex. "I need to speak with you alone first. Just for a minute."

Alex glanced at Tyler, who nodded reluctantly. After the boys stepped out of the visiting room, Snags gestured for Alex to lean closer. His breath was labored, each word an effort. "That boy... Ethan. I need to be sure... where's he from?"

"Why?" Alex's cop instincts were on high alert.

"His mother's name. Do you know it?"

Alex hesitated. "What does that have to do with anything?"

"Please." For the first time, Snags sounded genuinely desperate rather than manipulative. "I'm dying. I need to know."

"Elena," Alex said finally, remembering what Betty Jean had mentioned. "Elena Ross."

Snags' face crumpled. "Jesus. I knew it. The moment I saw him..."

"Knew what?"

"He's mine," Snags whispered. "Elena and I... we had an affair. Right before she left town. She was pregnant when she went."

Alex felt the world tilt. Another secret. Another family revelation that would shatter everything. "Are you sure?"

"Look at him. Really look at him. He's got my jaw, my build. And the timing..." Snags coughed, a harsh sound that seemed to tear through his chest. "I need to tell them. Both of them."

"Snags, this will destroy Tyler. Finding out his father had another child—"

"No." Snags' voice grew stronger, more insistent. "It will give him something I never could. A brother. Family that isn't tainted by what I did."

Alex stared at the dying man, already burdened with Lucas' secret, and now this. "Why now? Why tell them this?"

"Because I'm dying, and they deserve to know. Tyler deserves to know he's not alone in carrying my sins. And Ethan..." Snags' voice broke. "Ethan deserves to know where he comes from."

Returning to the visiting room, both young men looked expectantly at Alex and Snags. Tyler could see something had changed—Alex looked stricken, and his father seemed to have aged another decade in just a few minutes.

"Boys," Snags began, his voice barely audible. "I have something to tell you. Something that's going to change everything."

He looked directly at Ethan. "Son, Alex said your mother's name was Elena Ross?"

"Yes," Ethan said slowly. "Why?"

"Twenty-six years ago, Elena and I... We were together. Briefly. She left town right afterward. I was married, and she said it was wrong." Snags stopped gathering strength. "But I found out later that she was pregnant and had you."

The silence that followed was deafening. Ethan's face went completely white, while Tyler's mouth opened and closed soundlessly.

"That's impossible," Ethan whispered.

"Look at me, son. Really look. You've got my hands, my build. Well, when I looked like myself. The timing fits." Snags' voice was growing weaker. "Your mother never told you about your father?"

"She said... she said he was someone who couldn't be part of our lives. Someone who would only bring trouble." Ethan's voice was hollow.

Tyler was staring at Ethan as if seeing him for the first time. "You're my brother," he breathed, as if testing the words.

"Half-brother," Snags corrected. "But blood is blood."

Tyler's face crumpled then, and tears started flowing. Not tears of grief, but something more complex—joy mixed with anger, gratitude tangled with rage. "All this time," he whispered. "I had a brother all this time."

Ethan was still in shock, but he reached over instinctively to put a hand on Tyler's shoulder. "I... I don't know what to say."

"Say you'll be brothers," Snags said, his breathing becoming more labored. "Say you'll look out for each other. It's the only good thing I ever did—giving you each other."

Tyler looked at Ethan through his tears. "I always wondered what it would be like to have a brother."

"Me too," Ethan said softly, and suddenly he was crying too.

Snags watched them with something that might have been satisfaction. "Tyler, I know you hate me. You have every right to. But don't let that poison what you could have with Ethan. He's innocent in all this."

"I know," Tyler said, his voice thick. "I know he is."

Alarms started beeping then, and suddenly the room was full of medical personnel. Snags was having some kind of episode, his already shallow breathing becoming erratic.

"Time to go," a guard said firmly, as medical staff began working on Snags.

As they were escorted out, Tyler caught one last glimpse of his father being wheeled away on a gurney. The man looked more dead than alive, and Tyler knew with certainty that this was the last time he would ever see him.

In the parking lot, the three men stood in stunned silence. The morning sun felt too bright, the normal world too surreal after what they'd just experienced.

"So," Alex said finally, "I guess we need to figure out how to process all this."

Tyler wiped his eyes and looked at Ethan—his brother. "Are you okay?"

"I don't know," Ethan admitted. "Everything I thought I knew about myself just changed. But..." He paused, considering. "I'm glad it's you. If I had to have a half-brother, I'm glad it's you."

Tyler's smile was watery but genuine. "Same here."

Alex watched the two young men—brothers now—and felt the weight of yet another secret settling on his shoulders. How many revelations could one small town handle? And how was he going to explain to Betty Jean and Joseph that the boy they'd welcomed as family was actually connected to the man who'd murdered Iris?

But as he watched Tyler and Ethan talking quietly, supporting each other through the shock, Alex realized that revealing some secrets was worth the chaos they created at first. Some truths, no matter how complicated, were better than the lies that came before them.

Maybe that was how Serenity and Sam would react when he told them about Lucas. He could only hope that for them it would be good news.

The question now was how and when to tell them and how to help these two young men navigate their new reality. He hoped that was the last of the secrets in Lazy Rivers. But, of course, he was wrong.

# Thirty Five

P ete stood in Alex's kitchen, nursing his second cup of coffee and watching the morning light stream through the windows. The house felt empty with Alex gone, though Pete had to admit he was getting used to the comfortable rhythms of living here. Still, something was bothering him about the way Alex had looked when he'd left for the prison.

It wasn't just worry about Tyler facing his father—though that was certainly part of it. There had been something else in Alex's eyes, a weight that Pete recognized from his own mirror during the harder times in his life. The look of a man carrying secrets that weren't his to carry.

When the phone rang, Pete was grateful for the distraction.

"Pete? It's Tom from the nursery. Alex mentioned you might be willing to host a men's night at the house Friday night?"

"Absolutely," Pete said, settling into one of Alex's kitchen chairs. "I'd be happy to put something together. Been a while since I've had the chance to play host."

"Great! Brad and I were thinking we could help you get whatever you need. Food, drinks, maybe some card tables and chairs if Alex doesn't have enough seating."

Pete smiled, warmed by the offer. "That would be wonderful. It's perfect timing. I think he wanted to have something good happening right after the prison visit."

"Wonderful! How about we come by this afternoon and help you plan it out?"

After hanging up, Pete wandered around Alex's house, taking mental inventory of what they'd need. The basement had a pool table and some comfortable seating, and the main floor could accommodate the rest. It would be good to have the house full of voices and laughter.

But his mind kept drifting back to Alex's expression that morning. And to something else that had been nagging at him—those two strangers at the diner.

Something about both of them felt off, though Pete couldn't put his finger on what exactly. Maybe it was just the timing, right after the flood when people might be vulnerable. Or maybe it was just his many years of watching the world, and people at the diner. He had learned to read situations, to sense when something wasn't quite right.

When Tom and Brad arrived that afternoon, they came loaded with supplies: folding chairs, card tables, and enough snacks to feed a small army.

"Betty Jean insisted on making her famous chili," Tom said, setting down several containers. She said it tastes better heated up.

"And Mama says she'll make enough desserts to put everyone in a food coma."

"You folks are too kind," Pete said, genuinely touched. "I haven't hosted a big party since Nancy passed away." He dropped his head for a minute, thinking about how much he missed his wife. He thought she would be happy with his getting together with this many men.

As they set up the basement, arranging furniture and testing the pool table, Pete relaxed for the first time in days. This was what he'd missed most about farm life—not the hard work or the isolation, but the sense of community that came with it.

"Pete," Brad said during a break in their preparations, "can I ask you something personal?"

"Shoot."

"Tom and I were talking, and we're wondering about your plans. Long-term, I mean." Brad paused, choosing his words carefully. "Are you thinking about selling the farm?"

Pete set down the stack of paper plates he'd been arranging and looked at both men. "Funny you should ask. I've been thinking about exactly that."

"Really?" Tom leaned forward. "What's got you considering it?"

"Well, I'm not getting any younger, and the place is getting to be more than I can handle alone. Been leasing the farmland for years, anyway." Pete gestured around Alex's kitchen. "Staying here during the flood got me thinking—maybe it's time for something smaller. Something in town where I'd be closer to people."

"Have you thought about what you'd want to happen to the land?" Brad asked. "I mean, there are developers who'd probably love to get their hands on that much acreage close to town."

Pete's face darkened slightly. "That's exactly what I don't want. The farm's been in my family for generations. I'd hate to see it turned into a subdivision with houses packed together like sardines."

"So you'd want it to stay agricultural?" Tom asked.

"Ideally, yes. Or maybe conservation land. Something that preserves what it is." Pete sighed. "Problem is, I don't know how to go about finding the right buyer. Someone who'd respect the land instead of just seeing dollar signs."

Tom and Brad exchanged a look. "We might be able to help with that," Tom said. "First thing would be getting it appraised, figuring out what it's actually worth. Then we could put out some feelers, see if there are any young farming families looking to expand, or maybe conservation groups interested in preserving open space."

"You'd do that?" Pete asked, surprised by the offer.

"Of course," Brad replied. "You're family, Pete. We take care of our own."

The word 'family' hit Pete harder than he'd expected. He'd spent so many years thinking of himself as alone in the world, but somehow, in the space of just a few days, he'd found himself surrounded by people who cared about his welfare. And he realized they'd been there all along.

"I'd appreciate that more than you know," he answered.

As they continued setting up for the gathering, Pete felt a lightness he hadn't experienced in years. The decision to sell the farm, which had seemed so daunting when it was just an abstract idea, suddenly felt manageable with help from friends.

"You know," he said as they tested the sound system for Tom's playlist that he brought, "I'm looking forward to tomorrow night. Been too long since I've had a house full of people having a good time."

"It'll be good for Alex too," Tom said. "He's been carrying the weight of the world lately. Between the flood response and whatever's going on with Tyler..."

"And the strangers at the motel," Brad added. "Betty Jean mentioned they were asking odd questions."

Pete nodded grimly. "I've been thinking about that too. Timing seems suspicious, right after a crisis when people might not be thinking clearly."

"Should we mention it to Alex when he gets back?" Tom asked.

"He probably already knows, but we could let him know we noticed too." Pete glanced at his watch. "Speaking of which, they should be back from the prison soon. I hope whatever Tyler learned was worth the trip."

"Tyler's tougher than he looks," Brad said. "And having Ethan with him will help. Those two have become good friends."

As the afternoon wore on, the three men continued their preparations, the conversation flowing easily between practical matters and gentle gossip about the town. It felt good to Pete to be useful again, to have a purpose beyond just existing.

By the time Tom and Brad left, Alex's house was ready to host a proper gathering. Pete stood in the kitchen, looking at the evidence of their preparations, and smiled. Tomorrow night was going to be special—a celebration of friendship and community that would hopefully help everyone decompress from the week's stresses.

He just hoped that whatever was weighing on Alex's mind would be resolved by then. And that those mysterious strangers would be nothing more than innocent travelers who'd simply overstayed their welcome.

But Pete's instincts, honed by decades of country living, told him that things were rarely that simple. In his experience, when strangers showed up and didn't share who they were, trouble usually followed.

Still, that was a worry for another day. Tonight was about making sure Alex had a warm welcome when he returned from what was bound to have been a tough day. And tomorrow would be about celebrating the good things in life—friendship, community, and the simple pleasure of good company.

*Thankfully,* Pete reflected, *that was usually enough to get through whatever storms were coming.*

# Thirty Six

The Rivers family kitchen had been transformed into wedding planning headquarters. Fabric samples, flower catalogs, and recipe cards covered every available surface while Serenity, Sam, Lizzy, and Mama Ruth worked with the focused intensity of a military operation.

"The yellow roses or the white?" Sam held up two photographs, trying to decide between centerpiece options.

"Yellow," Lizzy said immediately. "They'll be beautiful against the green of the backyard, and they're cheerful. This should be a joyful celebration."

Mama Ruth looked up from the guest list she'd been reviewing. "How many people are we talking about realistically?"

"Maybe thirty or forty?' Sam said, sounding more confident now. 'Family, close friends, a few of my author colleagues if they can make the trip..."

"That's perfect for a backyard wedding," Serenity said, though her mind seemed elsewhere. She kept glancing at her phone, checking for messages that hadn't come.

"Mom, you're distracted," Sam observed gently. "Everything okay?"

Serenity set down the catering menu she'd been pretending to read. "I haven't heard from Alex since this morning. I know he said the prison visit might take a while, but..."

"You're worried about him," Lizzy finished.

"I am. He's been carrying something heavy lately. I could see it in his eyes yesterday, even during all the flood chaos. There's something weighing on him beyond just the normal stress of his job."

Mama Ruth reached over and patted Serenity's hand. "Honey, that man's been in love with you for months. Maybe he's just trying to work up the courage to tell you."

"Or maybe," Sam added with a knowing smile, "he's planning his own proposal."

Serenity felt her cheeks warm. "I don't think... I mean, we haven't..."

"Oh, sweetheart," Lizzy laughed. "You two have been circling each other like lovesick teenagers. Everyone in town can see it."

As if summoned by their conversation, a memory flickered in Serenity's mind—Alex just two days ago, standing in her kitchen after they'd learned about the flooding. The way he'd looked at her when she'd reached for his hand, the mixture of hope and fear in his eyes, as if he were trying to decide whether to say something important.

"He almost said something the other day," Serenity said quietly. "During the flood preparations. I could feel him working up to it, but then the emergency calls started coming in."

"See?" Sam said triumphantly. "I told you. Mom, that man is head over heels for you."

Mama Ruth nodded sagely. "The question is, what are you going to do about it?"

Before Serenity could answer, her phone buzzed with a text. Her face lit up as she read it. "It's Alex. They're on their way back from the prison. Says we'll talk later."

"That's good news," Lizzy said. "At least you know they're safe."

"But he didn't say how it went," Serenity noticed, her worry returning. "A prison visit with Tyler's father... that couldn't have been easy."

Sam looked up from the flower photographs. "Tyler's stronger than he looks. And having Ethan with him will help. Those two have become really close friends."

"It's sweet watching their friendship develop," Mama Ruth agreed. "Ethan needed friends his own age, and Tyler needed someone who wasn't constantly walking on eggshells around him."

Another memory surfaced in Serenity's mind then, this one from just yesterday at the diner. Tyler and Ethan working together behind the counter, moving in sync like they'd been partners for years. There had been something almost familial about the way they communicated without words, understanding each other's rhythms instinctively.

"You know," Serenity said slowly, "watching Tyler and Ethan together reminds me of something. The way they work together, it's like they're..."

"Like they're what?" Lizzy prompted.

"I don't know. Connected somehow. More than just friendship." Serenity shook her head. "Maybe I'm imagining things."

"The Rivers women don't imagine things," Sam said with a grin. "We see what's really there, even when other people miss it.

Which reminds me, Mom, are you ready for your opening at the art gallery in Spring Falls?" Sam's question seemed to come out of nowhere, but Serenity thought she knew what she meant.

"How did you get to that?" Serenity asked anyway.

"'Seeing what others don't see. Painting. Your art shows people things they might have missed. Kinda the same thing as our gift, right?'"

"You mean like writing books?" Serenity teased back. "But to answer your question, it's going well. I just have one more painting to finish. Jan is putting it together, as she always does. She's working with Cindy, the gallery owner.

"They make a great team, and Jan always knows exactly how to present my work. I still have a few weeks left to finish this painting, and then my part is done. And are you still open to having your books there too?"

"A mother and daughter show? Of course I am! Jan has already picked out the books she wants to feature. I don't have to do anything but show up," Sam exclaimed, her enthusiasm building.

Serenity smiled, thinking how wonderful this show was going to be. "But it's only a week after your wedding. You might be on a honeymoon."

"Nope. We're going to take our time and have a long trip later."

Mama Ruth and Lizzy exchanged knowing smiles. Was it really less than a year ago that Serenity and Sam had come home to Lazy Rivers? Had all this happiness and change happened in such a short time? And both of them thought about their own men, wondering if perhaps it was time to stop waiting for the "right" moment.

As Lizzy looked at her daughter, she caught a memory that surprised her since she didn't see memories as often anymore, for which she was grateful. Seeing other people's memories had been one reason she had been a recluse for so many years. Now that her life was filled with people she loved and trusted, the unwanted intrusions had become rare. Perhaps love and acceptance created a kind of barrier, a mutual respect that her gift honored.

Lizzy wondered if that was true for Serenity and Sam, or if the fewer memories was a sign of getting old. She'd ask them later. But for now, she wondered why she was seeing one of Serenity's memories. She rarely saw her family's memories. She considered that a good thing.

So she had to think that it was important that she saw this one. A gallery opening, and a young man. Watching the memory unfold, she realized that the young man in the scene was probably Lucas—Samantha's father. He was standing close to Serenity, both of them young and radiant, looking at a painting together as if they were the only two people in the world.

*Why would I be seeing this?* Lizzy asked herself, now feeling a pang of worry instead of joy. She pushed the worry aside. This was supposed to be a time of celebration, not worry. Except she knew something must be happening, something coming, and she wasn't sure it was going to be a good thing.

Lizzy glanced around the kitchen at the women she loved most in the world—her daughter, granddaughter, and Mama Ruth—and felt a protective instinct rise in her chest. Whatever was coming, they would face it together. But she couldn't shake the feeling that the happiness surrounding them was about to be tested in ways they couldn't yet imagine.

# Thirty Seven

A cross town, Matthew, John, and Randy were having their own planning session at the men's clothing store, though theirs involved significantly less paperwork and significantly more good-natured ribbing.

"This one," John said, holding up a charcoal gray suit. "Classic, but not stuffy. Perfect for a spring wedding."

Randy examined himself in the three-way mirror, tugging at the jacket. "It feels weird, getting fitted for a wedding suit. Six months ago, I thought Sam would run away if I even mentioned the word "commitment." Now here I am, buying a suit to marry her in."

"Sometimes people just need time to realize what they want,' Matthew said, adjusting Randy's collar. 'And sometimes they need to stop being afraid of what they might lose and start focusing on what they could gain."

"Speaking of getting what you want," John said with a meaningful look, "when are you going to ask Lizzy to marry you, Matthew? You two have been dancing around it for months, and you're not getting any younger."

Matthew's face reddened slightly. "We've talked about it. Maybe after Sam's wedding. One celebration at a time."

"And what about Alex and Serenity?" Randy asked. "Please tell me someone's going to push him to finally make a move."

"Oh, I think he's working up to it," Matthew said. "Though with everything that's been happening lately, he might need a little encouragement to focus on his own happiness."

The tailor finished pinning Randy's jacket and stepped back to admire his work. "There. You'll be the handsomest groom Lazy Rivers has ever seen."

Randy grinned, looking at himself in the mirror. "I still can't believe this is really happening. That Sam said yes." Randy's voice carried a note of wonder. "Sometimes I wake up thinking I dreamed the whole thing."

"Believe it," John said, clapping his son on the shoulder. "And enjoy every minute. These are the good times, son. The ones you'll remember when you're my age."

As they left the shop, Matthew's phone rang. It was Lizzy updating him on the women's planning session.

"How's it going over there?" he asked.

"Wonderfully chaotic," Lizzy replied. "Though Serenity's worried about Alex. She says he's been carrying something heavy lately."

Matthew glanced at John and Randy, who were listening with interest. "Prison visits aren't easy. I'm sure that's weighing on him. He takes everyone else's problems to heart."

"Maybe. Or maybe," Lizzy's voice carried a hint of mischief, "he's trying to work up the courage to propose and doesn't know how to do it without upstaging Sam and Randy."

"That would be just like Alex," John said when Matthew relayed the comment. "Always putting everyone else first."

"Well, maybe it's time someone reminded him that his happiness matters too," Randy said. "Sam and I want everyone we love to be as happy as we are. Life's too short to wait for the perfect moment."

As they walked back to where they'd left their trucks, the late afternoon sun casting long shadows on the sidewalk, the three men fell into a comfortable conversation about weddings, love, and the strange way life had of working out when you least expected it.

None of them noticed the man sitting in a dark truck across the street, watching their easy camaraderie with calculating eyes. Raymond had spent the day observing the rhythms of Lazy Rivers, learning who was friends with whom, mapping the social connections that bound this community together, figuring out the best way to approach the situation with Pete.

Tomorrow night's gathering would be perfect. All the men in one place, relaxed and off guard after a few drinks and some friendly games. It would be the ideal time to approach Pete directly, and claim what he'd come for. He'd make a scene. No one could deny that he was claiming his rights. There would be all those witnesses.

But as he watched Matthew, John, and Randy laughing together like old friends, sharing in each other's joy without reservation, Raymond felt a sharp pang of something he didn't want to name. Loneliness, maybe. Or envy of the uncomplicated relationships he'd never quite managed to build, always too focused on what people could do for him rather than what he could offer them.

He pushed the feeling aside. Sentiment was a luxury he couldn't afford. He had a job to do, and Pete Jones had something that belonged to him by right. That Pete seemed to have built a life surrounded by people who cared about him was irrelevant.

Tomorrow night, Raymond would get his answers. And if Pete didn't like what he had to say, well, that wasn't Raymond's problem. He'd waited too long and come too far to let sentiment stand in the way of what was rightfully his. He was about ready to test the happiness of Lazy Rivers.

# Thirty Eight

E than, Alex, and Tyler made a decision on the way home from the prison. Actually, the two boys made it, and Alex agreed, understanding that some news was too important to let others hear through gossip. There were two people who needed to know what happened at the prison before anyone else found out. It was Joseph and Amy. And that meant Betty Jean, too. Joseph would need her to be there.

Then they had to decide how and where. If they closed the diner early, everyone would know something was up. They had been training more help at the diner for the past month, and both Tyler and Ethan thought the new people could handle the last few hours on their own. Tyler made the phone calls since Alex was driving, and Ethan was still processing the shock of learning he had a brother—and that his father was the man who'd killed Tyler's grandmother.

They agreed to meet at Betty Jean and Joseph's house. When Tyler asked them to have Amy come with them, Betty Jean put her hand on her heart, fear evident in her voice. "Why?" she asked, dreading the answer.

"Please," Tyler said, and Betty Jean nodded at the phone, said a quiet "okay," and leaned against the counter. There were only a few people in the diner, so she thought Tyler was right about them not needing to be there. First, she took one of the new waitresses aside and told her she was responsible for cleaning up and closing the diner. The girl looked nervous but determined. Betty Jean had to give her credit—she simply nodded and said yes, rising to the challenge.

Joseph was already at home, so all she had to do was collect Amy. Like Betty Jean, Amy was worried, her face pale with anxiety. "Is something wrong? Is Tyler okay?"

Betty Jean could only shake her head, wishing she knew more, while praying it wasn't something terrible. It was possible it was good news, but the gravity in Tyler's voice told her otherwise. Alex dropped the two boys off at Betty Jean and Joseph's house. They didn't need him to be there for this family conversation. It was between them and the people who'd been like parents to both boys. Relieved of his duty regarding Snags, Alex's mind immediately turned to the other burden he carried—telling Serenity about Lucas.

He decided that if there was ever a time to add to the current chaos, now was it. Get both terrible secrets out in the open before they festered any longer. And the person who had to know about Lucas first was the woman he loved.

Alex was terrified. What if she blamed him for not telling her immediately? What if seeing Lucas reminded her that she'd loved him first, more deeply than she could ever love Alex? Sure, Lucas was dying, but that might make it worse—guilt and old feelings could be a powerful combination. Whatever she felt might make her not love him anymore because he was sure that she did. At least at the moment.

But waiting would not make it better; it was going to make it worse. Afraid Serenity would hear the terror in his voice, he texted her instead, asking if he could pick her up in an hour. He didn't explain why, hoping she would assume he needed to talk about the prison visit. She would never guess that he was about to tell her something that would change both of their lives forever.

Meanwhile, at Betty Jean and Joseph's house, Ethan sat across from Amy at their kitchen table, Tyler beside him for moral support. Joseph and Betty Jean stood beside Amy, their hands on her shoulder to let her know they were there.

To Ethan, the words felt impossible to say out loud. "Amy, there's something I need to tell you about my father. I found out who he is today. And Joseph, this affects you too." Betty Jean's heart started beating so fast she thought it would pop out of her chest.

Just a few months ago, Joseph had found out that Lizzy was his half-sister, and Tyler was his nephew. After absorbing the shock that his father, Big Mike, had been a busy man, he had been happy to finally find his family. Was this about something else his father had done?

After helping Ethan tell his story, Tyler needed air. He walked toward the woods behind Betty Jean's house, his mind reeling with everything that had happened. He had a brother. His father was dying. And somehow, despite all the pain Snags had caused, Tyler felt a strange sense of completion—like a missing piece of himself had finally been found.

Inside the house, Betty Jean felt a wave of relief. This wasn't about Joseph fathering another child or more secrets about Big Mike. It was another man's wrongdoing. Snags. But at least Snags had finally told the truth.

And as the news settled in, she realized that Ethan being Tyler's half-brother meant he was officially family too. She didn't know what the exact term would be for their relationship to Joseph—step-nephew maybe?—but the family tree was getting wonderfully complicated. What mattered was that Ethan was officially part of their chosen family now.

Ethan, who was terrified about what everyone would say, discovered that there was nothing to worry about. Amy gasped, tears came to her eyes, and said, "This is so wonderful, Ethan. You have a brother, and it's Tyler. Could anything be any better?"

"Agreed," Joseph and Betty Jean said simultaneously, all three of them hugging Ethan at once. Betty Jean whispered in his ear, "Welcome to the family, officially this time," while Joseph added, "You were already ours, son. This just makes it legal."

Outside in the woods, Tyler smiled as he heard the sounds of celebration through the kitchen window. For the first time in his life, his father had given him something good—a brother. It was more than he'd ever dared hope for.

# Thirty Nine

A lex pulled into his driveway and sat for a moment, gathering his courage. Through the windows, he could see Pete moving around the kitchen with Tom and Brad, the three of them clearly deep in party preparations. The normalcy of the scene—friends helping friends, laughter and easy conversation—made what he was about to do feel even more surreal.

Inside, he found his house transformed. The living room furniture had been rearranged to create better conversation areas; card tables were set up in the dining room, and the basement had been turned into a proper game room.

"This looks incredible," Alex said, genuinely impressed. "You guys have outdone yourselves."

Pete beamed with pride. "Tom and Brad did most of the heavy lifting. I just supervised and made sure there will be enough beer."

"It's going to be a great night," Tom said, folding up the last of the extra chairs. "Everyone needs this after the week we've had with the flooding."

Alex thought they didn't know the half of it. *Wait until they learn about Snags and Lucas.*

Brad nodded, then glanced at Pete. "We should probably head out and let you get some rest. But Alex, before we go—Pete mentioned he's thinking about selling his farm. We offered to help him find the right buyer, someone who'd respect the land."

Alex looked at Pete, surprised. "You're really serious about selling?"

"I am," Pete said. "Staying here with you, it's shown me what I've been missing. I'm tired of being alone out there."

Tom and Brad exchanged a look. "We'll start with getting an appraisal," Tom said. "Then we can put out some feelers, see if there are any conservation groups or young farming families interested."

After they left, Alex found himself alone with Pete in the kitchen. The older man was wiping down counters that were already clean, clearly nervous about hosting duties.

"Pete," Alex said carefully, "have you thought about what you'd do after you sell? Where will you live?"

Pete paused in his cleaning. "A place in town for sure. Nothing fancy, just something smaller, more manageable, and close to people."

Alex took a breath. "What if you didn't have to look? What if you just... stayed here?"

Pete's head snapped up. "What are you saying?"

"I'm saying this house is too big for one person, and I enjoy having you around. Good company, someone to share meals with." Alex felt his cheeks warm. "I'm asking if you'd consider making this permanent. We'll be roommates."

Pete's eyes filled with tears. "Alex, I... are you sure? I don't want to be a burden."

"You're not a burden. You're family." The word felt right as soon as Alex said it. "Think about it, okay? No rush."

Pete nodded, too emotional to speak.

Alex headed upstairs to change clothes, his mind already shifting to the conversation ahead. He put on a clean shirt and jeans, then checked his reflection in the mirror. He looked like a man about to deliver life-changing news, which, he supposed, he was.

The drive to the Rivers' house was too short and too long at the same time. Alex's palms were sweating as he pulled into the driveway, and he had to force himself to get out of the truck.

Serenity was waiting on the porch, having seen him arrive. She looked beautiful in a simple blue sweater and jeans, her red hair catching the late afternoon light. Behind her, through the window, Alex could see Lizzy and Mama Ruth still surrounded by wedding planning materials.

"Hey," Serenity said, studying his face with concern. "How did it go at the prison?"

"We'll talk about that," Alex said, his voice already strained. "But first, I need to tell you something else. Something important."

For a moment, Serenity panicked. Was he breaking up with her? But then, they had never really officially been together. Still, she was scared, but tried not to show it.

Serenity waved goodbye to her mother and Mama Ruth, both of whom waved back. As they drove away, Alex could feel their curious gazes following them.

"Where are we going?" Serenity asked, as Alex turned away from town, trying to keep her voice light as if she wasn't terrified of what was about to happen.

"The river landing. I need somewhere quiet for this conversation."

The worry in Serenity's voice was clear. "Alex, you're scaring me. What's going on?"

Alex pulled into the small parking area at the river where people launched small boats and canoes. It was still wet from the flood, but the water had receded enough to park. It was a spot where countless Lazy Rivers residents had come to think, to talk, to make important decisions.

The water was calm now, reflecting the sky like a mirror, the sun almost to the horizon. It would be dark soon. He turned off the engine and sat for a moment, his hands gripping the steering wheel.

"Alex," Serenity said softly, "whatever it is, just tell me."

Alex turned to face her, this woman he loved more than he'd ever thought possible. Should he tell her first, that he loved her? *No,* he thought. *That wouldn't be fair.*

He took a deep breath, reached out to hold her hand, and said, "Serenity, do you remember that man at the diner. A few days ago? He was driving away as we came in."

"Yes. He seemed familiar somehow. Seeing him triggered that memory I saw. I told you about it. About my art show thirty years ago."

"That's because he was at your art show. He has been telling people his name is Philip Brown, but it isn't." Alex's voice was barely above a whisper. "His real name is Lucas Ng."

The silence that followed was deafening. Serenity's face went completely white, and for a moment, Alex thought she might faint.

"That's impossible," she whispered. "Lucas is dead. Sam's agent found his obituary."

"He faked his death. He's been living under the name Philip Brown for a long time." Alex reached for her hand, but she pulled away.

"Serenity, he's dying. Terminal cancer. He came to Lazy Rivers because he found out about Sam, about you. He wants to meet his daughter before he dies."

Serenity's breathing became shallow, rapid. "You're telling me that Lucas—Sam's father—is alive? And he's been in town, watching us?"

"Yes."

"How long have you known?" Her voice was sharp now, cutting.

Alex flinched. "Since yesterday. He came to the station, showed me proof of who he was. Medical records, old photographs of the two of you together. I wanted to tell you right away, but—"

"But you didn't." Serenity's eyes flashed with anger and hurt. "You let me sit through wedding planning, let Sam continue grieving her dead father, while you knew he was alive and a few miles away."

"I was trying to figure out the best way to handle it. And I had to take Tyler and Ethan to the prison. I wanted to wait until that was done."

When Serenity said nothing to ease his guilt, he continued. "Lucas is sick, Serenity. Really sick. And he's terrified of disrupting your lives."

"Disrupting our lives?" Serenity's voice rose. "Alex, my daughter thinks her father is dead! She's been mourning him, planning a wedding without him, and all this time he's been in town watching us?"

Alex felt his heart breaking as he watched the woman he loved process this betrayal. "I'm sorry. I know I should have told you immediately, but…"

"But what? You decided you knew better than I did about how to handle my own life? My daughter's life?"

"I was trying to protect you."

"From what? From the truth?" Serenity turned away from him, staring out at the river. "Where is he now?"

"At the motel. He's been staying there, trying to work up the courage to approach you."

"I need to see him."

"Serenity, maybe you should take some time to process this first."

"No." She turned back to him, her eyes blazing. "I've lost thirty years with him because of our stupid Rivers women tradition of not telling the fathers about their children. I'm over all that. I'm not losing another minute because you think you know what's best for me."

The words hit Alex like a physical blow. This was exactly what he'd been afraid of—that learning Lucas was alive would remind Serenity of what they'd once had, what they'd lost.

"Take me to him," Serenity said. "Now."

Alex started the truck, his hands shaking slightly. As they drove toward the motel, he couldn't help but wonder if he'd just destroyed the best thing that had ever happened to him. But some truths couldn't be hidden forever, and Lucas Ng was very much alive, waiting to reclaim his place in the lives of the two women Alex loved most in the world.

The only question now was what would be left when the dust settled.

# Forty

Serenity's fury kept her silent as Alex drove her to the motel. The anger radiated from her in waves, filling the truck cab with a tension so thick it felt suffocating. Alex had never seen her like this—not hurt, not disappointed, but coldly, righteously furious.

When they pulled into the motel parking lot, Alex could see Lucas's car parked outside room twelve. The sight made his stomach clench with dread and something that felt uncomfortably like jealousy.

"Serenity," he started, but she cut him off.

"Don't." Her voice was ice. "Just don't."

Alex got out and knocked on the motel room door, his heart hammering against his ribs. When Lucas opened it, his face went pale at the sight of Serenity standing behind Alex by the truck.

"She knows," Alex said simply.

Lucas nodded, his green eyes—so much like Sam's—filled with a mixture of hope and terror. "Thank you for bringing her."

Through clenched teeth, Serenity turned to Alex. "Go now, Alex."

He looked at her one more time, hoping to see some softness, some forgiveness in her expression. Instead, he saw only the cold fury of a woman who felt betrayed by the person she'd trusted most. Alex got back in his truck and drove away, leaving the two of them to face thirty years of unfinished business.

As he drove through the familiar streets of Lazy Rivers, Alex felt something breaking inside his chest. This was the worst day of his life, and he'd had some terrible days. His father's drunken rages that had left him with scars both visible and hidden. His younger brother Zach's disappearance for most of his life, and then losing him again to cancer only a few months ago, the grief of finding and losing his brother again had nearly broken him.

The job had brought its own horrors. Domestic violence calls that ended in tragedy. Car accidents that stole young lives. The night he'd had to tell the Morrison family that their son wasn't coming home from deployment. Being a cop in a small town meant carrying the weight of everyone's worst moments.

But today felt different. Today, he'd lost something he'd never actually had but had dared to hope for. A future with Serenity, a life built on trust and love and the quiet certainty that they belonged together.

The last forty-eight hours had been like a roller coaster. The flood crisis that had brought the whole town together. The engagement of Randy and Sam, the preparations for tomorrow night's gathering, Pete's obvious happiness at having a purpose again. Then the prison visit, watching Tyler and Ethan discover they were brothers, helping them navigate that shocking revelation.

After he dropped them off at Betty Jean and Joseph's, Tyler had let him know that the family had rallied around them, accepting Ethan's parentage as just another thread in the complicated tapestry of their lives. That should have been a good thing, watching love triumph over the sins of the past.

Instead, it had only highlighted how spectacularly he'd failed with his own secret. Tyler and Ethan had chosen honesty, immediate disclosure to the people who mattered most. Alex had chosen deception, thinking he could manage the situation, control the outcome.

Now Serenity was in that motel room with the man she'd once loved, the father of her child, learning the truth about his survival from his own lips instead of from the man who claimed to love her. The betrayal in her eyes when she'd looked at him in the truck would haunt him forever.

Alex stopped at the police station, needing to check on things, needing something normal and routine to ground him. Deputy Wilson was handling the evening shift, and everything was quiet.

"You okay, Chief?" Wilson asked, studying Alex's face. "You look like you've been through a war."

"Long day," Alex said, forcing a smile. "Just checking in before I head home."

"Everything's under control here. Go get some rest."

But rest felt impossible. Alex drove home through the gathering dusk, dreading the moment he'd have to walk into his house and face Pete's questions. The older man had become like a father to him, and Alex wasn't sure he could handle Pete's disappointment on top of everything else.

Pete was waiting in the kitchen when Alex walked in, his face creased with concern. "Alex? What happened? You look like death warmed over."

Alex slumped into a chair at the kitchen table, suddenly exhausted. "I told her about Lucas."

And then, seeing Pete's face, he realized he didn't know what he was talking about. After giving him a brief explanation that the man in the diner with the dark hat claiming to be Philip Brown was actually Lucas Ng, Sam's father, Pete's eyebrows shot up in shock.

"Ah." Pete poured two cups of coffee and sat down across from him, setting down his coffee cup hard. "Well, that explains the tension I've been feeling around here. I take it that didn't go well."

"She's furious. And she has every right to be." Alex rubbed his face with his hands. "I handled it all wrong, Pete. I thought I could manage the situation, figure out the best way to tell her. Instead, I just made everything worse."

"Did you tell her because you wanted to, or because you had to?"

Alex looked up at Pete, surprised by the question. "What do you mean?"

"I mean, did something happen that forced your hand? Or did you finally realize that keeping secrets from someone you love is a recipe for disaster?"

Alex was quiet for a long moment. "Both, I think. I couldn't carry it anymore. But also... I kept thinking about what would happen if she found out some other way. If Lucas approached her directly, or if someone else saw him and recognized him."

Pete nodded slowly. "You were in an impossible situation, son. Damned if you did, damned if you didn't."

"I should have told her immediately. The moment I knew."

"Maybe. Or maybe you were trying to protect her from more pain after everything with Sam and the grief she was carrying and now her excitement about the wedding. Plus, you were dealing with a flood, and the Snags situation." Pete leaned forward.

"Alex, you're a good man. Maybe it was a mistake, but really, it was only twenty-four hours that you kept the secret. In the grand scheme of thirty years, that's nothing."

"It doesn't matter now," Alex said, his voice hollow. "She's with him. And after thirty years apart, with him dying... I don't know if there's room for me in that story."

"There's always room for love, Alex. Real love. The question is whether you're going to fight for it or give up."

Alex looked at this man, who'd become so important to him, who'd seen him at his worst and still offered wisdom and support. "I don't know how to fight for something I never really had."

"Yes, you do," Pete said firmly. "You fight by being honest, by being present, by showing her that what you have together is worth saving. And you don't give up just because it gets hard."

Alex nodded, though he felt too broken to believe it. "I'm going to try to get some sleep. Tomorrow's going to be another long day." He paused, thinking about the party preparations. "And we still have to host that gathering tomorrow night. The last thing I want is a party at my house, but everyone's counting on it."

He climbed the stairs to his bedroom, each step feeling like it weighed a thousand pounds. Behind him, he could hear Pete moving around the kitchen, probably cleaning up from the party preparations that now felt like they'd happened in another lifetime. The last thing he wanted was a house full of people when his world was falling apart, but he was committed now. Pete had worked so hard to make it special.

Alex lay down fully clothed on his bed, staring at the ceiling. Across town, Serenity was having the conversation she should have had thirty years ago. And tomorrow, he'd have to face whatever came next—whether that was losing the woman he loved or finding some way to rebuild the trust he'd shattered.

Either way, he knew he'd never forget the look in her eyes when she'd told him not to wait. It was the look of someone who'd been betrayed by the person they'd trusted most, and Alex wasn't sure he'd ever forgive himself for putting it there, but tonight, he just wanted to disappear.

# Forty One

After Alex left, Serenity and Lucas stood in the doorway for a long moment, simply staring at each other. He looked older, of course, and much thinner than she remembered, his face gaunt with illness.

But his eyes were the same—those distinctive green eyes that Sam had inherited, eyes that had once looked at Serenity like she was the most important thing in the world. Her breath caught in her throat. This was real. He was really alive.

"Hello, Serenity," he whispered.

"Hello, Lucas."

He stepped aside to let her into the small motel room, and she hesitated only briefly before crossing the threshold.

Back at the Rivers house, Lizzy and Mama Ruth were cleaning up the wedding planning materials when Serenity's text came through: "Don't wait up. See you in the morning."

Lizzy smiled, showing the message to Mama Ruth. "She must be having a good conversation with Alex. About time those two stopped dancing around each other."

"Good for them," Mama Ruth said, gathering her purse. "Maybe we'll have another engagement to celebrate soon. I should head home and get some sleep."

"Don't forget we're shopping for Sam's wedding dress tomorrow," Lizzy called as Mama Ruth headed for the door. "Serenity wants to go to Spring Falls so she can check on her gallery opening too."

"I wouldn't miss it," Mama Ruth replied. "It'll be fun, all of us girls together."

Neither woman could have imagined that Serenity's text had nothing to do with a romantic evening with Alex, and everything to do with the ghost of her past come back to life.

Hours later, Lucas dropped Serenity off at the end of her driveway, both of them emotionally drained from their conversation. They'd talked about everything—why she'd sent him away all those years ago, why he'd never tried to find her, Sam's existence and what that meant to all of them, his illness and how little time he had left, the decades of separate lives they'd built without each other.

It hadn't been a reunion either of them had expected. There had been tears, anger, regret, and finally, a kind of sad acceptance of what they'd lost and what they couldn't reclaim. Years of Sam having a father.

"I'm sorry," Lucas had said as his car idled in front of her house. "I'm sorry for coming here and disrupting your life. I can see you're happy with Alex."

"I was happy," Serenity had replied, the past tense hanging heavy between them.

Now, as she quietly let herself into the house, Serenity felt the weight of what lay ahead. The house was dark, everyone asleep, trusting that she was safe and happy. If only they knew.

She went to her room and lay down fully clothed on her bed, staring at the ceiling just as Alex was doing across town. Sleep felt impossible. Her mind kept replaying the conversation with Lucas, the hurt in Alex's eyes, the impossible situation they'd all found themselves in.

This morning she'd have to tell Sam that her father was alive. The daughter, who'd spent the last few days mourning a man she'd never met, would learn that he was not only alive but had been in their town, watching them. How do you explain that to someone? How do you take back grief and replace it with... what? Joy? Confusion? Anger?

And what about Alex? As the hours passed and her initial fury cooled, Serenity began to understand the impossible position he'd been in. Lucas was dying. He'd begged Alex to help him figure out how to approach his daughter without destroying her life.

What was Alex supposed to do—tell her immediately and shatter the happiness she'd just found with Randy? Or try to find a gentler way, a way that might preserve everyone's hearts while still revealing the truth?

She'd been so angry at being kept in the dark, but now she was terrified that she'd reacted exactly wrong. Alex had been trying to protect her, trying to protect Sam, and she'd turned on him like he was the enemy instead of the man caught in the middle of an impossible situation.

What was the right thing? Was there even a right thing in a situation like this?

As she lay there, she thought about a memory of Alex's that she had seen the moment her fury had erupted at him. It was the day ten-year-old Zach had crept up to his brother's bed and told him he loved him. The next day, Zach was gone, vanished without explanation. She knew that memory had haunted Alex his whole life—the fear that people who loved him would disappear without warning.

She knew that to Alex, her walking away with Lucas must have felt like history repeating itself. Another person he loved choosing to leave him behind. Would she ever be able to make it right? The thought of Alex lying awake, believing she'd chosen Lucas over him, made her stomach clench with guilt.

And she still had to tell Sam. Should she tell her before they went shopping for a wedding dress? Or wait? And in that moment, she fully understood why Alex hadn't told her the moment he knew.

It was an impossible choice. Either way, there was pain and regret.

Across town, Lucas lay in his narrow motel bed, staring at the water-stained ceiling and wondering if he'd made the biggest mistake of his life by coming to Lazy Rivers.

Seeing Serenity tonight had been everything he'd hoped for and nothing like he'd imagined. She was still beautiful, still the woman who'd captured his heart thirty years ago. But she wasn't his anymore. Maybe she had never really been.

The way she'd talked about Alex—even in her anger—Lucas could see the love there. Genuine love, the kind he and Serenity had never quite achieved.

Theirs had been passion and youth and intensity, but it hadn't been the deep, abiding partnership that Serenity had clearly built with Alex. What he and Serenity had shared was the bright flame of first love—beautiful, but unsustainable. What she had with Alex was a steady warmth that could last a lifetime.

Lucas had destroyed that. In coming here, by insisting on revealing himself, he'd shattered something precious and real. Alex and Serenity belonged together in a way that he and Serenity never had, and now his selfish need to meet his daughter before he died had ruined it.

The question was: could he fix it? Was there a way to undo the damage he'd caused, to restore what Alex and Serenity had before his arrival?

Lucas had spent months thinking about what he owed his daughter, but maybe who he really owed was the man who'd tried to help him and the woman who'd built a life worth protecting. Maybe the most loving thing he could do was find a way to repair what his presence had broken.

He had so little time left. The cancer was advancing, and soon the pain medication wouldn't be enough anymore. But maybe, in whatever time he had remaining, he could figure out how to give Serenity back her happiness.

Even if it meant sacrificing his own chance to know Sam.

As dawn crept through the motel room curtains, Lucas decided. He would meet his daughter—he'd come too far and had too little time left to give up on that entirely. But he would also find a way to repair the damage he'd caused to the people he'd inadvertently hurt. Somehow, he would make this right. He just had to figure out how to do it before his body gave out entirely.

Neither Serenity nor Lucas slept that night. Both lay in the darkness, wrestling with regret and responsibility, trying to figure out how to move forward when every choice seemed to hurt someone they cared about.

And across town, Alex stared at his own ceiling, wondering if he'd lost the only woman he'd ever truly loved because he'd tried too hard to protect her from a truth that wasn't his to hide.

Tomorrow would bring new challenges, new conversations, and fresh pain. But it would also bring the possibility of redemption, if any of them were brave enough to reach for it.

The question was whether love—in all its complicated forms—would be enough to heal the wounds that secrets and good intentions had opened.

# Forty Two

Tyler had been awake for hours before his phone rang. When he saw Ethan's name on the screen, relief flooded through him.

"I was going to call you," Tyler said by way of greeting. "But I wasn't sure if you'd want to hear from me after everything that happened."

"Are you kidding?" Ethan's voice was warm with concern. "I was worried about you all night. How are you holding up?"

Tyler looked out his kitchen window toward the woods, trying to process everything that had happened. A brother. He had a brother, and he was the one person in Lazy Rivers who'd become his closest friend before either of them knew about the blood connection.

"I don't know," Tyler admitted. "Happy, confused, angry at Snags for waiting until he was dying to tell us. But mostly... grateful. Is that weird?"

"Not weird at all. I feel the same way," Ethan paused. "Want some company? I could come over; we could talk through this together."

"Yeah, I'd like that. Actually, I was thinking about taking a walk down to the river. There's something I want to show you."

An hour later, Ethan pulled into Tyler's driveway, and they set out toward the tree line behind the house. The morning air was crisp and clean, washed fresh by the recent rain, and Tyler felt his head begin to clear for the first time since leaving the prison yesterday.

"So this is the trail Pete mentioned?" Ethan asked as they pushed through the overgrown brush.

"Yeah. He said Big Mike originally cut it, probably fifty years ago or more." Tyler held back a low-hanging branch so Ethan could pass. "I'm thinking about clearing it out properly, making it walkable again. It could be a nice project for the summer."

"I'd help you with that," Ethan offered immediately. "Might be good to have something to work on together. Something positive."

As they walked, Tyler found himself talking more freely than he had since learning about Snags' illness. Having Ethan there—his brother—made everything feel more manageable somehow. They talked about the prison visit, about Snags's motivations, and about what it meant for their futures.

"I keep thinking about timing," Tyler said as they navigated around a fallen log. "If we hadn't become friends first, if we'd just been told we were brothers out of the blue..."

"It would have been different," Ethan agreed. "But maybe this was better. We chose to be friends. The family part is just a bonus."

When they reached the river, Tyler led Ethan along the shoreline toward the ruins he'd discovered. The water was still higher than normal from the recent flooding, but it was receding steadily, leaving behind the usual debris of branches and leaves.

"There," Tyler pointed toward the tree line. "See that pile of old boards? I found it a few days ago, just after it flooded."

Ethan followed him into the brush, his curiosity piqued. "What is it?"

"Foundation stones. Someone built a cabin here decades ago." Tyler walked the perimeter, pointing out the layout. "Look, you can still see where the rooms were. And that's an old wood stove."

Ethan whistled softly. "Who do you think lived here?"

"That's what I'm trying to figure out. The trail leads right to it, so Big Mike definitely knew about it. Maybe he used it as a retreat, or maybe someone else built it and he just found it later."

As they explored the ruins together, Tyler felt a sense of connection to the past that he'd never experienced before. This place represented something lasting, something that had survived decades of weather and neglect. It felt symbolic somehow—proof that people could build things that mattered, that endured.

"Look at this," Ethan called from the far corner of the foundation. He was crouched next to what had once been an interior wall, brushing dirt and leaves away from something that was partially buried.

Tyler joined him and saw what looked like a small metal box, wedged between two foundation stones. It was old and tarnished, but still intact.

"Should we…" Ethan started.

"I don't know," Tyler said, studying the box. "It feels like we'd be intruding on someone's privacy."

"But whoever left it has probably been dead for years. And we found it fair and square." Ethan worked the box loose from its hiding place. "Besides, maybe it's something important. Something someone wanted to be found, eventually."

The box was locked, with a small metal clasp that had rusted shut over the years. Tyler shook it gently and heard things shifting inside—papers, maybe, or small objects.

"We should probably ask Pete about this," Tyler said. "He might know more about who lived here."

"Good idea. We could bring it to the men's night tonight." Ethan stood, brushing dirt off his knees. "Speaking of which, are you looking forward to that?"

Tyler nodded, surprised to realize he genuinely was. "Yeah. A few months ago, the idea of being in a room full of men playing cards and telling stories would have terrified me. Now... it sounds exactly like what I need."

"Same here. Joseph and Alex and all the others, they've been so good to us."

As they made their way back up the trail, Tyler carrying the mysterious box, both young men felt a sense of anticipation that had nothing to do with whatever was inside the locked container. Tonight's gathering represented something important—acceptance, belonging, the kind of casual male friendship neither of them had ever experienced.

"You know what's funny?" Tyler said as they emerged from the woods. "Yesterday I thought talking to Snags was going to be the day ever. Instead, it gave me a brother, and that made everything else make more sense."

"Think we'll ever understand why things happen the way they do?" Ethan asked.

Tyler looked back toward the river, thinking about the cabin ruins and the trail Big Mike had cut so many years ago, about the box they'd found and the secrets it might contain. "Maybe not. But maybe that's okay. Maybe it's enough just to deal with things as they come and trust that it will work out somehow."

Back at Tyler's house, they set the box on the kitchen table and studied it from different angles. Neither of them suggested trying to force it open—that felt like it was something they should do together with the other men, the family that had embraced them both.

"Tonight," Ethan said, and Tyler nodded.

Whatever secrets the box contained, whatever stories it might tell about the people who'd lived and loved and built things in Lazy Rivers decades ago, they would discover them surrounded by friends. And somehow, that felt exactly right.

The mystery could wait a few more hours. They had a lifetime to uncover truths together.

# Forty Three

S erenity had made her decision sometime before dawn—she
would tell Sam today, while they were surrounded by family,
in the safety of their own home. Everyone would be together,
happy and relaxed, and maybe that would soften the blow of what
she had to reveal.

She could hear voices downstairs—Sam's laughter mixing with
Lizzy's gentle teasing and Matthew's deeper chuckle. The sounds
of her family starting their day, completely unaware that their
world was about to shift on its axis again.

Serenity sat on the edge of her bed, still in yesterday's clothes,
and tried to gather the strength to leave her room. The doors to
her studio were open, and she could see the painting she had just
finished for the gallery opening—an image of the river in autumn
that had taken her months to complete. She had been planning

to take it to the gallery herself today to check on the installation. Now, that didn't seem important at all.

She had ruined her chances with Alex, and now she was about to make Sam either really happy or devastate her all over again. Which would it be? And both these outcomes were out of her control, even though it was her choices, her secrets, her failures to handle the most important relationships in her life, that had brought them here.

She'd managed maybe an hour of sleep, and that fitfully. Every time she'd closed her eyes, she'd seen either Alex's hurt expression or Lucas' desperate hope, and both images made her chest ache with guilt and confusion.

The sound of a car in the driveway told her Mama Ruth had arrived, right on schedule for their shopping expedition. Serenity closed her eyes and took a deep breath. There was no more delaying this.

Leaving her room, she found exactly the scene she'd expected—Sam and Lizzy at the kitchen table with their coffee, Matthew reading something on his phone and making occasional comments that made the women laugh. Mama Ruth was just coming through the door, her face bright with excitement.

"There's our bride-to-be!" Mama Ruth announced, giving Sam a hug. "Ready to find the perfect dress?"

"I can't wait," Sam said, practically glowing with happiness. "I've been thinking about it all morning. Something simple but elegant, something that would make Randy forget how to breathe when he sees me walking down the aisle."

Lizzy laughed. "That boy already forgets how to breathe when he looks at you. But I know what you mean."

The easy joy in the room made what Serenity had to say feel especially cruel. These people she loved were having a perfect morning, planning a perfect day, and she was about to shatter it all.

"Good morning," Serenity said quietly from the kitchen doorway.

The conversation stopped immediately. Four pairs of eyes turned to her, and she watched their expressions shift from welcome to concern in the span of seconds.

"Honey," Lizzy said carefully, "you look exhausted. Are you feeling alright?"

Matthew set down his phone, his reporter's instincts clearly picking up on the tension. "Did something happen with Alex last night?"

Sam was studying her mother's face with growing alarm. 'Mom? What's wrong? You look like you've been crying."

Mama Ruth moved closer, her maternal instincts kicking in. "Serenity, you look like you haven't slept at all. Sit down. Let me get you some coffee."

"I need to tell you something," Serenity said, her voice barely above a whisper. "All of you. Something that's going to change everything."

The room went completely silent. Sam's face went pale, and Lizzy reached instinctively for Matthew's hand.

"Is it Alex?" Sam asked. "Is he okay?"

"Alex is fine. This is about..." Serenity's voice caught. "This is about your father, Sam."

"My father? But we already know—he died. Jan found his obituary."

Serenity shook her head, tears flowing again. "He didn't die, sweetheart. He's alive. And he's here. In Lazy Rivers."

The silence that followed was absolute. Sam stared at her mother as if she'd spoken in a foreign language, while Lizzy's hand flew to her chest and Matthew leaned forward in his chair.

"That's impossible," Sam whispered.

"The man at the diner," Serenity continued, the words tumbling out now. "The one with the black cap. Philip Brown. His real name is Lucas Ng. He's your father, Sam. He faked his death when he got sick, so he could be alone. Then he found your book and realized he had a daughter."

Sam's coffee mug slipped from her hands, shattering on the kitchen floor. The sound seemed to break whatever spell had held the room frozen.

"He's here?" Sam's voice was barely audible, her hand pressed against her chest as if she couldn't breathe. "My father is alive, and he's been here, in our town, watching us?"

"He wanted to meet you, but he was afraid of disrupting your life. He asked Alex to help him figure out how to approach you."

"Alex knew?" The betrayal in Sam's voice was sharp. "How long has Alex known?"

"Since Wednesday afternoon. He was trying to find the right way to tell us."

Sam stood up abruptly, her chair scraping against the floor. "'My father is alive. He's been alive this whole time, and I've been mourning him. I've been planning a wedding without him, thinking he'd never get to walk me down the aisle, and he's been sitting in our diner watching me grieve for him?"

The pain in her daughter's voice cut through Serenity like a knife. "Sam, I know this is a shock..."

"A shock?" Sam's voice rose. "A shock is finding out Randy likes his eggs scrambled instead of over easy. This is... this is..." She couldn't finish the sentence, dissolving instead into tears that seemed to come from somewhere deep in her soul—tears of relief, anger, confusion, and overwhelming joy all mixed together.

Mama Ruth moved immediately to comfort her, while Lizzy sat frozen in her chair, trying to process what she'd just heard. Matthew was the first to speak.

"Where is he now?" Matthew asked quietly, his mind already working through the implications of what this meant for all of them.

"At the motel outside town. He's very sick, Matthew. That's why he came—he's dying, and he wanted to meet Sam before it was too late."

Sam looked up through her tears. "I want to see him. Right now."

"Honey, maybe you should take some time to process this first..." Lizzy began.

"No." Sam's voice was firm despite the tears. "I've lost thirty years with him already. I'm not losing another minute."

Serenity nodded, understanding. "I'll call him. Ask him to come here."

"Here?" Mama Ruth looked around the kitchen. "Are you sure that's wise? Maybe somewhere more neutral?"

"Here," Sam agreed. "If he's my father, then he should come to our family home. I want him to see where I grew up, where I became the person I am. I want him to meet all of you properly."

Then, sitting back in her chair, Sam crossed her arms, stared at her mother, daring her to make the call, and waited, not letting herself cry more. She was a woman now, not a child. *I can handle this*, she thought, hoping that maybe if she said it to herself enough she could.

# Forty Four

As Serenity called Lucas, her hands shaking, the others moved around the kitchen in a kind of shocked silence. Matthew helped Mama Ruth clean up the broken coffee mug while Lizzy made fresh coffee, trying not to think at all.

"Lucas?" Serenity said, when he answered. "She knows. Sam knows. She wants to meet you... Can you come to the house?"

"Are you sure?" Lucas asked, and Serenity could hear the hope and terror warring in his voice.

"No. But it's what Sam wants, and I've learned that keeping her from what she wants only makes things worse."

"'I'll be there," Lucas said so quietly that Serenity felt the words rather than hearing them. She was afraid and relieved at the same time, and missing Alex so much it physically hurt.

When Serenity hung up, she turned to see Sam staring out the kitchen window as if she could will her father's car to appear in the driveway.

"He's coming," Serenity said. "He should be here in about twenty minutes."

"Twenty minutes," Sam repeated, wonderingly. "In twenty minutes, I'm going to meet my father for the first time."

The family fell into an anxious silence, each lost in their own thoughts. The morning that had started with such joy and anticipation had transformed into something none of them had been prepared for.

When Lucas's car finally pulled into the driveway, they all froze like deer in headlights. Through the window, they could see him sitting in his car for a moment, gathering courage just as they were.

"That's him?" Sam asked, pressing her face to the glass.

"That's him," Serenity confirmed.

Lucas looked even frailer in the morning light than he had the night before. His black cap was pulled low, and he moved slowly up the front walk, each step carefully planned.

When the doorbell rang, no one moved for a moment. Then, Sam straightened her shoulders and walked to the front door.

"Hello," she said when she opened it, her voice barely steady. "You must be my father."

Lucas looked at her. The daughter he hadn't known he had. She had his eyes and hair, his grandmother's cheekbones, but everything else was uniquely hers.

"Hello, Sam," he said, his voice as frail as he looked.

Sam stared at the man she had wanted to meet her whole life. Nothing about him felt familiar, and yet she knew without a doubt it was true. This man was her father. She had imagined someone strong and sturdy she could run up to and embrace, but this man looked as if he could be knocked over with a feather.

"May I come in?" Lucas asked.

Sam hadn't realized she had been frozen in the doorway, blocking his entrance. She put her hand to her chest, apologizing as she stepped aside and led him into the living room.

The awkwardness in the living room was evident as everyone tried to figure out where to sit, what to say, and how to behave in a situation none of them had ever imagined. Lucas looked overwhelmed by the crowd of people, while Sam couldn't seem to stop staring at him, as if she were afraid he might disappear again.

But gradually, as Lucas answered Sam's questions about his life, his illness, and his decision to find her, the tension eased. He told them about his years as an art dealer, traveling the world but never feeling like he belonged anywhere.

Lizzy made more coffee. Matthew asked gentle questions about the places Lucas had lived and the art he'd collected for his clients.

Mama Ruth, in her infinite wisdom, simply accepted this new reality and began treating Lucas like family.

By the time the morning was over, something had shifted. Lucas was no longer a stranger who'd disrupted their lives. He was Sam's father, returned from the dead with stories to tell and love to give in whatever time he had left.

As Lucas prepared to leave, promising to return the next day to continue getting to know his daughter, Sam hugged him for the first time. It was tentative and brief, but it was a beginning.

"'I can't believe you're real," she whispered against his shoulder, breathing in the unfamiliar scent of him—medication and aftershave and something uniquely him.

"I can't believe you turned out so beautifully," he whispered back, his voice breaking.

Watching Lucas struggle to his car, each step clearly painful, Sam turned to look at her mother. Serenity, understanding what was about to happen, nodded with tears in her eyes. Sam ran out to stop him before he could get away again.

"Let me go to the motel with you to get your stuff. You can stay here."

Lucas had to keep himself from crying as relief washed over him. He looked up to see Serenity standing in the doorway, smiling at him through her own tears. He hadn't dared dream this would happen, but now that it had, he felt a weight he'd been carrying for months finally lift from his chest.

After Sam and Lucas left, the family sat in the living room, emotionally drained but somehow lighter than they'd been before.

"Well," Matthew said finally, "that wasn't what I expected when I woke up today."

"Poor Alex," Lizzy said suddenly. "He must have been carrying this alone, trying to figure out what to do. Serenity, you have to talk to him."

Serenity nodded, already reaching for her phone. "I know. I owe him the biggest apology of my life."

As she called Alex's number with trembling fingers, Serenity realized that finding Lucas again hadn't diminished her love for Alex—it had only made her more certain of it. Lucas was her past, but Alex was her future. Now she just had to hope it wasn't too late to make things right.

# Forty Five

Raymond was cleaning the dirt from under his fingernails at the motel room sink when he heard car doors slamming outside. Through the thin curtains, he could see Philip Brown—or whoever he really was—standing beside his car while a young woman helped him load a suitcase into the trunk.

The woman looked familiar, and it took Raymond a moment to place her. The diner. She'd been there, talking and laughing with her mother and the sheriff. Pretty girl, with distinctive green eyes and long black hair shining in the morning light.

Raymond stepped outside as they were finishing up, making a show of checking his truck. The man in the black cap looked up and gave him a tentative wave—the kind of polite acknowledgment strangers give each other in small towns.

"Morning," Raymond called out, his voice carefully friendly.

"Morning," Philip replied, though he seemed nervous. He moved closer to the young woman, as if she were his protection.

As they drove away, Raymond noticed the woman looking back at him through the passenger window, her expression thoughtful and slightly puzzled.

In the car, Sam was quiet for the first few minutes, processing everything that had happened in the past few hours. Her father was alive. He was sitting right next to her, real and breathing and telling her again about finding her books, loving them, and then realizing she must be his daughter. It felt surreal, like a dream she might wake up from at any moment.

Sam realized then how much she needed Randy to meet Lucas. It couldn't wait. She texted him to come to the house, saying simply, "Something amazing happened. Come now. It's important."

He texted back that he'd be right there. This was another thing she loved about him—she could always count on him to drop everything when she needed him. Now she couldn't wait for her father to meet the man she was going to marry. Despite that, the man at the motel worried her.

"That man at the motel," she said suddenly. "Do you know him?"

Lucas glanced in the rearview mirror, though Raymond was no longer visible. "Not really. He got there a day or two after I arrived. Keeps to himself mostly, but..." He paused, choosing his words carefully. "There's something angry about him. Like he's carrying a grudge against the world."

"I've seen him at the diner," Sam said, frowning. "Something about him seems familiar, but I can't place it. I wish I knew why he is in Lazy Rivers."

Lucas adjusted his grip on the steering wheel, his hands shaking slightly from the medication, doing his best to hide the wave of pain that shot through his side.

"Maybe he's just passing through and got stuck because of the flooding."

Sam looked back one more time, though the motel was long out of sight. "Maybe. But something about him bothers me. The way he was watching us just now, like he was taking notes."

Lucas nodded grimly. "I noticed that too. But let's not worry about strangers today. I'd rather talk about you. Tell me about your writing, about Randy, about the life you've built here."

As they drove toward the Rivers house, both father and daughter pushed thoughts of Raymond aside, more interested in making up for thirty years of lost conversations.

Raymond waited until their car disappeared around the corner before getting into his truck. He'd planned to spend the day researching property records at the courthouse, but his appetite had been sharpened by the morning's encounter.

The diner seemed like the best place to gather information, as it had been since he'd arrived. Betty Jean had a talent for knowing everyone's business, and if he timed it right, he might overhear something useful during the lunch rush.

When he walked into the diner, he found Betty Jean and Joseph huddled together near the coffee station, their voices low but animated. Raymond took a booth within earshot and pretended to study the menu he'd already memorized.

"I still can't believe it," Betty Jean was saying, shaking her head. "Philip Brown is Sam's father, and I served him coffee every day without knowing. That poor man was watching his daughter from across the room."

"Lucas Ng," Joseph corrected. "It was good of Serenity to call and let us know what was happening."

Betty Jean nodded in agreement, wiping the counter down with more force than necessary before answering, "That poor girl. Thinking her father was dead all this time and then finding out he's been staying at the motel. I should have trusted my instincts. Something about him seemed familiar, but I couldn't place it."

Raymond's attention sharpened. So Philip Brown was Sam's father, and his real name was Lucas Ng. That explained the protective stance, the careful way he'd moved around her.

"Is he staying at the Rivers' place now?" Joseph asked.

"That's what Serenity said. Sam insisted on it." Betty Jean glanced around the diner, then lowered her voice further. "Joseph, what do you think this means for Alex? He and Serenity were getting so close, and now..." Her voice trailed off with worry for the man who'd become like family to all of them.

"Now her old love shows up, dying and desperate to know his daughter. It's a mess." Joseph shook his head. "But if anyone can handle it, it's Alex. He's tougher than he looks."

Raymond filed this information away as he ordered his usual lunch. He knew the police chief was involved with this Serenity woman, who was apparently the mother of Philip/Lucas' daughter. The family dynamics were getting interesting.

As he ate, Raymond reconsidered his plan for tonight's men's gathering. He'd intended to show up uninvited and force a conversation about what was rightfully his. But now he realized that would be a mistake. The timing was all wrong.

Tonight, all attention would be on this family drama—the dying father, the reunited daughter, the love triangle with the police chief. Raymond would be just another interruption, another problem to be managed. He needed everyone's full attention, not a distracted audience trying to juggle multiple crises.

Besides, showing up uninvited at a police chief's house might raise the wrong questions. Raymond had worked too hard to maintain his cover as just another traveler to blow it now with aggressive tactics. No, he needed a different approach. Something more subtle, and yet more direct. Something that would get him what he wanted.

As Raymond paid his bill, nodding politely to Betty Jean, his mind was already working on a new plan. He'd been patient this long. He could be patient a little longer.

But his patience wasn't infinite. One way or another, he was going to get what he'd come for. Raymond had no intention of leaving Lazy Rivers empty-handed.

The family drama unfolding around Lucas Ng and his daughter might actually benefit him. While everyone was focused on their emotional reunions and romantic complications, Raymond could move more freely, plan more carefully.

By the time the dust settled on their personal crises, Raymond would be ready to claim what was rightfully his. And if it hurt the people in this cozy little town, well, that wasn't really Raymond's problem. Some people deserved what was coming to them.

# Forty Six

The basement of Alex's house buzzed with the comfortable energy of men gathering for an evening of cards, conversation, and the kind of easy camaraderie that small towns do best.

Pete had outdone himself with the preparations—card tables were set up with perfect precision, Mama Ruth's chili simmered in slow cookers, and coolers full of beer sat strategically placed around the room.

Alex descended the stairs with Randy and Lucas, the latter moving carefully but determinedly down each step. The conversation in the room quieted for a moment as the other men took in the sight of Sam's father—alive, present, and clearly welcomed into their circle.

"Gentlemen," Alex said, his voice carrying only a slight strain, "I'd like you to meet Lucas Ng. Sam's father."

The introductions went smoothly, each man stepping forward to shake Lucas' hand with the respectful warmth that Lazy Rivers extended to family members. Because that's what Lucas was now, regardless of the complicated circumstances that had brought him here.

Pete pulled Alex aside while the others were settling Lucas into a comfortable chair near the pool table. "How are you doing, son?" he asked quietly. "This can't be easy."

Alex glanced toward Lucas, who was already deep in conversation with Joseph about Sam's writing career. "I'm managing. Serenity and I talked this afternoon. She apologized and explained everything. But..."

"But it still stings that she turned on you instead of trusting you to handle it right," Pete finished.

"Something like that." Alex accepted a beer from John, grateful for the distraction. "I know she was shocked, angry. I know I probably should have told her immediately. But the look in her eyes when she told me to leave..." He shook his head. "I've never seen her like that."

"Give it time," Pete advised. "Love doesn't disappear overnight, even when it gets bruised."

Randy appeared at Alex's elbow, his face bright with excitement that seemed to radiate from every pore. "Can you believe this? Sam's father is here, alive, and he gets to be at our wedding. He can walk her down the aisle!"

The joy in Randy's voice was infectious, and Alex genuinely smiled for the first time all day. "That's wonderful, Randy. Sam must be over the moon."

"She is. We all are." Randy paused, his expression growing more serious. "Though... well, he doesn't look very strong, does he? Do you think he'll be okay for the wedding?"

Alex looked across the room at Lucas, who was laughing at something Tom had said, but clearly struggling to hide his fatigue. The man's color wasn't good, and he moved with the careful deliberation of someone managing significant pain.

"I hope so," Alex said quietly. "For Sam's sake."

Meanwhile, Tyler and Ethan had found themselves in the corner near the old upright piano, both carrying the weight of their own recent revelations. The box they'd discovered by the river ruins sat locked away in Tyler's truck, but its presence seemed to hover between them like an unspoken question.

"Should we mention the box?" Ethan asked quietly, nodding toward the group of men.

Tyler shook his head. "Not tonight. This is supposed to be about celebrating Lucas being here, about all of us just being together. About Randy and Sam getting married. The box has waited decades—it can wait one more night."

"Besides," Tyler added with a small smile, "we're still processing the whole brother thing ourselves. I think that's enough family revelations for one week."

Ethan grinned. "Fair point. Though I have to say, having a brother is pretty great, even if we found out about it in the worst possible way."

"Snags finally did something right," Tyler agreed. "Even if he waited until he was dying to do it."

Joseph approached them, carrying three bottles of beer. "How are my boys doing?" he asked, the pride in his voice unmistakable. "Still getting used to being brothers?"

"It's weird," Ethan admitted. "But good weird. Like finding out you've had a best friend your whole life, you just didn't know it."

"That's exactly right," Joseph said, clapping them both on the shoulders. "And now you're both officially part of this crazy extended family. Tyler through Big Mike, Ethan through Tyler. It all works out."

The evening progressed with the peaceful rhythm of men who genuinely enjoyed each other's company. Card games started and stopped, stories were told and retold, and the conversation flowed from work to sports to gentle ribbing about relationships.

Lucas, despite his obvious fatigue, seemed to come alive in the warmth of male friendship. He told stories about his years as an art dealer, the famous pieces he'd handled, and the eccentric collectors he'd worked with. In return, the men of Lazy Rivers shared their own tales—Pete's farming wisdom, Tom and Brad's nursery adventures, John's construction mishaps.

"You know," Lucas said during a quiet moment, "I spent thirty years thinking I'd never be part of something like this. A community, a family. I convinced myself I didn't need it."

"What changed your mind?" Matthew asked.

"Getting sick, partly. But mostly Sam." Lucas's voice grew soft. "Reading her books, realizing I had a daughter out there living a life I knew nothing about. It made me understand what I'd been missing."

Randy leaned forward in his chair. "She's incredible, isn't she? Your daughter?"

"She is." Lucas smiled, and for a moment his illness seemed to fade into the background. "And she chose well with you, Randy. I can see how much you love her."

"I do. More than I ever thought possible." Randy's voice carried the wonder of a man still amazed by his good fortune. "I just hope..." He stopped, glancing around the room.

"What?" Lucas prompted gently.

"I hope you'll be strong enough to walk her down the aisle, I know it's only a few months away, but..."

The room went quiet. Everyone could see what Randy was seeing—Lucas was clearly declining, each day a little weaker than the last.

Lucas met Randy's eyes. "I'll be there," he said with quiet determination. "Even if they have to wheel me down that aisle, I'll be there for my daughter's wedding."

Pete raised his beer bottle. "To Lucas," he said simply. "Welcome to the family."

"To Lucas," the other men echoed, and the toast carried with it all the warmth and acceptance that Lazy Rivers could offer.

As the evening wound down, Alex watched Lucas with a mixture of admiration and sadness. The man was dying, but he was spending his last weeks trying to be the father Sam had always needed. It was both heartbreaking and inspiring.

"Thank you," Lucas said to Alex as they prepared to leave. "For bringing me tonight, for accepting me into this. I know it can't be easy, given everything with Serenity."

Alex studied the man who had once been Serenity's love, the father of the young woman he thought of as family. "Sam needed you here," he said simply. "That's all that matters."

As they climbed the stairs from the basement, Alex realized that tonight had been exactly what they'd all needed—a reminder that families came in all shapes and sizes, that love could survive complications, and that sometimes the best thing you could do was simply show up for the people who mattered.

The road ahead was still uncertain—for Lucas's health, for Alex and Serenity's relationship, for all the secrets that Lazy Rivers seemed to specialize in keeping. But tonight, surrounded by friends and filled with the warmth of acceptance, those uncertainties felt manageable.

Some problems were too big to solve in one evening. But some moments of grace were too precious not to savor, and this had been one of them.

# Forty Seven

Saturday morning brought the kind of crisp, clear weather that made everything seem possible. Ethan and Tyler arrived at Alex's house just after nine, Tyler carrying a small metal box that had spent decades hidden in the ruins by the river.

Pete was making pancakes when they walked into the kitchen, his face brightening at the sight of the two young men. "Perfect timing," he said, flipping a golden pancake with practiced ease. "I made enough to feed an army."

"Actually, Pete," Tyler said, setting the box carefully on the kitchen table, "we found something yesterday. Something we thought you might know about."

Alex looked up from his coffee, noting the serious expressions on both young men's faces. "What kind of something?"

"We were exploring some old cabin ruins by the river," Ethan explained. "They were near the trail Big Mike cut years ago. Tyler found this box wedged between some foundation stones."

Pete wiped his hands on a dishtowel and moved closer to examine the box. It was old, clearly weathered by decades of exposure, but still intact. "I remember that cabin," he said slowly. "My father mentioned it once or twice when I was young. Said the cabin had been there long before him."

Tyler had managed to work the rusted lock open that morning, but he hadn't looked inside. Something about it felt too private, too important to examine alone. "We thought maybe you'd know who might have left it there."

"There's only one way to find out," Alex said, pulling up a chair.

With careful hands, Tyler opened the box. Inside, wrapped in oilcloth that had somehow survived the years, were several items: a few pieces of simple jewelry, a pressed flower that had long since turned to dust, and a sealed envelope with "To My Son" written across it in faded ink.

Pete's breath caught. "That handwriting looks familiar." His voice was barely a whisper, as if speaking louder might make the recognition false.

Tyler lifted the envelope carefully. The paper was yellowed and fragile, but the seal had held. "Should we...?"

"Yes," Pete whispered. "If it's been waiting this long, it needs to be read. Would you read it? I can't see that good." Pete's admission was quiet, almost ashamed, as if his failing eyesight was just another reminder of all the things he was losing.

Tyler opened the envelope with the care of someone handling a butterfly's wing. Inside was a single sheet of paper, covered in the same delicate handwriting. He cleared his throat and read:

> My dearest son, If you are reading this, then somehow fate has brought you to the place where you were conceived in love, even if that love had to remain secret. I don't know if I will survive bringing you into this world. But I know I will have to give you away to keep you safe. But I need you to know that you were wanted, that you were loved before you took your first breath. Your father is a good man, though the world might not see him that way. He has responsibilities, a family, a life that cannot include us openly. But he loves us both, in his way. This cabin has been a safe place for us, and we meet when we can, though now I know it must stop. He has to return to his wife, and I to my husband. We love them. It's just that we loved each other too. I pray that someday you will understand why you will have to grow up without knowing who your birth parents are. It's not that we don't want you—it's that we want to protect you. Your father's name is Michael Clarkson, though

everyone calls him Big Mike. He's strong and kind and stubborn, maybe you will be all that too. I know you will grow up not knowing where you came from, but I hope you feel you come from love. Secret love, complicated love, but love nonetheless. I hope you grow up to be as good a man as your father. I hope you find happiness that doesn't have to hide in the shadows.     All my love, always, your mother, Annie — February 1948

The silence that followed was profound. Tyler's hands were shaking as he set the letter down, and Ethan looked like he'd been struck by lightning.

Tyler, who had only a few months before learned that his grandfather was Big Mike, couldn't believe what he had just read. Another secret child, another family connection hidden for decades. Ethan, who had just learned that his father was Snags, stared at the letter, overwhelmed by how tangled these family trees had become.

But it was Pete's reaction that alarmed them most. The older man had gone completely white, his eyes wide with shock. He gripped the edge of the kitchen table as if it were the only thing keeping him upright.

"Pete?" Alex said, hurrying to his side. "Are you okay?"

"I have a brother," Pete whispered, his voice barely audible. "Somewhere out there, I have an older brother."

Pete stared at the letter again, his hands trembling. "My mother," he whispered. "My mother had an affair with Big Mike." His voice broke on the words. "All these years, I thought she was just... fragile. Delicate. The way my father talked about her after she died, like she was this perfect angel who'd been too good for this world.

"She died when I was eight," Pete continued, his voice barely audible. "I always wondered why she seemed so sad, so distant sometimes. Now I know—she was carrying this secret, knowing she had a son out there somewhere that she'd given away. Maybe that's what really killed her. Not her heart giving out, but her heart breaking.

"But she lied to me my whole life," Pete said, his voice growing stronger with hurt. "Every time I talked about wishing I had a brother, she knew I had a brother who was out there somewhere, maybe wondering about his family."

Tyler and Ethan exchanged uncomfortable glances. This was more than just discovering a brother—this was Pete's entire understanding of his mother being rewritten.

"She was protecting her son—your brother," Alex said gently.

"But she never told my father, did she" Pete said, his voice growing hollow. "He raised me never knowing there was another boy out there. A boy who should have been my brother."

Pete's eyes filled with tears. "My father died never knowing he had a stepson who might have needed him."

The words seemed to echo in the quiet kitchen. Pete's legs gave out, and Alex caught him just as he started to collapse, helping him into a chair.

"Easy, Pete. Just breathe."

"All these years," Pete said, his voice hollow. "All these years I thought I was alone. My mother said nothing, never mentioned... How could she not tell me?"

Tyler reread the date on the letter. "1948. If the baby survived, he'd be... what, seventy-six now?"

Pete shook his head slowly. "My mother would stare out the window for hours, and I always assumed it was because she never wanted to be a farmer's wife. But now..." He gestured to the letter. "I think she was mourning. She was grieving for the son she'd given away."

He looked at the letter again. "She had two children in two years. I was born only a year later. I thought I was her first and only child, but I was actually her second baby."

The kitchen fell silent again as they all grappled with the magnitude of what they'd discovered. Pete had a half-brother he'd never known existed, the product of a secret relationship that had been hidden for over seventy years.

Alex's mind was working through the implications. "Pete, if your brother is Big Mike's son, that means he's also...'

"Half-brother to Joseph, Lizzy, and Snags," Pete finished, his face going even paler. "Can you believe it? There is another one of Big Mike's children."

The weight of that settled over the room. Joseph had turned out to be a good man. Lizzy was beloved by everyone. But Snags had been a murderer.

"What if he's like Snags?" Pete asked quietly, voicing what they were all thinking. "What if Big Mike's blood runs dark in him too?"

Pete stood up abruptly, pacing to the window. "What kind of man is he? Did he grow up angry about being given away? Is he out there somewhere, bitter and resentful?"

He turned back to face them. "What if he's dangerous? What if he blames our family for abandoning him?"

"Pete, you're borrowing trouble," Alex said, though he could understand the fear. "We don't even know if he's alive, let alone what kind of person he became."

"But what if he is alive?" Pete pressed. "What if he's been looking for me? What if he already knows about me and just hasn't made contact?" Pete's voice was rising with anxiety.

"What kind of man is he? Did he grow up angry about being given away? Did he spend his whole life wondering why his parents didn't want him?" Pete's voice cracked. "Is he out there somewhere, blaming me for having the life he should have had?"

Alex watched Pete pace, his mind already working on the implications. He thought about the angry stranger in town and wondered if it was possible that he was not out there somewhere, but was already in Lazy Rivers.

# Forty Eight

"What do we do now?" Randy asked quietly.

Before anyone could answer, Alex's phone rang. He glanced at the screen and felt his stomach clench. Serenity.

"I should take this," he said, stepping into the living room.

"Alex?" Serenity's voice was strained. "I'm sorry to bother you, but I'm worried about Lucas. He's gotten so much weaker since yesterday, and he's trying to hide it, but..." Her voice broke slightly. "I think he's failing faster than he thought he would."

Alex closed his eyes, feeling the weight of another crisis settling on his shoulders. "How bad is he?"

"He can barely stand for more than a few minutes. He's in pain, even with the medication. Alex, I don't think he's going to make it to the wedding."

The words hung between them, carrying all the weight of unfulfilled promises and time running out too quickly.

"I'll be right over," Alex said.

"You don't have to..."

"Yes, I do." Alex's voice was firm. "Whatever's between us, Sam needs support right now. And so do you."

After he hung up, Alex returned to the kitchen to find Pete still staring at the letter, as if reading it again might change what it said.

"I have to go," Alex said. "Lucas is getting worse. Pete, are you going to be okay?"

Pete nodded slowly, though he looked anything but okay. "I need some time to process this. A brother. After all these years..."

Tyler and Randy exchanged glances. "We'll stay with Pete," Tyler offered. "Help him figure out what to do next."

As Alex drove toward the Rivers' house, he couldn't help but think about the cruel irony of the morning. Pete had just learned he had family he'd never known about, while across town, Sam was losing the father she'd just found.

Remembering his brother Zach and how he lost him just after finding him again, he felt that perhaps life specialized in giving people exactly what they needed at precisely when it might be too late to matter.

But as his phone buzzed with another call from Serenity, Alex pushed aside his own hurt and focused on what was important. Sometimes love meant showing up even when your heart was still bruised. Sometimes it meant putting someone else's crisis ahead of your own pain.

And sometimes, it meant racing toward the woman you loved, even when you weren't sure she still loved you back.

# Forty Nine

Alex pulled into the Rivers' driveway, and the sight of several cars already there filled him with dread. Either Lucas had taken a dramatic turn for the worse, or the family was rallying for something equally serious.

He found them all gathered in the living room, their faces etched with worry and exhaustion. Lizzy sat beside Matthew on the couch, her hand clasped tightly in his.

Randy was pacing by the window while Sam sat curled in an armchair, her eyes red from crying. Serenity stood near the doorway to the hall, looking like she hadn't slept in days.

"How is he?" Alex asked quietly.

"Sleeping," Serenity replied, her voice barely above a whisper. "I moved him into my room downstairs so he wouldn't have to climb the stairs. Every step seems to exhaust him now. I'll sleep in one of the guest rooms upstairs for now."

Matthew looked up from his phone. "We called the doctor. He was here about an hour ago."

The silence that followed told Alex everything he needed to know, but he asked anyway. "What did he say?"

Sam's voice was hollow when she answered. "Maybe a week. If we're lucky."

The words hit the room like a physical blow. Randy stopped pacing and moved to Sam's side, taking her hand in both of his.

"A week," Sam repeated, as if saying it again might make it less real. "I just found him, and now I'm going to lose him again."

Alex felt his own throat tighten. Despite everything—the complications Lucas' arrival had caused, the strain it had put on his relationship with Serenity—he genuinely liked the man.

Lucas had shown up at the men's gathering with dignity and grace, sharing stories and accepting the friendship offered to him. He didn't deserve to die alone and afraid.

"There has to be something..." Randy said.

"There isn't," Serenity interrupted gently. "The cancer has spread everywhere. The doctor said, the only thing we can do now is keep him comfortable."

Lizzy wiped her eyes with a tissue. "That poor man. To find his daughter after all these years, only to have so little time with her."

The room fell into another heavy silence, each person lost in their own thoughts about the cruelty of timing and the fragility of life. Serenity dropped her head, feeling a crushing guilt. This was all her fault. She was the one who had sent him away and never told him about Sam. Just because it had been the Rivers women's way, didn't make it right.

Then Sam stood up, her jaw set with determination. "We're having the wedding tomorrow."

Everyone stared at her. Randy's eyes widened. "Sam, honey, maybe we should wait."

"No." Sam's voice was firm, though tears streamed down her face.

"My father is dying. He came here because he wanted to be part of my life, and I refuse to let him die without seeing me get married." Sam's voice cracked on the last words, but her determination was absolute.

Randy studied her face, seeing the fierce love and desperation there. "Are you sure? We could wait until he's feeling better."

"He's never going to feel better," Sam said, her voice breaking. "This is as good as it's going to get. If we want him to be able to walk me down the aisle, it has to be now."

Matthew leaned forward. "Sweetheart, planning a wedding in one day, how can we do it?"

"I don't care if it's perfect," Sam interrupted. "I don't care if we have to get married in the backyard with paper plates and grocery store flowers. I just want my father there, conscious and able to see me happy."

Serenity moved to her daughter's side, pulling her into a fierce hug. "Then that's what we'll do."

Randy looked around the room at the faces of the people who'd become his family. "What do we need?"

Lizzy was already reaching for her phone. "First, we call Mama Ruth. If anyone can pull off a wedding in twenty-four hours, it's her."

As if summoned, the front door opened and Mama Ruth walked in, her arms full of grocery bags. "I brought supplies for lunch," she announced, then stopped short when she saw the expressions on everyone's faces. "What's happened?"

"We're having a wedding tomorrow," Sam said simply.

Mama Ruth set down the bags slowly, her eyes taking in Sam's tear-streaked face and Randy's protective stance beside her. "Because of Lucas," she said, understanding immediately.

"He has maybe a week," Serenity explained. "Sam wants her father to walk her down the aisle."

Mama Ruth nodded once, decisively. "Then we're having a wedding tomorrow. Where?"

"I was thinking of the backyard." Sam said.

"The nursery," Mama Ruth interrupted. "Tom and Brad have been working on the new garden area behind the greenhouse. It's perfect for a spring wedding."

Randy's face lit up with the first smile Alex had seen from him all morning. "The nursery would be perfect. And I bet that Tom and Brad would love to host it there."

"I'll call them," Matthew offered, already dialing.

As the room suddenly filled with purpose and planning, Alex watched Serenity. She was coordinating with Lizzy about flowers, making lists on the back of an envelope, but he could see the exhaustion in every line of her body.

She caught him looking and gave him a tentative smile—the first genuine smile she'd directed at him since their fight. But behind it, he could see fear. Not just fear for Lucas, but fear that she'd damaged something between them that couldn't be repaired. Alex felt his own heart clench, wanting to reassure her but not sure he was ready to bridge that gap yet.

"We'll need help with everything," Mama Ruth was saying, pulling out her own phone. "Food, decorations, chairs, music..."

"Betty Jean and Joseph will handle the food," Lizzy said confidently. "And I'll bet John can round up tables and chairs from somewhere. He did it for the men's gathering."

"What about Sam's dress?" Serenity asked suddenly.

Sam looked down at her jeans and sweater. "I don't care what I wear."

"You will care," Mama Ruth said firmly. "Every bride cares. We'll figure something out."

As the planning continued around him, Alex felt a sense of déjà vu. This was what Lazy Rivers did when a crisis struck—they rallied. They dropped everything and showed up for each other, whether it was sandbagging during a flood or pulling together a last-minute wedding for a dying man's daughter.

"Alex," Randy said, pulling him aside. "Will you be my best man? I know we planned on Tyler, but with everything happening, maybe it's too much."

"Tyler should still do it," Alex said immediately. "He needs this right now. Something good to focus on instead of worrying."

Randy nodded, understanding. "You're right. But I want you there too. Will you help officiate? You're qualified, right?"

Alex was indeed qualified to perform marriages in his capacity as police chief. His answer, "I'd be honored," filled him with a sense of peace. He really was part of this family. Something he never thought he'd get to experience until Serenity came back to town.

As the afternoon wore on, the house filled with the controlled chaos that comes with attempting the impossible. People came and went—Tom and Brad arriving to discuss transforming the garden space, Betty Jean appearing with notebooks full of catering ideas, John showing up with a truck full of folding chairs he was taking directly to the nursery.

Through it all, Lucas slept in Serenity's room, unaware that his mere presence was galvanizing an entire community into action.

His daughter was getting married tomorrow, and everyone who loved her was determined to make it beautiful.

For the first time since opening the box that morning, Alex felt something approaching hope. Yes, Lucas was dying. Yes, Pete was dealing with the shock of discovering a long-lost brother. Yes, his relationship with Serenity was still fragile and uncertain. But love was happening. Family was being chosen and celebrated and protected. And sometimes, that was enough to tip the scales toward grace, even in the darkest of times.

Tomorrow would bring its own challenges. Alex, Pete, Tyler, and Ethan had decided not to share yet what they found in the box, because today, they had work to do and a wedding to plan.

And in Lazy Rivers, that was exactly the kind of impossible task that brought out the best in everyone. When love was on the line, miracles had a way of happening.

# Fifty

Lucas woke on Sunday morning to sunlight streaming through Serenity's bedroom windows, and for a moment he forgot where he was. Then the familiar ache in his bones reminded him—Serenity had given him her bedroom so he didn't have to climb the stairs.

She had left the doors open to her studio, and he could see her latest painting on an easel.

The painting took his breath away. It was a picture of the river, but not as it appeared to the casual observer. This was the river as seen through an artist's soul—layers of light and shadow that revealed depths invisible to the naked eye, colors that seemed to pulse with their own inner life.

"It's the most beautiful thing you've ever done," he said softly as Serenity appeared in the doorway with a cup of tea.

She looked surprised. "You really think so?"

"I know so." Lucas struggled to sit up, his body protesting every movement. "It's... it's like you've painted the secret life of water. The way it remembers everything it's touched."

Serenity's eyes filled with tears. "I wanted to finish it for the gallery opening next month." Her voice carried both pride and sadness—pride in the work, sadness that Lucas wouldn't be there to see it displayed.

"I'm sorry I'll miss seeing it displayed properly," Lucas said, genuine regret in his voice. "But maybe that's fitting. Your art should outlive all of us."

A gentle knock interrupted them, and Matthew appeared in the doorway. "Morning, Lucas. Ready to help your daughter get married?"

Hours later, they saw the transformation of Tate's Nursery. It was nothing short of miraculous. Tom and Brad had worked through the night, turning their new garden area into something from a fairy tale.

White fabric draped between the trees created natural cathedral walls, while strings of lights twined through the branches cast everything in a warm, golden glow.

John had arranged rows of chairs in a perfect semicircle facing an arch formed by two flowering dogwood trees. The aisle between them was carpeted with cherry blossom petals that Mama Ruth had somehow procured from her vast network of gardening friends.

"I can't believe we pulled this off," Brad said, adjusting one final light string.

"Mama Ruth pulled this off," Tom corrected, nodding toward the woman who was currently directing the placement of floral arrangements with the precision of a military commander. "We just followed orders."

The flowers were indeed spectacular—early spring blossoms, all arranged in simple glass vases that caught and reflected the filtered sunlight. Everything looked effortlessly elegant, as if it had grown naturally from the garden itself, which much of it had.

Betty Jean and Joseph had set up their catering station near the greenhouse, with Amy and Ethan helping to arrange platters of food that would make any restaurant jealous. Although they had stayed up almost all night preparing the food, they weren't the slightest bit tired. Love had a way of sustaining people beyond their normal limits. They knew exhaustion might catch up with them later, but for now all they felt was pure joy.

Several waitresses from the diner moved between the tables, making final adjustments to place settings and ensuring everything was perfect.

"Where did the china come from?" Amy asked, admiring the delicate plates and crystal glasses.

"Don't ask," Betty Jean replied with a mysterious smile. "Mama Ruth has connections we can't even imagine."

Near the entrance to the garden, Pete stood ready to greet guests, yesterday's shock about the letter temporarily set aside in favor of wedding duties. He'd insisted on handling this job, saying he needed something normal to focus on, something that celebrated life instead of dwelling on secrets from the past.

The soft sound of a harp drifted through the garden as the musician Mama Ruth had somehow located began her prelude. The music seemed to make the very air shimmer, adding an ethereal quality to the already magical setting.

Back at the Rivers house, Serenity and Lizzy were helping Sam into her dress—a simple but elegant creation that had appeared as if by magic.

"I still can't believe Mrs. Henderson had this in her shop," Sam said, smoothing the silky fabric. The dress was perfect—classic lines that complemented her figure without being fussy, with delicate lace details that caught the light.

"She's been saving it for the right bride," Lizzy explained. "When Mama Ruth called and described you, she insisted it was meant to be yours."

The dress fit as if it had been made for Sam, which Mrs. Henderson swore it might have been, given how perfectly everything aligned. With Serenity's pearl earrings and a simple veil, Sam looked radiant despite the circumstances that had rushed them all to this moment.

"How do you feel?" Serenity asked, stepping back to admire her daughter.

"Like I'm about to marry the love of my life while my father watches,' Sam replied, her voice steady despite the tears threatening to spill. 'Scared and grateful and so, so happy I can barely breathe."

At the nursery, guests were arriving. The gathering was small—just the people who had become family to Sam and Randy over the past months.

Tyler stood near the altar in his role as best man, having spent the morning helping Randy with his nerves and his tie. Alex, resplendent in his dress uniform, reviewed his notes one final time while Randy paced nearby.

"You sure about this?" Tyler teased. "It's not too late to run."

"Never been more sure of anything in my life," Randy replied, then grinned. "Though if you'd asked me a year ago if I'd be getting married to Samantha Rivers, I'd have said you were crazy. Now I can't imagine my life without her."

"Funny how life works out," Tyler said, thinking about his own recent revelations about family and brotherhood.

The harp music shifted to a more formal processional as Matthew appeared, pushing Lucas in the wheelchair they'd arranged for him. Lucas was dressed in a borrowed suit that John had somehow found in his size, and despite his obvious weakness, his eyes were bright with joy and determination.

But as they reached the aisle, Lucas surprised everyone by slowly standing up. Matthew moved to help him, but Lucas waved him away.

"I'm walking my daughter down the aisle," he said quietly but firmly. "Even if it kills me."

The gathered guests held their collective breath as Sam appeared at the entrance to the garden, radiant in her wedding dress, carefully linking her arm with her father's. Only she could feel how much he was leaning on her for support, and she was determined to be strong enough for both of them. Lucas moved slowly, clearly using every ounce of strength he possessed, but he was walking.

Step by careful step, father and daughter made their way down the petal-strewn aisle. The harp music seemed to carry them forward, and by the time they reached Alex and Randy, there wasn't a dry eye in the garden.

"Who gives this woman to be married?" Alex asked, his voice carefully controlled.

"I do," Lucas said, his voice strong despite his physical frailty. "With all my love and all my pride."

He placed Sam's hand in Randy's, then whispered something in his daughter's ear that made her smile through her tears. With Matthew's help, he took his seat in the front row, having accomplished what he'd come to Lazy Rivers to do.

The ceremony itself was beautiful in its simplicity. Alex spoke about love that transcends time and circumstance, about the choice to build a life together despite uncertainty. Randy and Sam exchanged vows they'd written themselves, promises that acknowledged both joy and sorrow, health and sickness, presence and loss.

When Alex pronounced them husband and wife, and Sam and Randy kissed—a gentle, reverent kiss that spoke of promises kept and dreams fulfilled—the small gathering erupted in cheers and applause. The harp music swelled as the new couple walked back down the aisle, their faces radiant with happiness.

As guests moved to the reception area, where tables had been set up under a white canopy, Alex surveyed the scene with deep satisfaction. Everything was perfect—the food, the flowers, the gentle music, the faces of people he thought of as family.

But as he looked beyond the garden toward the horizon, he noticed dark clouds beginning to gather in the distance. Storm clouds, heavy and ominous, suggested that the recent clear weather might not last.

He caught Pete's eye across the garden and saw that the older man had noticed the approaching weather as well. Their eyes met for a moment, and Alex knew they were both thinking the same thing—about Annie's letter, about Pete's unknown brother somewhere out there, about the way secrets in Lazy Rivers had a habit of surfacing just when life seemed most peaceful.

But for now, in this moment, there was joy. There was love celebrated and family gathered and promises made under an open sky. Sam and Randy were married, Lucas had lived to see his daughter's happiness, and the community of Lazy Rivers had once again proved that miracles were possible when people came together.

The storm clouds could wait. Today was for celebration.

# Fifty One

As the guests gathered around the buffet tables, the garden filled with the warm sounds of celebration—laughter mixing with the gentle harp music, the clink of glasses, and the comfortable chatter of people who genuinely cared for each other. Lucas sat in his wheelchair near the head table, surrounded by well-wishers, his face radiant despite his obvious exhaustion.

Serenity was refilling her coffee cup when the memory hit her with unexpected force. But this time, something was different—instead of seeing one person's memory, she was experiencing two simultaneously, as if her gift had suddenly doubled in intensity.

She saw the memory of Pete's shock as Tyler read Annie's letter aloud in Alex's kitchen, felt his knees giving out as the weight of discovering a brother crashed over him.

At the same time, she experienced Alex's perspective—his concern for Pete, his mind racing through the implications, his growing worry about what this unknown brother might mean for the man he'd come to love like a father.

The dual memory was so vivid that Serenity had to grip the edge of the table to steady herself. She'd never experienced anything like this before—seeing the same moment through two different sets of eyes, feeling two different emotional reactions to the same revelation.

When the memory faded, she looked across the garden to where Pete was greeting late arrivals, then to Alex, who was finishing his official duties. Both men looked troubled beneath their celebratory smiles, carrying a burden that none of the other guests could see.

Meanwhile, John was watching the celebration with a heart full of conflicting emotions. His son was married to a wonderful woman, surrounded by friends who'd become family. Randy looked happier than John had ever seen him, and that should have been enough.

But watching the joy on Randy's face made John think about Mary, about how much she would have loved this day. She'd always said Randy would know when he found the right woman, and she'd been right. Mary should have been here to see their son's happiness, to welcome Sam into their family properly.

His eyes drifted to Mama Ruth, who was directing the serving of cake with her usual efficiency and warmth. She'd thrown herself into planning this wedding with such love and enthusiasm, treating Sam like her own daughter and Randy like her son, making sure every detail was perfect.

John had been carrying their marriage license in his wallet for three weeks now. They'd filled out all the paperwork, but kept it a secret between them, not knowing when they would find the perfect time to make it official.

But watching Randy and Sam glow with newlywed happiness, seeing the way love had transformed both their lives, John realized that the perfect time was now. Life was uncertain—Lucas's presence was proof of that. You couldn't wait for ideal circumstances when love was standing right in front of you.

He made his decision. Walking over to Alex, who was putting away his officiant's notes, John cleared his throat nervously. "Alex, could I ask you for another favor?"

Alex looked up, noting John's serious expression. "Of course. What do you need?"

"I need you to perform another wedding," John said, pulling the folded license from his wallet. "Ruth and I could never find the perfect time. But well... I figured today might be the perfect day."

Alex's face broke into a wide smile—the first completely unguarded expression Serenity had seen from him in days. "John, that's wonderful. Does Ruth know you're about to propose this plan to her in front of everyone?"

"I'm about to find out," John said with a grin that made him look twenty years younger.

He walked over to where Mama Ruth was cutting cake, took her flour-dusted hands in his, and dropped to one knee right there beside the dessert table.

"Ruth Tate," he said loud enough for everyone to hear, "will you marry me right now, in front of all our friends and family?"

Mama Ruth's face went through about six different expressions in the span of two seconds—surprise, joy, exasperation, and finally, pure love. "John Carver, I've been ready to marry you for months. What took you so long?"

"I was waiting for the perfect moment," John replied, standing up and kissing her soundly.

"And you think this is it?" Ruth asked, gesturing to her slightly disheveled appearance.

"I think any moment I get to marry you is perfect," John said simply.

Randy, who had been watching this exchange with growing delight, picked up his champagne glass and tapped it with his fork.

"Ladies and gentlemen," Randy announced, his voice carrying across the space, "it seems we have one more wedding to celebrate today."

Everyone turned to see Alex standing with John and Mama Ruth, while Randy moved to stand beside his father and Lizzy appeared at Ruth's side.

"Since we're all here," John said, his voice carrying a note of wonder, "and we've got the perfect officiant, we've got a marriage license, the most beautiful setting, and all the people we love... why not take advantage of the situation?"

The garden erupted in cheers and applause as Alex opened his notes again, this time with a smile that reached his eyes. Within minutes, they were ready for their second ceremony of the day.

This wedding was even simpler than the first—no music except for the excited murmur of guests, no formal processional, just two people who'd found love later in life and decided not to waste another moment waiting for it.

When Alex pronounced John and Ruth husband and wife, their kiss was met with even louder cheers than Randy and Sam had received. There was something particularly joyful about seeing love triumph at any age, about witnessing two people brave enough to start over together.

As the celebration continued, Matthew and Lizzy stood together near the edge of the garden, watching the joyful chaos around them.

"We could, you know," Matthew said quietly.

"What?" Lizzy asked, though she knew exactly what he meant.

"Make it three weddings in one day. I've got a ring in my truck, been carrying it around for weeks."

Lizzy smiled and took his hand. "Ask me tomorrow," she whispered. "Today has been perfect, but I want our moment to be just ours. Not shared with anyone else, no matter how much we love them."

Matthew nodded, understanding. "Tomorrow, then."

"Tomorrow," Lizzy agreed.

But even as the second round of celebrations began, the storm clouds that had been gathering on the horizon were growing darker. What had started as wispy gray clouds was building into something that looked threatening.

The first fat raindrops began to fall just as the cake cutting was finishing, sending everyone scrambling to help pack up the remaining food and decorations. Within minutes, the gentle spring afternoon had turned into a proper downpour.

Guests rushed to their cars, laughing and calling out goodbyes as they ran through the rain. The magical garden setting was quickly abandoned for the dry safety of vehicles and buildings.

Randy and Sam made their rounds, hugging everyone goodbye and promising to see them in the morning at Lizzy's house for a celebration brunch.

"No honeymoon trip?" someone called out.

"Later," Sam replied, glancing toward her father, who was being helped into Matthew's car. "We'll have our honeymoon later. Right now, family comes first."

As the last of the guests departed, Alex found himself alone in the garden for a moment, helping Tom and Brad secure the remaining decorations against the wind and rain. Through the downpour, he caught sight of a dark truck driving slowly past the nursery entrance.

There was something deliberate about the way it moved, as if the driver was observing rather than simply passing through. Alex couldn't make out the driver through the rain and the truck's tinted windows, but something about it made him uneasy.

He thought again about the stranger he'd seen in the diner, about the questions that had been asked around town, about the way some problems had a habit of appearing just when life seemed most perfect.

The truck disappeared around the bend, but Alex continued to stare after it long after it was gone. In his experience, when strangers lingered in small towns asking the wrong kinds of questions, it usually meant trouble was coming.

But for today, there had been enough joy to balance whatever darkness might be approaching. Two weddings, a father who'd lived to see his daughter's happiness, and a community that had once again proved that love could conquer almost anything.

The storm could rage all it wanted. They'd weather this one too, just like they had all the others.

But as Alex finally ran for his truck through the pelting rain, he couldn't shake the feeling that the actual storm was still ahead of them.

# Fifty Two

R aymond sat in his truck outside Tate's Nursery, watching as the wedding celebration unfolded. Even from the road, he could see the canopy near the greenhouse, and the guests talking, laughing and hugging.

For just a moment—a single, traitorous moment—he wondered what it would be like to be part of something like that. To belong somewhere, to have people who celebrated your happiness and mourned your losses. To be invited instead of always watching from the outside.

The feeling lasted maybe thirty seconds before the familiar anger crashed back over him like an icy wave. These people had what should have been his. That land, that community, that sense of belonging—it had all been stolen from him when his mother gave him away and his father pretended he didn't exist.

When Raymond saw Alex look his way, he pulled away from the nursery, but not before noting how happy everyone looked, how easy their lives appeared. Well, that was about to change. He'd been patient long enough, watching and waiting and planning. Tomorrow, when all the celebrating was over and the hangovers had set in, it would be time to claim what was rightfully his.

The party was over. Now the real business could begin.

Monday morning arrived, gray and drizzling, the previous day's storm having settled into a steady rain that made everything feel damp and gloomy.

Pete was making coffee in Alex's kitchen, lingering as he tried to process everything that had happened in the past few days. A brother he'd never known about. A letter that rewrote his understanding of his mother. Two weddings that should have been pure joy but felt overshadowed by secrets and approaching threats.

Alex was at the kitchen table, reviewing reports from the weekend's activities, when the knock came at the front door. It was sharp, insistent, and somehow aggressive in its rhythm.

"I'll get it," Alex said, but something in his tone made Pete look up with concern.

Through the front window, Alex could see a man standing on his porch—tall, broad-shouldered, with the stillness that suggested barely controlled violence. This wasn't a social call.

Alex opened the door to find himself face-to-face with the stranger from the diner and realized it was probably the man whose truck he'd seen driving past the nursery yesterday. Up close, the man looked a little like Pete, although his face was harder, marked by resentment and anger.

"Alex Williams," the man said, his voice carefully controlled. "Police chief. I'm Raymond Harmon. I think you and Pete Jones need to hear what I have to say."

"About what?" Alex kept his voice level, his police instincts on high alert.

"About property that's been in the wrong hands for too many years."

Pete appeared behind Alex, drawn by voices, and stopped dead when he saw Raymond. The resemblance was like looking in a funhouse mirror—similar features, but twisted by bitterness into something harder and more dangerous.

"You're him," Pete said, his voice steady. "You're my brother."

Raymond's smile was sharp and cold. "Half-brother. And I'm here to collect what's mine."

Alex stepped back reluctantly, letting Raymond into the house. Every instinct he had screamed that this was a mistake, but Pete had a right to hear what his brother had to say.

In the living room, Raymond pulled out a folder thick with documents. "Birth certificate," he said, slapping papers onto the coffee table. "Adoption records. Death certificates for my adoptive parents. Legal documentation proving that I am Raymond Miller Harmon, born to Annie Jones in February 1948, given up for adoption to Harold and Margaret Harmon of Pittsburgh."

Pete stared at the documents, his face pale. "Annie Jones. My mother."

"Our mother," Raymond corrected harshly. "The mother who kept you and threw me away."

"She didn't throw you away," Pete said quietly. "She was trying to protect you."

"Protect me?" Raymond's voice rose. "From what? From having a family? From having a home? From having land that should have been mine by right of birth?"

Alex observed the exchange, noting the way Raymond's anger seemed to build with each word. This wasn't just about property—this was about resentment and perceived abandonment.

"The farm belongs to me now," Pete said. "My father left it to me when he died."

"Your father," Raymond spat. "The man who married our mother and never even knew I existed, did he? She kept me a secret from everyone, didn't she? Had me and then threw me away like garbage.

"Half that farm was my mother's, and she would have left it to me," Raymond corrected harshly, hoping that what he said was true. That she would have loved him enough to do so, even though she didn't know where he would end up. "Which means half of it should have been mine. And you've had it long enough."

Raymond pulled Annie's letter out of the folder—the same letter Tyler had read aloud just two days earlier.

Pete's eyes widened as he recognized the letter. "How did you get that? We found that in the old cabin ruins."

Raymond's laugh was bitter. "You found a copy. I've had the original for months. Found it in my adoptive mother's papers after she died. Turns out she kept everything—birth certificate, correspondence with the adoption agency, even this letter that our mother gave to her to keep for me. But she never gave it to me while she was alive, so I had to find out the hard way who I really am."

Alex felt his blood run cold. "You've been watching us. You knew about Pete before you came here."

"I've been planning this for months," Raymond confirmed. "Tracking down my real family, learning about the property, figuring out what was owed to me." His voice turned harder. "And what I found was that the farm is half mine, and I want it. Now."

"Pete is your brother," Alex said firmly. "That makes him family."

"Half-brother," Raymond corrected again.

Pete was staring at the letter in Raymond's hands, his voice barely a whisper. "You want me to sign over the farm."

"Yes," Raymond said, his face hard. "You've had seventy-five years of a life that should have been mine. Consider this my inheritance, finally coming due."

"And if I don't?"

Raymond's smile was cold and predatory. "Then I'll take it, anyway. Accidents happen to old men living alone on isolated farms. House fires. Falls down stairs. Heart attacks from too much stress...' He shrugged. "Life is so fragile at your age."

The threat hung in the air like poison. Alex's hand moved instinctively toward his service weapon, but Raymond noticed and shook his head.

"I'm not threatening anyone, officer. Just pointing out that life is uncertain, especially for elderly people. Pete here looks like he's been under a lot of stress lately. All this excitement about brothers and family reunions... it could be too much for a man his age."

Pete suddenly straightened, a memory clicking into place. "You," he said, staring at Raymond. "The day of the flood. You bumped into me on the diner steps. You were watching me even then."

"I've been watching all of you," Raymond confirmed. "Learning about your little community, figuring out who matters to whom, understanding the connections." His voice turned

313

mocking. "Such a close-knit family. Would be a shame if something disrupted all that happiness."

Alex stood up, his voice carrying all the authority of his badge. "I think this conversation is over. You need to leave. Now."

Raymond gathered his papers calmly. "I'll be in touch, Pete. You've got twenty-four hours to think about my offer. Sign over the farm, and I'll disappear from your life forever. Keep trying to hold on to what isn't yours..." He shrugged. "Well, we'll see what happens.

"Oh. And one more thing. I know who my real father was. Says right here on the birth certificate—Michael Clarkson. Big Mike himself. He abandoned me too, just like everyone else.' Raymond's eyes glittered with malice. "I might just go after that part of my inheritance too. The diner, all of it."

After Raymond left, Pete slumped into his chair as if all the air had gone out of him. "He's going to kill me for that farm," he said. "I can see it in his eyes. The same look Snags used to get when he wanted something."

Alex watched through the window as Raymond's truck disappeared down the road. "We need to call the others," he said grimly. "This isn't something you can handle alone, Pete. And this isn't over—not by a long shot."

# Fifty Three

After Raymond left, the house felt as if it had been poisoned. Pete slumped in his chair, looking every one of his seventy-plus years.

They had both read the birth certificate. Raymond was Annie's son, and his father was Big Mike.

Alex shook his head, wanting to tear the copy of the birth certificate Raymond had left into shreds. Wishing Big Mike were around so he could punch him in the face. What was that man thinking? Had Big Mike even known about Raymond? Something told him that somehow Annie had kept it secret from both him and her husband.

He wondered how she had made sure no one knew about her baby. Perhaps she had gone to visit family for a few months. That seemed like the logical explanation of how she'd hidden the pregnancy from everyone.

"I'll give him what he wants," Pete said quietly.

"No," Alex answered. "Absolutely not. You give in to him now, he'll just take more. And Pete, this isn't a man who would take care of the land or be part of the community. This is someone who destroys things."

"But if I don't..."

"If you don't, we'll deal with it. Together. As a community." Alex's voice was firm, but inside, his own fear was growing. Raymond reminded him too much of Snags—the same bitter anger, the same willingness to hurt people to get what he wanted.

He silently cursed Joseph's father, Big Mike, and all the trouble he had caused even from the grave. It was too bad he wasn't around to pay for his mistakes, but he had died before all his misdeeds had surfaced. Before he could face the consequences of all the lives he'd damaged.

Until just a few months ago, everyone had thought that Joseph was Big Mike's only child. Then they discovered Lizzy was his half-sister, Snags was his half-brother, and now this.

How was he going to tell Joseph that he had yet another sibling? Joseph had been grateful to discover that Lizzy was his sister and Tyler was his nephew, but this was different. Raymond was dangerous. And he wanted the diner that Joseph had worked his whole life to build.

Raymond reminded him of Snags, two brothers who'd never met but shared the same capacity for violence.

Pete looked out the window thinking of his farm, the land that had been in his family for generations.

"After all these years," he said, his voice hollow. "After surviving floods and droughts and my parents' deaths and my wife's death and everything else... now I'm going to lose it all to a brother I never knew existed."

Alex wanted to offer reassurance, but the words wouldn't come. Raymond wasn't bluffing—Alex could see it in his eyes, in the careful way he'd laid out his threats. This was a man who'd spent months planning, who had nothing left to lose and everything he thought he deserved to gain.

The storm clouds that had gathered yesterday were nothing compared to what was coming now. And Alex wasn't sure any of them were prepared for the destruction Raymond seemed capable of unleashing.

But they'd weathered things before, and they'd do it again. This was not something he could do alone, though. They needed to gather people who could help. And they needed to tell Joseph, Lizzy, and Tyler that there was another member of the family.

That's when Alex realized that there was one thing they had missed. Something that might make Pete smile.

"Pete, I know this is a mess, but you know we'll work it out as a community. And there is a silver lining."

"What," Pete said, his voice filled with tears.

"Well, if Big Mike was Raymond's father, and Annie was his mother, then that makes Joseph your half brother."

"That means I'm related to Lizzy and Tyler too?" Pete asked, hope creeping into his voice despite everything and starting to smile.

"Looks like it."

Pete's smile grew wider. "Wow, that's confusing as all get out. But I'll take it. I'm really part of the family."

"Yep," Alex answered, his mind racing ahead. He had a plan forming, but first he needed legal advice. If Raymond wanted to claim inheritance rights, there were proper legal channels for that. Threats and intimidation weren't among them. Once again, they all needed to gather; this time it would be at his house.

But first, he had a few calls to make. Leaving Pete to call everyone to meet in a few hours, Alex went into his study and made his first call to his friend David, the best attorney he knew in the county. After explaining the situation, Alex felt the first glimmer of genuine hope he'd had since Raymond's visit.

"Alex, listen carefully," David said. "Even if Raymond can prove he's Annie's son and Big Mike's biological child, that doesn't automatically entitle him to anything. Big Mike never acknowledged him, never provided for him, and never left him anything in his will, so it's ridiculous that he is threatening the diner. The farm belonged to Annie and her husband, not Big

318

Mike. Raymond would have to file a formal claim in probate court and prove his case legally for both properties."

"What about his threats?"

"You know that's criminal intimidation. Document everything. If he threatens Pete again, arrest him." David's voice was firm. 'This isn't the Wild West, Alex. He can't just show up and demand property based on a birth certificate and a few documents. The law doesn't work that way.'

Alex made two more calls—one to the county courthouse to research property records, and another to an old friend in the state police who owed him a favor. By the time he finished, he had the beginnings of an actual plan.

"They'll be here in a few hours," Pete said.

"We'll be ready for them," Alex answered.

# Fifty Four

Alex's house had never felt so small. What had been a comfortable gathering space for the men's night just two days earlier now seemed to shrink under the weight of nearly twenty people crowding into the living room and kitchen. The atmosphere was a strange mix of post-wedding joy and growing anxiety—everyone could sense that this wasn't a social call.

The folding chairs were back, and people perched on the arms of the couch and leaned against walls. The last two times the group had called emergency gatherings like this, the news had changed lives.

The first meeting had been about what Alex's brother Zach had been doing with Joseph, Betty Jean, and Big Mike for years to help ten-year-old boys escape abuse families. The next meeting had revealed Big Mike's relationships with two women other than his wife, and the children that had resulted from those affairs—Lizzy and Snags.

Now, seeing the serious expressions on Alex and Pete's faces, everyone suspected they were about to hear something that would shake their world again. But no one expected it was once again going to be about Big Mike and his connection to another woman that produced yet another child, Raymond.

Serenity watched Alex from across the room, noting how he still held himself apart from her despite their tentative reconciliation. She wanted to go to him, to offer support for whatever burden he was carrying, but the careful distance he maintained told her she hadn't yet fully earned back his trust. The knowledge sat heavy in her chest.

She glanced toward her mother and Matthew, who stood close together near the kitchen doorway, and suddenly saw a memory that made her breath catch.

It was Matthew's memory from decades ago—the first time he'd seen Lizzy at a community meeting, how he'd been struck not just by her beauty but by the intelligence in her eyes, the way she listened with her whole being. It was the moment he'd fallen in love, though it had taken him years to find his way back to her.

The memory faded as Lucas appeared at her elbow, moving slowly but determinedly with his walker. When they were preparing to leave the house, he demanded to go with them. "I don't want to be left alone," he said quietly when she tried to protest. "Whatever's happening, I want to be here for it."

Serenity hovered anxiously beside him after helping him to the couch, adjusting cushions and making sure he was comfortable. Alex felt his heart clench at the sight. She was doing exactly what she should do—caring for a dying man, putting his needs first. But it still hurt to watch her attention focused so completely on someone else.

When everyone had finally settled, Alex stood in the center of the room, Pete beside him for moral support.

"Thank you all for coming on short notice," Alex began, his voice carrying the authority of his office. "I wish this were another celebration, but we have a problem. A serious one."

He told them about Raymond's visit, about the documents and threats, about the connection to Big Mike that made him Pete's half-brother and therefore part of their extended family network. As he spoke, he watched faces change from confusion to understanding to anger.

"He threatened Pete," Joseph said, his voice tight with fury. "This man threatened one of our own." It didn't matter to Joseph that Raymond was claiming to be his half-brother. He was like Snags, and Joseph wanted nothing to do with him. Pete was more family to him than Raymond could ever be.

"He wants the farm," Tyler said, working through the implications. "But if Big Mike was his father too, does that mean he could go after the diner as well?"

"He could try," Alex confirmed. "But I have a plan."

He paused, looking around at the faces of people who'd become his chosen family. "You all know about my brother Zach. Maybe you remember that when he died, he left me everything. A substantial inheritance that's been sitting in trust while I figured out what to do with it."

Alex's voice grew stronger, more determined. "I'm going to buy Pete's farm. I'll give half the money to Pete for his retirement, and half to Raymond as settlement of any claim he thinks he has. Pete will come live with me permanently, and Raymond will have no reason to stay in Lazy Rivers."

The room erupted in surprised murmurs. Pete looked stunned, while others began talking over each other about the logistics and implications.

"Alex, that's incredibly generous," Mama Ruth said, "but what if Raymond doesn't take the deal?"

"Then we'll deal with that when it happens," Alex replied. "But this gives us a legal, clean solution that protects Pete and gets Raymond what he thinks he wants. And the deal will include that he leaves the diner alone."

"So, Joseph," Tyler said, trying to work out all the family connections. "You are Raymond, Lizzy, and Snags' half-brother. And of course, since Snags is my father, you are my uncle."

Joseph, who was still processing that his father had yet another child—one who seemed as dangerous as Snags—nodded, wondering where Tyler was going with this.

"And Pete is Raymond's half-brother," Tyler continued. "Then in a very roundabout way, Pete is kind of my uncle too?"

Everyone laughed. "Very convoluted reasoning, Tyler," Alex said, "but I think Pete would be glad to be your uncle, and in someway Pete and Joseph could be brothers."

Pete grinned widely. 'Heck yeah!' he said, giving Tyler a high five that made everyone laugh again, the sound breaking some of the tension in the room.

"Something else to celebrate," Joseph said. A year ago he'd felt isolated from the community, keeping to himself at the diner. Now he had discovered sisters and nephews and friends who'd become family.

"'Yes, to family," Betty Jean said firmly. "Blood or not. We are family."

"Like the song," Matthew said, and hummed a few bars of "We Are Family." A few people joined in, their voices blending together, momentarily forgetting that they still had Raymond to deal with.

"Uncle Pete," Pete said. "I like the sound of that."

As embraces and congratulations filled the room, Alex felt some of the tension ease from his shoulders. This was what Lazy Rivers did best—turn strangers into family, find silver linings in dark clouds, support each other through whatever storms came their way.

But the reality of Raymond's threats tempered the celebration. He was still out there, still angry, still dangerous. And there was no guarantee he'd accept Alex's offer.

"When do we approach him?" Tom asked, ever practical.

"Tomorrow," Alex decided. "Tom, Brad, would you be willing to come with me? Since you already have the information about Pete's farm. Meet him at the diner where it's public, lots of witnesses."

"Absolutely," Brad said immediately.

"We'll make it clear this is a onetime offer," Alex continued. "Take it or leave it. And if he chooses to leave it..." He let the implications hang in the air.

As the gathering broke up, people headed home with promises to stay in touch and be ready if needed, Serenity lingered behind. When it was just her, Alex, Pete, and Lucas left in the living room, she finally approached Alex directly.

"Thank you," she said. "For protecting Pete, for bringing the family together, for..." She gestured helplessly. "For everything."

Alex studied her face, seeing the regret and love there. "We'll get through this, Serenity. All of it."

"I hope so," she replied. "I really hope so."

As she helped Lucas to the car and drove away, Alex felt the weight of the next day settling on his shoulders. Tomorrow would determine whether his plan worked, whether Raymond could be bought off and sent away, whether the peace of Lazy Rivers could be preserved.

But tonight, surrounded by the evidence of community and love, Alex allowed himself to hope. They'd faced worse odds before and come through stronger. Maybe with luck and determination and the bonds that held them all together, they could do it again.

The only question was whether Raymond Harmon would prove reasonable, or if they were about to discover just how far anger and resentment could drive a man when everything he thought he deserved was finally within reach.

# Fifty Five

Tuesday morning dawned clear and cool, exactly one week since the floodwaters had first threatened Lazy Rivers. Alex sat in his truck outside the diner, checking his phone one more time before heading inside. He'd texted Serenity earlier, asking if she could be at the meeting for moral support, and her immediate "yes" had eased some of the knots in his stomach.

Inside the diner, Betty Jean was wiping down tables with more energy than necessary, her nervous tension evident in every movement. Joseph stood behind the counter, methodically organizing things that didn't need organizing, while Tyler and Ethan worked quietly in the kitchen. Amy moved between tables, refilling salt shakers and trying to look busy.

Everyone was trying to act normal, but the undercurrent of anxiety was palpable. They all knew what this meeting meant, what was at stake for Pete and for their community.

Alex had just settled into the corner booth when his phone rang. The caller ID made his blood run cold: State Correctional Institution.

"Chief Williams," he answered, turning his back to the rest of the dinner.

"Chief, I'm calling to inform you that inmate Snags Clarkson died this morning."

Alex closed his eyes, feeling a complex mix of emotions wash over him. "Thank you for letting me know. I'll inform the family."

After hanging up, Alex stood for a moment, processing the news. Then he walked over to where Joseph, Tyler, and Ethan were standing together.

"That was the prison. Snags died this morning."

Tyler's face went completely blank, while Ethan reached out instinctively to put a hand on his brother's shoulder. Joseph's expression was unreadable.

Betty Jean, who had overheard, set down her cleaning cloth with shaking hands. "Thank God," she said, then immediately looked stricken. "Oh Lord, is that terrible of me to say?"

Amy moved closer to Betty Jean, their eyes meeting in understanding, happy that Snags was no longer in the lives of the men that they loved, and sad for them at the same time.

The three men stood together for a long moment, each processing the news in their own way. Finally, Joseph spoke.

"No, Betty Jean. It's not terrible." His voice was quiet but firm. "Thank God. Thank God it's over."

They all exhaled together, as if a weight they'd been carrying for months had finally been lifted. Tyler looked up at Joseph, his face vulnerable.

"I keep trying to think of one good memory of him," he whispered. "Just one. But I can't."

Joseph immediately pulled both Tyler and Ethan closer, wrapping his arms around them. "Then we'll make new memories. Better ones. As a family."

The diner door chimed as Serenity, Tom, and Brad arrived together, Pete right behind them. Alex quickly filled them in on the news about Snags, and they absorbed it with the same mixture of relief and complicated emotions.

"One less problem to worry about," Tom said simply, and everyone nodded.

The door chimed again, and Raymond walked in. The atmosphere in the diner immediately shifted, becoming charged with tension. He looked around at the gathered faces—some sympathetic, some wary, some openly hostile—and his jaw tightened.

Joseph surprised everyone by pulling up a chair to Alex's booth. "Raymond," he said simply. "Sit."

Raymond hesitated, clearly not expecting this gesture, then slowly took the offered seat. Alex spread the legal documents across the table, along with a cashier's check that represented more money than most people in Lazy Rivers would see in a lifetime.

"This is my offer," Alex said without preamble. "A full buyout of any claim you think you have to Pete's property and the diner. Clean, legal, and generous. Take it, and you never have to see any of us again."

Raymond stared at the check, his face cycling through several emotions. "You think you can just buy me off? Send me away like I'm some kind of beggar?"

"I think I'm offering you a solution that benefits everyone," Alex replied calmly. "You get compensation for what you feel you're owed, Pete gets security, and Lazy Rivers gets peace."

"What if I don't want your money?" Raymond's voice was rising. "What if I want what's rightfully mine?"

That's when Serenity saw the memory. Raymond as a boy, maybe eight years old, laughing as his adoptive father pushed him on a swing. The joy on his face was pure and uncomplicated; the love in his adoptive parents' eyes unmistakable.

"You had a good life," Serenity said softly, surprising everyone. "I can see it. Your adoptive parents loved you. You were happy."

Raymond's head snapped toward her, his eyes narrowing. "What would you know about it?"

"I know what I see," Serenity said gently. "And I see a little boy who was loved, who had birthday parties and bedtime stories and parents who would have done anything for him. That's not nothing, Raymond. That's everything."

For a moment, Raymond's carefully constructed anger seemed to waver. But then he looked around the table at the faces surrounding him—Alex's determined protectiveness, Tom and Brad's solid presence, Joseph's wary concern, Serenity's caring—and something shifted.

He was outnumbered, and he knew it. More than that, he was alone in a way that had nothing to do with numbers and everything to do with the bonds these people shared.

"Fine," he said finally, his voice flat. He signed the documents with sharp, angry strokes. "Give me the money."

Alex slid the check across the table. "It's done."

But Pete, who had been quiet throughout the exchange, suddenly leaned forward. "It doesn't have to be, you know."

"What?" Raymond looked up, suspicious.

"You could stay," Pete said simply. "We're brothers, Raymond. Half-brothers, but still family. You could try being part of this community instead of fighting against it. There's room for you here if you want it."

The offer hung in the air, genuine and unexpected. For a moment, Raymond looked almost tempted, as if he could imagine a different version of his life.

But then his face hardened again. "I don't need your pity."

"It's not pity," Pete said sadly. "It's family."

Raymond stood up, folding the check and putting it in his wallet. "I don't know how to be family. Too late to learn now."

He walked toward the door, then paused and looked back. "For what it's worth, I'm sorry about your grandmother," he said to Tyler. "Snags was wrong to kill her. But that doesn't make us family."

Then he was gone, the door chiming softly behind him.

The diners sat in silence for several long minutes. Finally, people dispersed—Tom and Brad back to the nursery, Joseph and the others back to work.

Soon it was just Alex and Serenity sitting across from each other in the booth, the legal documents still scattered between them.

"I'm sorry," they said simultaneously, then looked at each other in surprise.

"You first," Alex said.

Serenity took a deep breath. "I'm sorry I didn't trust you. I'm sorry I turned on you when you were trying to do the right thing in an impossible situation."

Alex reached across the table and took her hand. "And I'm sorry I kept Lucas' secret from you, even for a day. I'm sorry I thought I knew better than you did about how to handle your own life. I'm sorry I let my fear of losing you make me act like I didn't trust you."

"Do you forgive me?" Serenity asked quietly.

"Do you forgive me?" Alex replied.

They smiled at each other across the table, and for the first time in days, the weight between them began to lift.

"I love you," Serenity said. "I should have said that first, before anything else. I love you, Alex Williams."

"I love you too," Alex replied, bringing her hand to his lips. "And I want to spend whatever time Lucas has left supporting you through this. All of it. Together."

Outside the diner windows, Lazy Rivers was beginning another day. The crisis had passed; the threat had been neutralized, and once again their small community had proven that love and loyalty could overcome almost anything.

But for Alex and Serenity, the most important victory was the simplest one: they had found their way back to each other.

# Epilogue

One month later...

Alex sat across from Serenity in their usual booth at the diner, watching her flip through the gallery catalog she had brought with her to share with him. The Spring Falls exhibition had been a tremendous success, with nearly every piece selling within the first week. The only painting that remained was the river landscape she'd finished the morning of Lucas's arrival—the one she'd dedicated to his memory.

"Still no interest in selling that one?" Alex asked, nodding toward the photo of the painting in the catalog.

"Not yet," Serenity said softly. "Maybe someday. But for now, it feels too much like letting go of him all over again."

Alex reached across the table and squeezed her hand. Lucas had passed away quietly three weeks earlier, surrounded by the family he'd found in his last days. The small ceremony they'd held had been perfect in its simplicity—just the people who'd known and loved him in those precious last weeks.

Randy and Sam had left for China a week later, carrying Lucas's ashes back to his homeland as he had requested. Their honeymoon had become something deeper—a pilgrimage of sorts, honoring the man who'd given Sam life and then found her just in time to see her happiness.

"Any word from the newlyweds?" Alex asked.

"Postcards from Beijing and Shanghai," Serenity smiled. "Sam says it's exactly what Lucas would have wanted—adventure, beauty, and the knowledge that his ashes are becoming part of something larger."

The diner door chimed, and Tyler walked in, his clothes dusty from working on the land that was now officially Alex's, but was going to be put in a trust for Lazy Rivers. He had spent the morning walking the property lines, making plans to turn it into a protected green space for the community—hiking trails, picnic areas, maybe even a small amphitheater for outdoor concerts.

"How's the land planning going?" Serenity asked as Tyler slid into the booth beside them.

"Good. Really good." Tyler's face was bright with enthusiasm. "Alex and I think we can have the first trail open by fall. And I've been thinking..." He paused, suddenly looking younger than his twenty-five years. "I want to travel first. See some of the world before I settle down completely. But I'll always come back to Lazy Rivers. This is home now."

Alex felt a surge of pride for the young man who'd transformed so completely from the lost soul who'd arrived in town just months earlier. "Where are you thinking of going?"

"Europe, maybe. Australia. Ethan suggested we take a trip together before he and Amy get married next year." Tyler grinned. "Speaking of which, I talked to Joseph yesterday. We think it's time to officially hand over the diner to them. They've earned it."

From behind the counter, Joseph looked up from the grill and nodded. The transition had been gradual and natural, with Ethan and Amy taking on more and more responsibility while he and Betty Jean focused on moving into their retirement years. It felt right—the diner would stay in the family, but with people who truly loved the work.

"Another wedding to plan," Serenity mused. "This town loves its celebrations."

Alex felt his heart speed up slightly. This was the opening he'd been waiting for, the perfect moment to say what he'd been thinking about for weeks.

"Speaking of weddings," he said carefully, "I've been wondering... that is, when you're ready... if you'd ever consider..."

He was fumbling with the words, making a mess of what he'd rehearsed a dozen times. But Serenity's face was lighting up with understanding and joy.

"Are you asking me to marry you, Alex Williams?"

"I'm asking if you'd be open to the idea of me asking you to marry me," Alex said with a nervous laugh. "When you're ready. When it feels right. When..."

"Yes," Serenity interrupted, her smile radiant. "Yes, to all of it. Yes to your asking, yes to saying yes, yes to spending the rest of our lives figuring this out together."

From across the diner, Betty Jean had been watching the exchange with the keen eye of someone who'd been observing human nature for decades. She approached their table with the coffeepot, a knowing smile on her face.

"Refills?" she asked innocently, but her eyes were twinkling with mischief.

"Betty Jean," Alex said, still holding Serenity's hand, "I think we're going to need to plan another celebration."

"About time," Betty Jean said, pouring coffee with a flourish. "I was wondering when you'd work up the courage." She leaned closer and whispered, "This is perfect timing, by the way. Everyone's going to be so happy."

As she walked away, Alex could already see the wheels turning in her head—another gathering, another chance for the community to come together and celebrate love.

Outside the diner windows, Lazy Rivers continued its quiet rhythm. The spring floods were a memory now. The town recovered and rebuilt stronger than before. Raymond was gone, his anger and resentment taken elsewhere. The secrets that had haunted families for generations had been brought to light and resolved.

At his house, Pete was tending the garden he'd planted behind Alex's kitchen, finally having the chance to grow things just for beauty instead of survival. Matthew and Lizzy, having slipped away to get married, were settling into married life with the contentment of people who'd waited long enough to appreciate what they'd found. John and Mama Ruth were doing the same, their late-in-life romance a reminder that love could bloom at any age.

"So," Serenity said, bringing Alex's attention back to the moment, "when are you officially going to ask me?"

Alex grinned, reaching into his jacket pocket for the ring he'd been carrying around for weeks, waiting for the right moment.

"How about right now?"

As he dropped to one knee beside the booth, the entire diner erupted in cheers and applause. Joseph came out from behind the counter, Tyler jumped up to clap, and Betty Jean started making plans out loud for yet another celebration.

And in that moment, surrounded by the people who'd become their chosen family, Alex asked Serenity Rivers to marry him in the same diner where they'd shared their first meal together, where secrets had been revealed and hearts had been mended, where a small town had proven once again that love—in all its complicated, messy, beautiful forms—was always worth fighting for.

"Yes," Serenity said, tears streaming down her face as Alex slipped the ring onto her finger. "Yes, yes, yes."

Outside, the spring air was soft with the promise of summer. Inside the diner, another love story was beginning, another celebration was being planned, and the community of Lazy Rivers was already making room for one more happily ever after.

Some stories end with dramatic flourishes. But the best ones—the ones that matter most—end with the quiet certainty that love endures, that family can be chosen as well as born, and that home is wherever people gather to take care of each other.

In Lazy Rivers, that would always be more than enough.

# Author Note

This book, and the entire *Rivers of Time* series, live within the same universe as my other fiction books.

Not just the same part of the world—southwest Pennsylvania—but in the same belief that good always overcomes evil, and community, no matter what it looks like, is powerful and is what makes life beautiful.

If you like these ideas too, you will also like *The Ruby Sisters* series, which takes place in Spring Falls, where the gallery Serenity mentions is located.

*The Stories from Doveland* series is a little more magical realism and not mentioned in this book, but the characters there have interacted with the community of Spring Falls and the Ruby Sisters.

If you like more fantasy, a few of the characters from the *Stories From Doveland* series move off into another dimension that includes some dragons and a lot of magic. You'll find them in the *Return to Erda* and *The Chronicle of Thamon* series.

One of my favorite books is the standalone *Follow Me Here*. It too, lives in this same universe of the power of good and community.

And yes, for those who have asked, I also have a non-fiction series about how to live in this world proving the power of good. Check out *The Shift Series* for that.

If you'd like to follow me, you can join my mailing list and also choose a free book or two at BecaLewis.com.

I thank you for reading my books, reviewing them if you can, and for choosing to live a good life for yourself and extending that to others.

Until we meet again, be well, and magnify good ...

*Beca*

# Acknowledgements

I could never write a book without the help of friends and family support. But for many years, both Jet Tucker and Diana Cormier have taken the time to do the final reader proof, and Laura Moliter provides fantastic book editing. I can always trust that they will tell me what I might have missed in my books. Which gives me peace of mind knowing, which is worth its weight in gold.

And thank you to all the people who tell me they love reading these stories. Comments from friends and strangers are more valuable than gold.

And as always, thank you to my beloved husband, Del, for being my daily sounding board, for putting up with all my questions, for my constant need to want to make things better, and for being the love of my life in more than just this one lifetime.

# Also By Beca

**The Rivers of Time Series: Women's Lit, Friendship, Small Town, Mystery, Magical Realism, Small Town Fiction**
*The Returning, The Awakening, The Rising*

***Follow Me Here:*** **Women's Lit, Friendship, Small Town, Mystery, Magical Realism, Small Town Fiction**

**The Ruby Sisters Series: Women's Lit, Friendship, Mystery, Small Town Fiction**
*A Last Gift, After All This Time, And Then She Remembered, As If It Was Real, Almost Innocent*

**Stories From Doveland: Women's Lit, Friendship, Small Town, Mystery, Magical Realism, Small Town Fiction**

*Karass, Pragma, Jatismar, Exousia, Stemma, Paragnosis,*
*In-Between, Missing, Out Of Nowhere*

**The Return To Erda Series: Fantasy**
*Shatterskin, Deadsweep, Abbadon, The Experiment*

**The Chronicles of Thamon: Fantasy**
*Banished, Betrayed, Discovered, Wren's Story*

**The Shift Series: Spiritual Self-Help**
*Living in Grace: The Shift to Spiritual Perception*
*The Daily Shift: Daily Lessons From Love To Money*
*The 4 Essential Questions: Choosing Spiritually Healthy Habits*
*The 28 Day Shift To Wealth: A Daily Prosperity Plan*
*The Intent Course: Say Yes To What Moves You*
*Imagination Mastery: A Workbook For Shifting Your Reality*
*Right Thinking: A Thoughtful System for Healing*
*Perception Mastery: Seven Steps To Lasting Change*
*Blooming Your Life: How To Experience Consistent Happiness*

**Perception Parables: Very short stories**
*Love's Silent Sweet Secret: A Fable About Love*
*Golden Chains And Silver Cords: A Fable About Letting Go*

## Advice / Journals

*A Woman's ABC's of Life: Lessons in Love, Life, and Career from Those Who Learned The Hard Way*

*The Daily Nudge(s): So When Did You First Notice*

# About Beca

Beca writes books she hopes will change people's perceptions of themselves and the world, and open possibilities to things and ideas that are waiting to be seen and experienced.

At sixteen, Beca founded her own dance studio. Later, she received a Master's Degree in Dance in Choreography from UCLA and founded the Harbinger Dance Theatre, a multimedia dance company, while continuing to run her dance school.

After graduating—to better support her three children—Beca switched to the sales field, where she worked as an employee and independent contractor in many industries, excelling in each while perfecting and teaching her Shift System and writing books.

She joined the financial industry in 1983 and became an Associate Vice President of Investments at a major stock brokerage firm. She was a licensed Certified Financial Planner for over twenty years.

This diversity, along with a variety of life challenges, helped fuel the desire to share what she's learned by writing and speaking, hoping it will make a difference in other people's lives.

Beca grew up in State College, PA, with the dream of becoming a dancer and then a writer. She carried that dream forward as she fulfilled a childhood wish by moving to Southern California in 1968. Beca told her family she would never move back to the cold.

After living there for thirty-one years, she met her husband, Delbert Lee Piper, Sr., at a retreat in Virginia, and everything changed. They decided to find a place they could call their own, which sent them off traveling around the United States. They lived and worked in a few different places before returning to live in the cold once again near Del's family in a small town in Northeast Ohio, not too far from State College.

When not working and teaching together, they love to visit and play with their combined family of eight children and five grandchildren, walk, read, study, do yoga or taiji, feed birds, and work in their garden.

www.ingramcontent.com/pod-product-compliance
Lightning Source LLC
Chambersburg PA
CBHW070050120726
47909CB00002B/342